THE HIGHLANDER'S

PROMISE

Books by Heather Grothaus

THE WARRIOR

THE CHAMPION

THE HIGHLANDER

TAMING THE BEAST

NEVER KISS A STRANGER

NEVER SEDUCE A SCOUNDREL

NEVER LOVE A LORD

VALENTINE

ADRIAN

ROMAN

CONSTANTINE

THE LAIRD'S VOW

THE HIGHLANDER'S PROMISE

HIGHLAND BEAST
(with Hannah Howell and Victoria Dahl)

Published by Kensington Publishing Corporation

THE HIGHLANDER'S

PROMISE

SONS OF SCOTLAND, BOOK 2

Heather Grothaus

LYRICAL PRESS
Kensington Publishing Corp.
www.kensingtonbooks.com

To the extent that the image or images on the cover of this book depict a person or persons, such person or persons are merely models, and are not intended to portray any character or characters featured in the book.

This book is a work of fiction. Names, characters, places, and incidents either are products of the author's imagination or are used fictitiously. Any resemblance to actual events or locales or persons living or dead is entirely coincidental.

LYRICAL PRESS BOOKS are published by

Kensington Publishing Corp.
119 West 40th Street
New York, NY 10018

Copyright © 2020 by Heather Grothaus

All Kensington titles, imprints, and distributed lines are available at special quantity discounts for bulk purchases for sales promotion, premiums, fund-raising, educational, or institutional use.

Special book excerpts or customized printings can also be created to fit specific needs. For details, write or phone the office of the Kensington Sales Manager: Kensington Publishing Corp., 119 West 40th Street, New York, NY 10018. Attn. Sales Department. Phone: 1-800-221-2647.

Lyrical Press and Lyrical Press logo Reg. U.S. Pat. & TM Off.

First Electronic Edition: March 2020
ISBN-13: 978-1-5161-0708-7 (ebook)
ISBN-10: 1-5161-0708-X (ebook)

First Print Edition: March 2020
ISBN-13: 978-1-5161-0712-4
ISBN-10: 1-5161-0712-8

Printed in the United States of America

For my Scots and English ancestors.
We will dwell forever in the Borderlands.

Prologue

He would go back for Harriet soon.

Thomas Annesley's huffing breaths swirled around his head in a thick, humid cloud, picking up the white moonlight and crafting his exhalation into a foggy hood. He took great, lunging strides up the rocky path, careful to avoid the seams of slick, cold mud between the sharp, wet slabs of stone, and was thankful for the moonlight that lit his track. Thankful, too, that the rain had finally stopped, but the bright glow bore none of the sun's heartening warmth, and he was soaked through his borrowed woolen shawl to his skin. It seemed so much colder here than at Tower Roscraig, just across the Forth from Edinburgh; as if the velvety Highland peat all around him hid a core of ice. He sought to distract himself from the deep ache in his bones by concentrating on the foreign terrain beneath his boots and by holding young Harriet Payne's sweet, rounded face in his mind's eye.

He would go back for Harriet soon; back to she who had saved his life by hiding him in her da's barn. She who had nursed his arrow wounds and the terrible injury inflicted by Vaughn Hargrave's arquebus. Harriet, who had only just crossed that budding threshold of womanhood and who had comforted Thomas in his anguish and his loss of Cordelia. Cordelia, and…

Thomas struggled along the slope of that frozen Highland mountain, imagining as he went the day he would return for Harriet on a horse not stolen, and take her and the child he suspected she carried away from that mean bit of farm to safety at Tower Roscraig on the Forth. He owed her his life, and his sanity, and he vowed to repay Harriet Payne's kindness by ensuring she spent the rest of her days in that strong, stone fortress that had belonged to his Scots mother's family.

Although elsewhere he might be called Baron Annesley, Lord of Darlyrede, Thomas wondered that he would ever return to England, let alone the great estate of his father. Darlyrede House had been soaked in so much blood, and not only Cordelia's, Thomas had learned on the fateful night Hargrave had tried to kill him. Thomas had been made a fugitive by that grand hold, by that night; a man wanted for the murder of the very woman who was to have been his wife.

The rushing of blood in his ears grew louder as the memories of that dank cellar thundered over him, and Thomas staggered to a halt, bracing his hand against the ruffled bark of a young birch as he caught his breath. He realized then it wasn't just his frenzied blood he heard; the sound of crashing water radiated through the trees.

The falls. They must be just over the shoulder of the mountain.

He straightened and turned on the path, pausing to peer across the long valley he'd just circled. Though earlier in the day the hills and vales had run with autumn's saffron and rust, made more barren by the unusually dry summer, now the treetops standing sentry around the bowl of scrubby land wore moonlight caps, their dripping skirts hidden in darkest shadow. Iain Douglas had directed him well, warning him to give wide berth to the dangerous Town Blair on the edge of Loch Acras.

Starving Lake...

Thomas shivered in his heavy, sodden clothes.

He shook the eerie feeling from his shoulders with a frown. After a fortnight of foot travel, he would reach the clansmen of his mother before dawn. He would show the Carson elders his father's dagger, kept safe at Tower Roscraig for so many years and ready now upon his calf, remind them of Iain Douglas's place of honor at Tower Roscraig, and then plead his kinship as just cause for requesting the town's fiercest warriors to help defend against the assault Thomas knew was coming. Vaughn Hargrave may have destroyed Thomas's life at Darlyrede, shattered the future he'd had always taken for granted, but Thomas had the hope of a new life to fight for; Hargrave would never take the Tower.

The Tower belonged to Harriet, and Thomas would return for her.

He turned to the wood again and strode on, the sound of the water swelling larger through the trees as he continued down the western slope of the mountain. He weaved through the trunks, navigating by ear toward the cascading heart of the roaring river, all other typical night sounds made mute. He didn't bother with stealth now, for even his crashing footfalls through the dense blanket of forest floor could not surpass the great wall of thundering water to reach even his own ears.

Follow the river downstream to the falls; there you shall find a footbridge. Once across, you are safely on Carson land...

His right boot slipped into a badger hole covered over with wet leaves, and Thomas only just managed to free his foot before his slide down the steep bank. He caught himself against the peeling trunk of another birch with a soundless *oof*, and then the moonlight revealed his sanctuary in the loud silence of the water.

The bridge appeared shamefully old and disused for such an essential channel, planked with only whole, once-young tree trunks. There was no railing, but a thick rope woven from vines stretched alongside the jagged-edged downstream side, tethered on either bank around sturdy ashes. The bridge was lit as brightly as at midday, the moonlight reflecting off the churning white foam exploding from the vertical granite slabs of the riverbed above it. The cylindrical treads of the bridge glistened with water and moss, belying the signs of long drought in the high valleys he'd passed through. Thomas vowed he could detect the faint odor of fish and the sea, and remembered that it was the time of the salmon running in from the wide, wild ocean.

His mouth watered at the thought of such fresh bounty; he'd not had a proper meal in days, surviving on the last shriveled crumbs of the provisions packed for him at Roscraig.

Thomas half-slid, half-leaped down the remaining curve of bank toward the footbridge, his pack flopping limply against the small of his back. As he stepped onto the first softened trunks, he realized the bridge was far longer than it had first appeared, and not nearly wide enough to suit him, considering the chaos of the water and the sheer drop it spanned over the sudden ravine. Thirty feet down it must be at the midpoint, and at least that far across, although the bridge was perhaps only six feet wide.

Six very slick feet. And the trunks were not lashed tightly together, leaving gaps that appeared to be just as wide as the very thickness of a grown man in several spots.

Do you nae good to bring a mount to such a place. The bridge isna meant for the crossing of those astride, my lord.

"It would seem as if the bridge wasn't meant for crossing at all, Iain," Thomas muttered aloud, his words lost beneath the weight of sound of the roaring falls. Already, his eardrums felt sore from the pressure.

The reverberations of the water against the rock rumbled beneath the soles of his boots, but the bridge held steady. He stepped carefully, testing each tread for the crumbly feel of rot, and pressing down firmly into the slick slime until he felt the bite of the softened wood. Stepping over the first gap caused hot beads of sweat to spring forth in the stubble covering his face. Then the planks shuddered, bucked, and the entire bridge swayed over the river. Thomas's stomach felt as if it fell into the pouch of his shawl as he froze in place, his gaze fixed on the sparkling fog of water misting over the trunks, his arms held to either side to steady himself, swiping blindly for the rope with his left hand.

He was halfway across; if the bridge failed, he was dead.

"Doona dare another step, lad," a deep voice called.

Thomas flinched and raised his eyes to find that the rickety span wasn't failing as he'd feared, but only occupied by other travelers. The north end of the bridge was now blocked by as many as eight rough-looking men, several of them bearing woven baskets on their shoulders. One switch-thin young man, gaunt and owl-eyed, juggled a bundle of long-handled, patched nets. The smell of fish now filled the ravine.

All of them save the owl-eyed man glared at Thomas, the distrust clear in their shadowed faces as the front man watched him expectantly, his posture tense.

Thomas willed himself to lower his hands slowly, then gripped them into sweaty fists as he stood over the highest point of the ravine. "We are well met," he said, shouting to project his voice over the roar of the falls. "I mean to gain the Carson town before dawn. My kin reside there. Perhaps you are one of them."

The leader of the group's brows rose in the moonlight, hollowing his temples further. "A Carson ye be, eh? Yer face isna known to me."

"My name's Annesley," Thomas called. "Thomas Annesley. My mother's family are Carsons." The wind changed then, blowing wet, flapping leaves and a wash of spray across the gulf, pressing against Thomas's chest as if warning him back. The men glanced at one another, their expressions unfathomable. "I claim a holding in Edinburgh, and have come requesting help to defend it against an enemy. I can pay. In silver."

When the gust had swept down the river valley toward the sea, the man replied, "Ye'd best back from the bridge, laird, whilst we cross; 'tis nae place to palaver."

Thomas glanced past the men to the slope of the night-cloaked wood he had been told led eventually to the sea, a frown forming on his face even as he spoke. "I mean to gain the town proper; I—" Thomas broke off as he realized the woods weren't nearly as black as they should have been on this western side of the highland hills, and not even as black as they had been when Thomas had started across the bridge. The far undersides of the firs and pines were now flickering with a faint yellow-orange glow… Thomas brought his gaze back to the leader of the group as he spoke once more.

"Nay, ye doona wish to carry on that way," the man advised with a slow shake of his head. "Back off the bridge now, lad."

Thomas felt as though his boots were mortared to the mossy treads. "Are you…Carsons?" he asked. "Are you my kin?"

The leader gestured toward Thomas. "Help him back, lads. The crossing seems to be giving him a wee spot o' trouble."

Two men from the group lifted their baskets to the shoulders of companions and then stepped around the leader with sure strides. Thomas lurched backward, the idea of escape coming to him too late as the smooth soles of his boots could find no purchase and he staggered to maintain his footing on the slick trunks. The orange glow beyond the woods grew, and the faintest smell of smoke wafted up the mountain to itch the back of his throat. A rumbling volley of what might have been thunder whispered through the trees.

The long, parched Acras valley above the falls; the laden baskets carried under the cover of darkness…

"You're poaching the salmon," he said as he realized the truth. "Did you set the town afire?" he croaked as the men wrapped hard hands around his biceps. They could swing him over the edge in a blink if they chose, but Thomas felt himself being dragged toward the bank.

"Nay, nae we, lad," the man said, following him across the bridge and over the gulf, the others stepping quickly in his wake with their baskets of gleaming, twitching fish. The men released him when his boots met the firm forest floor, and Thomas stumbled to keep his feet as the leader loomed over him. "It takes more clever tools than what the Blairs can boast to ensure a town of sodden houses should burn. It seems as though the enemy ye spoke of isna behind ye, but afore ye. A mighty foe he must indeed be."

The man paused and then gave Thomas a sly smile. "In fact, perhaps we've saved yer life. What will ye pay for that now, I wonder? *In silver?*" He looked to the men, waiting silently. "Run ahead up the valley, Geordie-boy, and wake the fine."

"Even the chief, Harrell?" the owl-eyed man asked with a bewildered expression on his slack, hound's face. His words were round and softened by speech impediment, and at this close distance, Thomas guessed he couldn't be older than a score.

"The chief, especial," Harrell said. "This is a day the Blairs will speak of for generations, and I'll warrant all in the town will wish to recount the moment they saw our arrival with their own eyes." Harrell stepped forward and swiped Thomas's dagger from his calf before raising up swiftly and bringing the point to dimple the skin beneath his chin.

His smile widened in the midst of his hollowed face, revealing gleaming teeth in the moonlight. "The fortune of Clan Blair, wrapped in a Carson shawl. 'Tis a hero I'll be." His chuckle sent a hot gust of breath, smelling of raw fish, into Thomas's nostrils.

"What, now? Have ye never wanted to be a hero, Thomas Annesley?"

Chapter 1

March 1458

Loch Acras, Town Blair

Scottish Highlands

Lachlan Blair lay his head back against the hard wood of the low chair and closed he eyes as he felt his time drawing near, the woman on her knees before him working her mouth so masterfully, so familiar with the territory she traveled, he knew he could last no more than a pair of moments before he—

His eyes snapped open again as he heard the door behind him scrape open across the dirt. "Lachlan, the chief is call—"

Lachlan reached down to the hatchet in his belt and flung it with a flick of his wrist, its resounding thud in the door frame assuring Lachlan he'd made his point, cutting off the man's words and heralding his exit by another scraping of the door.

Next time, he would remember to drop the latch.

He looked back down at the woman seated between his legs, disengaged from him now but still gripping him tightly with one hand as her lips, glistening and reddened by the friction of him, curved in a small smile. Her large breasts dangled free and bare above the folds of her crushed bodice.

"Shall I stop? It must be important."

Lachlan cursed aloud and then sighed and sat up in the chair, forcing Searrach to release him and move away with no more protest than a rueful pout. He stood, squatting to drop his manhood into his braies and lace up his codpiece while Searrach pushed her arms into her bodice and hid her breasts away from his admiring view. Now that his head was clearing of the impassioned fog conjured by the well-rounded brunette, Lachlan could better hear the sounds of commotion through the thick walls of the longhouse. He swiped his brush through his waving auburn locks, using his other hand to gather the length in a long tail at his nape.

"What could it be?" Searrach asked as she pulled the brush from his hand to tidy her own hair.

"I doona know," Lachlan said, securing the tail with a piece of leather and then rocking his hatchet free from the doorframe and returning it to his belt. "But if it's nae someone's death, it soon will be."

"Aye, and go see to it, Blair," Searrach cooed, and his eyes shot to her, his frown quirking despite himself at the woman's pandering allusion to the fact that Lachlan would soon be clan chief.

Lachlan wrenched open the door and stepped out into the bright light of midday. It seemed as though the whole of the town was gathered on the green before his grandfather's longhouse, clustered in a wary circle around a mounted rider who seemed as out of place in the fresh green Highland spring as a dagger clutched in the hand of a newborn babe.

The stranger was clad all in black, from his long, queued hair to his fine boots, nearly invisible against the flank of his equally black mount. He made no outward effort to control the beast crowded so by the obviously curious villagers, as there was no need; the man's horse stood as still as any mountain boulder, but its head was up, alert, and Lachlan had the impression that should any from the town attempt to lay a hand upon either the horse or its master, they would be stomped into the green in a blink.

The rider carried a long sword strapped across his back for transport, but the man was certainly armed well enough without it, as even from across the green Lachlan could spy no fewer than four blades of varying lengths, as well as a bow fixed in a tidy bundle across the back of the man's saddle. The rider's profile looked more out of place than even his fine mount, his long, pale face with its bony prominences seeming cold and detached here in the lush, humid green.

The townsfolk turned wary, frowning faces toward Lachlan as he neared, revealing the stooped and robed figure of Archibald Blair, Lachlan's grandfather, in their midst. Lachlan felt rather than saw the stranger's gaze fall upon him, but he would not dignify the man's presence with his attention as of yet.

"Is aught amiss?" Lachlan called out in an easy tone.

The old man was clearly distressed, the long, dirty-gray hair he was so proud of quivering and swaying like fluffy fleece over the shoulder of his long tunic, cut in the old fashion, his ancient shawl fastened over his concave chest.

"A stranger," he lisped, and jerked his head toward the black-clad man. "Englishman with wont to speak before the fine."

Lachlan stopped on the fringe of the group and at last turned up his face toward the man on the dark horse. He met the stranger's gaze, icy-blue and without the least hint of concern for his own safety in the midst of so many wary Highlanders.

He was either an idiot or the devil himself.

"We doona gather council upon the command of foreigners," Lachlan said.

The man raised a thin, black eyebrow in his pale face, as if amused, then dismissed Lachlan without a word, turning to look at his grandfather once more instead. "I bring news from the south that may be of great import to your clan. The fine will no doubt wish to—"

"*I said,*" Lachlan interrupted, his ire rising at the blatant disregard of the cool man, "we doona gather council at the command of a foreigner."

The rider didn't so much as glance at Lachlan as he continued. "Very well. If you give me leave to dismount, Blair, I will convey the word to you privately, and then you shall do with the information what you will. My only duty is to impart the facts as I have been given them."

"You doona have my leave," Archibald hissed. "Ennathin' you have to say to me, you can do it from your sack-of-bones horse and then take yer leave from this vale, lest 'tis yer hope never to see England again. That is my grandson ye offend."

At this, the man turned his head to Lachlan once more, his expression changed, his gaze now bright and earnest.

"You are Archibald Blair's grandson?" he asked, looking Lachlan up and down as if he were some animal at market. "Aged approximately one score, eight? Your mother was called Edna?"

"Aye," Lachlan said, feeling his head draw back slightly at both the accuracy of the information and the sound of his mother's name issuing from the man's lips; it had been so long since Lachlan had heard it spoken aloud. "I should think I know my own mother's name. Who are you to know of her?"

But before the stranger could reply, Archibald Blair seemed to erupt with anger, raising his arm to point a crooked finger at the man. "Ye get out of here! We doona wish to hear ennathin' from yer lyin' English lips! Go on, then!"

This time it was Archibald Blair the rider in black dismissed as he answered Lachlan's question. "I am Sir Lucan Montague, knight of the Most Noble Order of the Garter of His Majesty King Henry of England. Your name, sir?"

"Doona say ennathin'!" Archibald shouted, holding both hands skyward now as Lachlan glanced over at him. His grandfather's face had reddened, his yellowed eyes bulging. "You canna trust a bloody Englishman! *Hah, geddout!*" Archibald stepped toward Lucan Montague's mount, as if to shy the horse from the green, but the animal stood as if made from stone.

"I am Lachlan Blair, and aye, I am the only child of my mother Edna," Lachlan supplied calmly, his curiosity piqued despite his grandfather's distress.

"Is your mother present in the town, Master Blair?" the knight inquired in his crisp, southern accent.

"Master Blair now, is it?" Lachlan laughed. "My mother's been dead for a score and five. And as you're too young to have known her, I'd be answered as to your purpose at Town Blair."

"My condolences on your loss," Lucan Montague said with a slight bow in his saddle. "It is true that I claim no acquaintance with your mother; it is on your father's behalf that I travel."

"Tommy?" a townsman hidden within the crowd called out hesitantly, a faint reverence in the word that straightened Lachlan's spine. And yet he still found himself scanning the sea of faces for sight of Marcas or Dand as the gathered folk leaned their heads together, their murmurs rippling around the green.

"Ye get out of here now, I said!" Archibald shouted hoarsely, whipping his dagger from his belt and staggering forward so quickly that he tripped and would have fallen onto the horse had it not been for the men around him, catching the chief and struggling to assist him while he swung at them and cursed. "He canna be trusted! He canna be—" His words wheezed to a halt as Lachlan's grandfather clutched at his chest and closed his eyes, sagging within the grips of the two braw townsmen who supported him.

One of the men, Lachlan's friend Cordon Blair, met his eyes with a look of concern. Archibald's health had been failing for months, and the curious disquiet this English stranger was causing was a clear threat to the Blair chief.

"If by 'Tommy' you refer to Thomas Annesley," Lucan Montague called out over the din, "then yes; your father, Tommy."

Lachlan looked back up into the calm face of the stranger, who seemed not at all bothered by Archibald Blair's distress. "Perhaps you'd best say what you mean outright, Montague. You've caused my grandfather a great upset and I do find myself agreeing with his measure of your honesty: You are too young to have known my father either, for he, too, died many years ago. Before I was even born."

The knight inclined his head ever so slightly. "Forgive my disagreement, but that is not so, sir. I spoke at length with the man myself little more than a month ago in London."

The murmur of the crowd increased to a mumble and Lachlan felt his brows drawing together in a frown for the second time that day. He glanced at his grandfather and saw that Archibald's rheumy gaze was fixed determinedly on the ground before his feet as he continued to sag in the townsmen's arms. Lachlan thought he saw his grandfather's head shake ever so slightly. *Nay.*

Lachlan looked back to the knight. "Disagree all you like, but you have been played false. What would make you certain enough of an imposter's claim to make such a long and dangerous journey?"

"Thomas himself wasn't certain of your existence, true," Montague allowed. "But he wished for me to seek out Town Blair, and Edna Blair in particular, so that if he had indeed left issue behind, I could convey the truth to her."

"My father died in battle. *Before I was born*," Lachlan reiterated calmly, but a strange feeling sank into his guts with long, sharp spikes and Lachlan couldn't fathom why. "He sacrificed himself in order to save our town from an attacking clan. That is truth all here well know."

"Fabricated," Montague rejoined crisply. "Thomas Annesley deserted the Blairs' fight against the Clan Carson and has only just been hanged in London for murder."

Lachlan's breath caught in his chest as the air of the green filled with the ringing hiss of steel being withdrawn from sheaths. "Take care what you say about my father in the presence of his clan, stranger."

Lucan Montague quirked his brow again as he glanced around at the scores of weapons being pointed at him. Now, at last, his mount seemed wary, alert. The knight calmly reached inside his quilted doublet, then withdrew his hand slowly.

"Only a parchment," he announced, holding a square packet between his fingers so that those threatening him might see. He held it out toward Lachlan. "I am but a messenger, and a scribe of sorts. Here it is, put down in his own hand, meant for the Blair fine. But as your grandfather has refused to summon his council to order, I suppose…"

"Give it to me, then, ye bloody bastard," Archibald demanded hoarsely.

But Lachlan stepped forward as if in a dream, taking the wax-sealed packet into his own hands. It was smooth and warmed through from being held so long against the English knight's heart. The sounds of the spring day, the crowd around him, faded away, and even the warm breeze that blew his tail of hair over his shoulder seemed removed from Lachlan as he stood staring at the red wax seal.

"Council," his grandfather wheezed, breaking the spell of the parchment. "I call the council. Harrell, Harrell, where be ye? Turn me loose, Cordon. I must find—"

"Aye, Blair, I'm here." Searrach's father stepped to the old man's side, from where, Lachlan knew not. He leaned his ear near Archibald's head, listening. Then Searrach's father nodded and strode to Lachlan, holding out his hand. "Give it over, lad."

Lachlan looked at the older man and felt his fingers tighten on the smooth, waxy packet. Beyond Harrell's shoulder, Archibald was being helped away from the green—half-carried, half-dragged—toward his own door.

"It's meant for the fine," Harrell reiterated, and then plucked the parchment from Lachlan's reluctant grasp.

"You canna call a fine; Marcas hasna returned from the hunt."

"I'll send a runner," Harrell said, and then turned away from Lachlan to speak to the knight. "You've leave to dismount. See to yer horse in the chief's stable, then he'll hear ye."

Lachlan stood as if frozen for a moment, his hand still suspended as when it had gripped the square of parchment, as Montague swung down from his horse. Then he shook himself and marched toward his grandfather's longhouse after Harrell. He was about to duck through the doorway when the man turned and placed his hand against Lachlan's chest.

"Let me pass, Harrell," Lachlan said. "I've every right of the fine."

Searrach's father shook his head. "Nae this time, lad," he said solemnly. "The Blair's word."

Lachlan looked deeper into the long, dark room, his eyes straining to penetrate the gloom. Cordon Blair was lowering Archibald onto a pallet near the central fire, and Lachlan could see that his grandfather's face was now the same color as his fleecy hair. The Blair raised his hooded eyes to meet Lachlan's own for the briefest moment before his gaze skittered toward the banked coals.

Pressure on Lachlan's chest drew his attention once more to the man who would soon be his family in marriage, as Harrell pressed him back from the doorway. Lachlan had the sudden urge to break off the man's hand at the wrist. A black shape brushed by Lachlan's left, and he realized it was Montague. Although lean even in his black-quilted gambeson, the knight was taller than Lachlan would have guessed, besting his own height by half a hand, and it further increased Lachlan's already growing anger. Montague paused in the doorway to meet his gaze boldly. "You have my apologies."

Lachlan huffed as a young boy dashed from the longhouse between the two men—Harrell's runner. "What care have I for the empty courtesies of a scurfy Englishman?"

The knight's face was solemn, and Lachlan had the faint and ominous suspicion that he was missing a point of great importance.

"You have them any matter." Lucan Montague entered into the Blair's longhouse fully, and the last thing Lachlan saw was Harrell's grave face as he shut the door.

Lachlan turned back to the green and was startled to realize that the majority of the town was still gathered on the grassy lawn, some of the men still gripping the weapons they had readied at the insult to the name of Lachlan's legendary sire. They'd all witnessed his barring from the council and now seemed to be waiting for some explanation.

"Go on," Lachlan said in a voice full of bluster. "It's like as nae only a bit of political nonsense from the south. I'll keep watch for Marcas."

It wasn't entirely untrue, but it brought about his desired result of dispersing the curious crowd whose stares seemed to penetrate Lachlan. It wasn't as though he was unused to being the center of attention; as the son of the man who had managed to turn back the entire Carson clan single-handedly and saved Town Blair from massacre, Lachlan was accustomed to admiration.

But just now, the scrutiny made him feel uneasy, as if there was a hint of something…less than deferential in their gazes; questions and doubts in their eyes that Lachlan himself didn't understand.

He stood to the side of the door, resting his back against the sun-warmed wall, his arms crossed over his chest. His eyes darted from the wall of woods surrounding the basin of valley this north side of the loch to the alleys of the town that led to the water's edge, watching for signs of Marcas or Dand.

The sun grew ripe, orange, burnishing the low roofs with a golden glow, and the wall at his back fell into cold shadow. Lachlan slid to a squat, keeping his posture even when his feet tingled and the townsfolk went about their evening chores. He didn't rise until he at last saw the awkward shapes shudder free from the edge of the forest—his foster brother, Dand, followed closely by Marcas and the runner.

They disappeared for a moment as they drew near the town and were hidden by the houses, but a moment later, Dand's stormy expression was clear even from across the green, his pale face closed down in a glower, his red, curling lock falling over his forehead. Lachlan's junior by eight years, Dand hadn't even taken the time to unstring his bow as he charged across the common area, head lowered like a young bull.

"Is there an Englishman here?" he demanded incredulously as Lachlan rose to his feet on legs that felt showered with sparks from a fire. "Has he been given place over ye in the fine, Lach?"

"What took you so long?" Lachlan asked, not trusting himself to answer his brother's question without betraying the foreign humiliation he felt. "Harrell sent for you hours ago."

"We were way back." Dand panted, reaching Lachlan at last. "Da had to string up a buck." Dand nodded toward the closed door, then looked back at Lachlan with eyes still full of his fiery questions.

But Lachlan turned his gaze instead to the older man now nearing the longhouse with the runner. Marcas Blair was three score, his once rich, chestnut hair now gone white like Archibald's, but unlike the clan chief, Lachlan's foster father kept its length tamed from his face in a long braid. His features were solemn, like the side of Ben Nevis itself with his tall forehead and wide cheekbones below bright blue eyes. His hands swung free at his sides, stained a bloody brown, his sleeves rolled to his elbows; his shawl twisted around his waist, revealing the dampness of his light-colored shirt. Marcas had hurried to Lachlan's side, of that there could be no doubt.

And doubted him Lachlan seldom had, in all the years since he had come to live in Marcas's longhouse.

"I'll sort it," was all Marcas said in his low, calm voice as he passed Lachlan. He pushed open the door and paused, looking over his shoulder at Dand.

Dand shook his head, his chin raised. "I'll wait with Lach."

Marcas nodded once and ducked inside, the young runner fast on his heels.

But Lachlan would only be pushed so far. "Nae ye doon, ye schemin'—" he reached out and grabbed the runner's arm and swung him back from the door as it closed, shoving him toward the green. The boy gave Lachlan a sheepish grin before slumping off toward the maze of houses.

"Why are they barring you, Lach?" Dand pressed. "Who's the Englishman is said to've come?"

"A knight," Lachlan said grudgingly at last, sliding back down the wall again, this time to sit on the dirt, one leg stretched out before him. "He's brought a message to the fine."

Dand mimicked the posture. "From the English king?"

Lachlan shrugged. For some reason, he couldn't bring himself to repeat the blasphemous words Lucan Montague had said about Thomas Annesley. They were lies, any matter. 'Twould do no good to ire Dand further.

"But why would they bar you from—"

"Would ye shut up your blatherin', Dand?" Lachlan barked. "If I knew, d'ye think I'd be sitting here in the dooryard like some hound awaitin' his scraps?"

Dand didn't seem to take offense to the rebuke, crossing his arms over his chest, his bow still hooked over his shoulder. "You're nae hound, Lach, that's for certain. Tommy's own blood in yer veins. The wolf of Clan Blair. And my own brother."

Lachlan turned his head to look at Dand with a sigh. He huffed a laugh as he reached out to roughly scrub at the young man's orangey mop of hair, as he had when Dand had been only a boy, but Dand swatted away the juvenile attempt with a powerful blow. "And you're nae to forget it."

The door to the longhouse opened suddenly, and Marcas appeared, looking around the green until he noticed Lachlan and Dand rising from the dirt. Lachlan's spirits rose at the swiftness with which his foster father had apparently brought the fine to order.

"Dand," Marcas said, his gaze skittering away from Lachlan's, "run now, find Mother and tell her the fine shall be needing a meal."

"Aye, Da. How many will eat?"

"Eight; the Englishman's nae staying."

Dand frowned. "I ken he's nae welcome, but night is nearly upon us, and he a stranger to our land."

Lachlan hadn't taken his eyes from his foster father, and caught the tic of irritation in the older man's cheek. "'Tis his own decision," Marcas said, and glanced at Lachlan as if he couldn't help himself. "He doesna have far to travel." He looked back to Dand. "Hie, lad. Do as I say."

Lachlan felt his brows drawing together as his brother trotted away over the green. "There's naught for miles, Marcas. Where's he—?" Lachlan drew his head back as he realized the only logical answer. "Carson Town?"

"Go home, Lachlan," Marcas advised, the tic gone from his face now, but his eyes still hard. "We're nae likely to be done here any time soon."

"But I—"

"I'll send for you when you're needed," Marcas interrupted, and the finality of his tone was one Lachlan recognized from his boyhood; there would be no argument. "You ken I'll speak for your good."

"Why would there be need to speak for my good? What have I done to warrant speaking for me at all? I should be inside with the others, in my rightful place. What's that bastard said?"

"Naught," Marcas said. "You've done naught, and the Englishman's said naught against you. I swear it," Marcas insisted, the disbelief obviously clear on Lachlan's face. "You'll have nae grudge against Lucan Montague."

As if summoned, the dark knight ducked through the doorway and passed between Marcas and Lachlan.

"Pardon," Montague murmured, and Lachlan's glare followed the man as he walked swiftly toward the narrow run-in leaning against Archibald Blair's longhouse.

"Go home," Marcas repeated, "and wait for me there."

Lachlan continued to track the knight to the stable. "Aye, Marcas."

"Lach—"

"*I said aye, Marcas!*" Lachlan barked. He was still the Blair's grandson.

Marcas's mouth pressed into a grim line, but he gave Lachlan a single nod and turned to duck back into the longhouse.

A moment later, Lucan Montague rode onto the green atop his fine, black mount. He reined the horse to a dancing halt and stared boldly across the chilling twilight at Lachlan as if waiting for him, as if giving Lachlan the opportunity to decide to accompany him, assumedly to the town of the Blair's blood enemies, and the last place to which Lachlan would voluntarily journey: the Carsons.

Lachlan stared back. He thought of the hatchet at his side, the blade in his boot, and wondered if he should use them despite Marcas's warning. Lachlan didn't understand it, but he knew that this man—this interloper— had somehow ripped the orderly fabric of the town upon his arrival. Perhaps he had even disordered Lachlan's own life, although he couldn't see how that was possible. As the Blair's grandson, there was no one more powerful than he, set to take control of the town in only days—the youngest chief in all the highlands.

And yet, a voice whispered to him, *here you stand outside your own fine.*

Lucan Montague waited a moment longer, holding Lachlan's gaze, and then he gave a single nod and turned his mount's head west out of the village, chasing the sun that had already disappeared over the trees. Lachlan watched him go, the muffled hoof falls soon leaving a cold void that the early spring peepers rushed to fill with their enthusiastic calls.

The green was empty now. Lachlan was alone.

He loosened his shawl and rearranged it over his head and shoulders, tucking both ends into the front of his belt, then he, too, started westward across the green.

Chapter 2

"I've thought you a pome," Eachann Todde said, a smile in his voice. Finley could feel his gaze on the side of her face, as if he'd licked her, and the stench and moisture were evaporating in the cooling updraft of the falls.

"A what?" she said, turning her head to reluctantly look at him. They were both standing on the bridge with their forearms braced on the railing overlooking the deep, rippling river some ten feet below. She only needed give the awkward man another quarter of an hour, and then her parents—and the fine—should be satisfied.

His skull seemed misshapen beneath the thick, pockmarked skin of his face, his nose and upper jaw protruding while his brow and forehead sloped sharply into a bright orange hairline that didn't begin properly until past his crown. His eyelashes and brows disappeared against the fish belly color of his complexion, bracketed by ears that stuck from the sides of his head like scallop shells.

Finley thought he looked like a sea monster, if ever they existed. A prosperous and eligible sea monster who boasted the highest number of sheep in the town, but he smelled of brine all the same.

"A *pome*," Eachann said again, with what must have been meant as an indulgent grin. "A verse of song, you ken?"

"Ah," Finley said with a nod, and turned her gaze back to the water lest she visibly shudder. "A *poem*."

"Aye," he said. "A pome."

Finley watched the river roil and swirl, wondering if a quarter of an hour had yet gone. Perhaps she should carry a glass with her in the future. A small one, that might fit in her pouch and could be looked at surreptitiously to—

"Do you wish to hear it?"

Finley started. "What?"

"Do you wish to hear the pome?"

"Oh," she said with a forced smile. "Why not?" She turned her face away toward the south and muttered, "Perhaps it will pass the time."

"What's that, love?" Eachann asked.

"I said, does it happen to rhyme?"

His graveled face brightened and he leaned toward her to press her forearm in delight. "It does indeed, my sweet."

Finley swallowed hard.

Eachann coughed and then was apparently forced to clear his throat of a rather large plug of mucus, expelling it with a wet exclamation into the churning water below. Then he wiped his mouth with his shawl and turned to her fully, splaying one stubby palm against his breast. He took a deep breath and opened his mouth.

He closed it again with a sheepish grin and sank to one knee. Eachann reached up and pawed at Finley's right hand, now gripping the railing as if it would save her life. She resisted his prying fingers until it became obvious that he would not relent. She let him take her hand into his damp, salmon-fat fingers.

He cleared his throat again and narrowed his eyes, staring intently into Finley's face.

"'Her hair is like the dawn; her eyes, a gentle fawn's.'"

"My eyes are blue, Eachann," Finely interrupted.

"Shh," he scolded. "Dammit all. Now, where was I?"

"A fawn's eyes are brown," she reasoned. "I just thought you'd—"

"I'll start over," Eachann interrupted pointedly. "'Her hair is like the dawn; her eyes, a gentle fawn's.'" He looked at her with warning, but Finley wisely held her tongue, wishing the whole thing over with.

"'My many bairns she'll spawn. From my own loins, so brawn. Unto her glistening prawn. The fair Finley Car-son.'"

Finley knew her mouth had dropped open as she stared down at him, but she couldn't help it. "Wh—what?"

Eachann grumbled in his throat and drew a breath. "'Her hair is like the daw—'"

"Nay, Eachann, I heard you well," Finley interrupted, snatching her hand from his slippery grip. "'*Glistening prawn'?*"

His cheeks speckled like a drunk's, and he rose to his feet. "'Tis a passionate phrase, aye. But only for your ears, my sweet." He took a step toward her, his arms held out as if he would embrace her. "And the only words that could express how I anticipate—"

"Anticipate this," Finley said, and swept her foot at his ankles, at the same moment taking hold of his sloped shoulders and levering him across the low railing.

Eachann Todde executed a lovely cartwheel on his way to the river, his bard's voice rising in a shrill howl before it was cut off by the splash of his arse striking the rippling surface. Finley stood at the railing, waiting for him to surface—not because she worried for his welfare, but solely to see the expression of shocked confusion on his gnawsome face as he came up, gasping and sputtering.

She thought she heard some sort of canine bark from the trees behind her and turned, her eyes scanning the tall, slender trunks with suspicion. Wolves were generally rare in this part of the Highlands, but they did wander close to Carson Town now and again, especially along the river. But there was little to see in the deepening gloom of the bowing sun.

"*Finley Carson!*" The bellow from the water below caused Finley to whip her head back around to find Eachann Todde now standing on the steep and jagged riverbank below. Gone was the benign, doughy look of lustful admiration from his face, his fuzzy, flame-colored hair now hanging in pathetic tendrils. "You did that a-purpose!"

Her brows lowered. "I did," she admitted. "And if you dare bring your bloated girth to stand too near me in the future, I'll take a stick to you, Eachann Todde, speaking to me so boldly."

He stabbed a stubby forefinger up at her. "You hellion. I was your last hope. There's not a man left in the town ye havena offended!"

"God help me, if you were the last man in all of Scotland, I'd never marry you!"

"I'd nae have ye!" he bellowed back.

Finley stuttered a moment and then shouted, "Your poetry is rubbish!"

"Your father shall hear of this straightaway," he threatened, waggling his finger at her again before he turned to begin the arduous struggle up the slippery rock shelves that made up the bank. "The fine, as well!" he tossed over his shoulder.

Finley drew her head back in surprise. "Are you threatening me?" she asked incredulously, more to herself than for the benefit of Eachann's ears. Then her brows lowered again and she stalked to the eastern side of the bridge and gathered up a handful of rocks. She ran back to the center of the span and began throwing them at Eachann Todde's wide, dripping backside, her aim true more oft than not. "Tell them this while you're about it, you...you rat-faced farmer of sheep shite!"

He yelped and ducked as she pelted him with the stones, and he finally staggered onto the path. Finley was rather surprised that he'd managed to scale the bank. His rough complexion was dark with exertion and rage and his head lowered as he marched toward her.

"Doona come any closer, Eachann," she warned, gripping a final stone in her hand.

"Your trouble is that your da never gave you the proper beatin' you've been askin' for since you were nine. I'll do the town the favor of it myself."

"I'll lay you flat," she vowed, shifting her weight from foot to foot. "I swear it. Stay away. *Eachann...*"

"Perhaps that's what you want after all, innit?" he said. "A strong man to take you in hand and show you what's proper? I vow I'm that man. You'll be—" He slowed his advance, and his gaze went to the woods behind her. "Who the bloody hell is that?"

"Ha. Nice try," Finley said with a smirk and let her final missile fly. The smooth, heavy rock struck him squarely in his long, undulating nose, and Eachann Todde made a slow descent onto his back on the bridge.

But then the sound of hooves in the thick detritus of the forest floor emerged over the rush of blood in her ears and Finley felt her eyes widen and her mouth draw down in a grimace. She turned slowly, slowly, to look behind her and, indeed, there was a black-clad stranger approaching on the bridge path, astride a magnificent, inky horse.

"Oh nae," she breathed.

The stranger was at the ingress of the bridge in but a moment, reining his mount to an obedient halt. He was striking in appearance, pale, tall, his costume exquisite and perfect, as if he'd just ridden out of a true bard's own heroic song. He barely glanced at the bridge behind Finley before addressing her.

"Bonsoir, mademoiselle. Is this the bridge that leads into Carson Town?"

Finley swallowed, thinking of the body of Eachann Todde lying on the planks in plain sight, and how both she and the man astride were patently ignoring the fact of him. "Aye. It is. Who are you to be asking?"

The man gave a bow from his saddle. "Sir Lucan Montague, Knight of the Most Noble Order of the Garter of His Majesty, King Henry of England, at your service."

Finley's knees went watery.

Thankfully, the man continued to speak. "I'm surprised to find such accommodating passage. My intelligence informed me that I would scarce be able to bring my horse into the town with me; I was much concerned for Agrios's welfare."

"The bridge is new. I mean, it's been here about ten years," Finley said, the words bursting from her mouth as her tongue seemed to have caught up with her brain at last. "The Blairs built it for when the salmon run. It was little more than a plank and a rope up against the falls before that," she assured him.

The knight seemed intrigued. "I see. Well, I've an important message from London to deliver to the Carson elders. Will you allow me to pass, or am I fated to end up like that poor fellow dare I attempt it? It appears as though he's had a swim as well."

"Oh, I'm nae—" Finley stammered, gesturing behind her awkwardly, just as Eachann Todde began to groan. "He was—we were..." She looked back up at Lucan Montague, could feel the tips of her ears tingling. "Please, go on. I'm afraid I canna move him, though."

"May I assist you in that endeavor?" the knight inquired. "I could easily carry him to the town across my saddle. My horse is trained to transport the wounded."

Now Finley's entire face felt afire. "I'm sure he'll be fine." Behind her, Eachann groaned again. "This happens all the time."

"To him, or to you?" The knight stared at her without any expression whatsoever.

Finley wanted to shrivel away to nothing. "I'll manage. Thank you."

Lucan Montague's thin lips quirked. "As you wish, mademoiselle." He gave her another bow from his saddle. "Au revoir."

Finley stood aside as the English knight clucked to his mount and urged the fine beast onto the bridge. She held her breath as horse and rider came to the sprawled body of Eachann Todde, but the magnificent Agrios lifted each hoof as daintily as a woman holding her skirts aloft to tread a muddied street, and a moment later, Lucan Montague was trotting around the bend of the trail and disappeared into the wood.

The man on the bridge was rousing in earnest now, and as her temper had cooled, Finley was not at all interested in reviving her row with the toady man. Let him run to the elders and tell them all how mean and ungrateful she had been to him. Finley was sure no one would be surprised, and the sooner Eachann Todde was on his own way, the sooner she could follow the intriguing English knight to find out what sort of message would needs come to the Carson fine all the way from London.

Finley gathered her skirts and turned back to the woods, ducking behind a wide oak tree just as Eachann pulled himself up into a seated position. She peeked around the trunk, watching him raise his hand to his face, gingerly testing his nose with his fingers. She ducked down further as he raised his gaze and looked about him.

"Finley Carson!" he bellowed, and then winced and clutched his head. Finley rested her back against the trunk and closed her eyes with a sigh. All bravado aside, she would hear about this from the elders. Probably for weeks. Not a word would be said against Eachann Todde for his vulgarity and familiarity with her, of that she was certain.

She opened her eyes and turned her face slightly to the right, listening intently for footsteps on the bridge, indicating that Eachann Todde had given up and was on his way back to the town. But her eyes caught a flash of white against the tree directly across from her.

There crouched a man wearing a Blair shawl about his head and shoulders, staring at her. He raised his forefinger to his lips in silent plea in the same moment as she, and Finley opened her fingers to stifle her incredulous giggle.

In all the twenty years of her life, Finley could not recall traders venturing to this remote part of the Highlands, nor merchants by ship into their tiny bay. But in the past hour, she had met two strangers just outside town.

At last, the echoing sound of erratic stomps could be heard on the bridge, and Finley dared to lean around the trunk of the tree just as the man across from her moved slowly at a crouch to watch for himself Eachann Todde weaving down the path toward Carson Town. In a moment, there was nothing on the air but the evening cries of the birds calling their mates home.

Finley looked back to the man and was shocked to see that he was already halfway across the distance separating them. Her heart knew a moment's fear.

"You're nae supposed to be here," he said, looking down at her sternly.

"I'm nae supposed to be here?" Finley scrambled to her feet and backed away a pair of steps but then stopped; he wasn't going to get away with trying to intimidate her. "Sure, you're violating the treaty just as much as I."

"I'm nae violating the treaty until the village," he argued, correctly, much to Finley's disappointment.

"Well, what are you doing here?" she asked, her fear melting away under the building heat of curiosity. He didn't mean her harm, obviously.

The man nodded toward the bridge. "The rider. He's caused upset with the Blair fine, and I'll wager he's set to stir trouble here, too." His brown eyes bored into Finley's. "Perhaps trouble between the clans."

"Oh, and so you thought you'd just walk into Carson Town after him with your shawl wrapped about your head and expect to be welcomed?"

Finley laughed as she raised an eyebrow. "In fact, if they discover you've been in the wood alone with me..."

* * * *

"They'll likely apologize and ask after my welfare, if what I saw of the other fellow is to be believed," Lachlan taunted, but he couldn't keep the admiration from his tone. And then he, too, laughed, much to his own surprise, remembering the trollish man's clumsy and gross courting.

The girl's milky complexion pinkened even as her wispy red brows knit together. "And here I thought 'twas a dog I heard in the wood."

The droll insult only increased Lachlan's mirth. "I myself took exception to the reference of his braw loins."

Her lovely pink lips disappeared into a grim line and she threw out a slender arm toward the bridge. "They actually expect me to marry him! Can you imagine the hair of our children?" she asked with a horrified squint of her eyes.

"Och," Lachlan huffed another laugh, louder this time, unable to help the grin that seemed to have taken up permanent residence on his face. "You'd do them a mercy to toss 'em over the bridge as well."

But rather than be offended, the girl's perfect, elfin face had relaxed. She was like a fairy woman, and Lachlan couldn't look directly at her for long without the unsettling feeling in his stomach that he would be enchanted by her. Then he realized he'd done naught but stand about the wood for the last several moments, laughing and making light, and wondered if she hadn't already cast some sort of magic upon him.

"You go before me so I know the way is clear," Lachlan ordered in a gruffer tone. "I'll wait for you to gain the bend to follow."

"Aye, that's a grand idea," she said with a roll of her eyes. "I might even run ahead and warn them you're coming."

"Sure, tell them," Lachlan said. "I'd know what that English snake is about."

"Why nae simply ask your own fine?" she challenged. "Or is the legendary Blair too fearsome to be approached by a mere...what are you? Some kind of shepherd?"

Lachlan felt his ire rising at being argued with so blatantly, and by a woman, no less. And she thought him a shepherd? "Now listen here, lass—"

"I'm nae your lass, you ham-headed sawbuck," she scoffed. "And furthermore—"

Lachlan cut off her chastening as he caught the faintest sounds of hooves upon the trail. He grabbed the girl about the waist and pulled her behind the oak, covering her mouth with his hand. She promptly sank her teeth into the flesh of his palm.

Lachlan stifled his cry and thrust her upper body clear of the trunk for a heartbeat so that she might see the bridge path, then he yanked her back behind the tree. She stilled against him, her breathing shallow, rapid. He loosened his grip on her slowly, and the pair of them watched the retreat of the party in silence, Lucan Montague leading the charge.

When they were gone, the red-haired pixie looked up at him with all the solemnity she could likely muster in those clear blue eyes. "Have you still a care to carry on to Carson Town when most of the fine has just departed for your own valley?"

He stared at her for a moment, wondering what unlawful thing she'd done for her town to saddle her with such a repulsive man as a husband. Oh, well; it was no concern of his.

"Good luck to your future husband," Lachlan said, walking backward away from her with a cheeky salute. "I have a feeling he shall need it."

She watched him without reply until Lachlan was forced to turn and trot eastward once more. And yet he thought he felt her gaze on his back until he disappeared over the ridge of the valley, and the weight of the sadness that followed him was startling.

Chapter 3

The sun was melting into the dark gray horizon of the sea by the time Finley emerged from the wood into Carson Town, and the longhouses below sprawled like soldiers on a battlefield dressed in long, funereal shadows. She was later than she'd wanted to be; and because she hadn't seen her father's figure among the other elders riding toward Town Blair, she knew Da must be waiting for her to return. She hurried through the streets toward home, noting the emptiness of the alleys, the doorways already shut tight against the night, when they would normally be thrown open to the balmy spring air, so welcome after the long, dark Highland winter.

The Blair clansman had been right: The handsome English knight had brought concern to the town. The families must be all snugged around their suppers, whispering and speculating. Finley only wished she knew what about.

Rory Carson was drawing the second bucket to the rock edge of the well as Finley came up the last bit of hill toward her family's stead. She paused for a moment, observing her father's stooped posture, his gray hair poking from beneath his old knit bonnet. His hands moved deftly, but she knew if she was closer, their tremble would be apparent.

She crested the hill with long, lunging strides and picked up the first bucket from the grass as her father turned. "Why did you nae wait for me, Da?"

"Ah, Finley, there ye be," he said, a stiff smile breaking through the worried expression Finley knew he hoped she hadn't seen. He lifted the bucket from the ledge and fell into step beside her. "Nae need to rush back. Ye had a fine time with Eachann, then?"

She looked at him from the corner of her eye. "As fine as could be expected with a man such as he. He takes liberties with his words, Da."

"Aye, I feared he would. He understood yer refusal of all the younger men in the town as a sign he had a chance with ye."

Finley stopped. "More like he had nae the courage before he was near the only unmarried man left."

"He *is* the only unmarried man left, Fin."

Finley pressed her lips together. "Good. Perhaps now I'll nae longer have the fine pestering me."

Rory Carson lifted one gray brow. "Ye think because you gave Eachann Todde a swim they'll nae longer expect ye to marry at all?"

Finley tried to keep her eyes from widening, but was obviously unsuccessful, judging by her father's rueful look. "You know."

"Sure, I do." He began walking again, and Finley fell into step with him. "As do the rest of the elders. You're nae a wee girl any longer, Fin. Yer mother and I have indulged you overlong, and the fine have in turn indulged your mother and me. But I'll nae be able to take care of the farm much longer on my own."

"I can take care of the farm just fine for the three of us," Finley said with a frown. "I might not have been the son you hoped for, but there is naught I canna do that requires a man. Did I nae help you build this very wall with my own hands? Stone by stone?"

"You know I've never regretted that you were nae a lad," her father chastised, stopping beside the boundary she'd mentioned. "We always wished for more bairns, aye, but it wasna to be. And, sure, I love you enough for ten children."

"Then why can't I simply carry on here on my own, taking care of you and Mam?"

Rory sighed and filled the first trough with his bucket. "It's too much for a…it's just too much."

"For a woman, you mean? Dorcas manages her own plot," Finley said, handing her bucket to her father and then lifting her chin. "And I'm younger and stronger than she."

"Dorcas is a widow, and you know as well as I that she goes in with the others in winter. She keeps nae stock."

"I'd be a widow soon, too, were I forced to marry Eachann Todde," Finley muttered.

"Well, ye may well be forced to marry someone," Rory said, no trace of jest in his voice as he stacked the empty wooden buckets and set them on the wall. "Ye've had your pick and yet ye've nae chosen. 'Tis past time for you to settle and start your own family for the town."

The shock of it put Finley to silence for a moment. "Da—"

"You'll be spared this night, though," Rory cut her off. "There's been a visitor."

Her heart was pounding in her chest even before she picked up the fork and began throwing the last of the limp, pale winter hay into the pen for the shaggy, thin cows. "The English knight," Finley said, relieved to have the topic of conversation moved from her own failings. "I saw him."

Rory paused, the pail of meager scraps poised in his hands. "You could tell from where he hailed by his looks, could ye?"

Finley threw herself into the chore. "He asked the way to the town. That's all." She waited in silence while, behind her, her father fed the sow, heavy with the litter she would soon bear. When Finley had given the cows as much as she dared, she turned around. "Well? What did he want?"

Rory shrugged.

"Something to do with the treaty, you reckon?" she pressed, hanging up the fork. "He'd already been to Town Blair?"

Her father looked up at her with exasperation clear on his face. "Only asked the way to town, did he? What else did you get up to at the bridge, Fin?"

Finley wanted to bite off her own tongue, thinking of the brawny Blair clansman who had held her behind the tree.

"Saw Murdoch and the others heading that way," she said with a shrug of her own, and the explanation sounded weak even to her own ears.

To her surprise, he didn't press her. "Aye, well, I'm certain we'll all know the more of it come the morrow." He turned over the pail against the shed wall and held out his arm, which Finley gladly ducked under, grasping his left hand with both her own as it hung over her shoulder. He pressed a kiss to her temple.

"Let's go home, me gel."

And Finley was glad, for it was the only place she ever wanted to go.

* * * *

By the time Lachlan jogged into Town Blair, the quiet darkness of the green at night had been thrust upward by the handful of lit torches ringing the grass, the flickering light slashed by the oblong shapes of the Carsons' mounts grazing before his grandfather's door. It had taken him longer to return to the town; the way was uphill and the spring night had fallen quickly, like a cool, moist blanket dropped over the land, making for a slippery, steep climb through the wood.

His breath misted before his face as he slowed to a striding walk, and between the horses, he saw the lanky shape of Dand come away from the wall.

"Lach?" he called. "Where've you been at?"

"I followed the Englishman," Lachlan said. "He went straight to the Carsons and brought them into our town. He'll answer my questions now, whether Marcas and the rest of the fine like it or nae," he said, heading straight for the door.

Dand placed his long-limbed form between his foster brother and the entry. "He's nae here, Lach."

"I saw him, Dand. He was—"

"He must've gone on, then," Dand interrupted. "I'm telling you, the Englishman didna return." His eyes flicked to the structure behind him. "Only Carsons inside."

Lachlan felt his brows lower. "Move, Dand."

"I canna." Dand shook his head and stepped toward Lachlan, going so far as to place his hand upon Lachlan's chest. "Da said he'll call for you when—"

Lachlan swiped at Dand's forearm, causing the young man to stagger. Then he pointed at the Blair's house. "There is a room full of Carsons addressing our fine—*my fine*." He said, leaning forward to place his nose close to Dand's. "My patience for this shite has run out." He pushed the door inward and charged through.

He came chest to chest with a stranger, a red-bearded man with deep lines radiating from the corners of his eyes as if his face was usually pressed into a smile—or a grimace. But the man was definitely not smiling as he came eye to eye with Lachlan, and neither were the handful of Carsons who backed him, including the toadish poet whose clothing appeared damp yet from his rendezvous with the river.

Lachlan knew he was blocking their exit, but he would be damned if he'd give way for a flock of Carsons in the house that would soon be his own. The red-haired man obviously recognized their disadvantages of location and number, for he nodded and stepped to the side, although he did not lower his gaze or soften his expression.

Enemies since long before Lachlan was born. Why were they here?

"Lachlan."

He turned toward the fire in the center of the room and saw Marcas standing on the far side of the blaze, surrounded by men Lachlan had known all his life. They all stared at him, their faces blanched by flames. Lachlan sensed the Carsons filing out the door behind him, but he paid them no heed as he took notice of Archibald Blair lying near the fire.

His grandfather, too, watched him, and if the Blair elders' complexions were ashen, the Blair himself seemed nearly without life. His skin was the color of the peeling birch bark in the wood beyond, his eyes sunken and dark. It seemed to Lachlan that he could see all his grandfather's scalp, his white hair now thin and dark, perhaps with sweat. The sound of the door closing behind him and the presence of Dand at his side brought Lachlan's attention back to his foster father.

"I demand to know what's going on, Marcas. Why the Blair's house was full of Carsons; why I was barred from my own fine."

Marcas nodded toward the empty seat near the fire, probably only recently occupied by the red-bearded Carson who had thought himself Lachlan's equal. "Come; sit down."

Lachlan moved forward but said, "I'll stand."

"*Ye'll do...what...yer tol'!*" The whispery barks came from his grandfather, and when Lachlan looked down at Archibald, he was surprised at the sudden red in his cheeks, his eyes. His grandfather had a wild look about him now, where a moment ago there seemed to lurk only quiet, white death.

"Aye, Blair," Lachlan said in a low voice, and then eased down into the short chair, his eyes never leaving Archibald's face. His grandfather was looking at him, had spoken to him as if he were some base stranger and not his only grandchild who would soon lead their clan. Lachlan's skin tingled, his ears strained for any sound, his eyes catching the tiniest flicker of movement in the house.

"Lach," Marcas said quietly. Lachlan's foster father was sitting on the edge of his woven seat with his hands clasped loosely between his knees. "The Englishman—Montague. He brought word from London. From Tom—" He paused, seemed to collect himself. "From your father."

Lachlan stared at Marcas for a long moment. "He's lying. Tommy died at—"

"Thomas Annesley died in London," Marcas interrupted, and the bitterness in his tone curled around each syllable and squeezed it like famine. "He'd been on the run for more than thirty years, evading capture for the murder of his young bride. He was to be hanged shortly after Montague left the city."

Lachlan frowned and squinted at Marcas. "He didn't murder my mother. I may have been but a wee thing when she died, but I still have memory of her."

Marcas shook his head. "Nae Edna. 'Twas before he came here. He had come into Scotland to hide from the man he said accused him, but his enemy followed. He ventured into the Highlands to beg help from his kin."

"Why would an Englishman think a Highland clan to be of any aid to him? Especially the Blairs? He was nae kin to us. Tommy was a lowland Scot without clan." Lachlan noticed now that most of the elder men of the council were no longer looking at him. Only Harrell, Searrach's father, whose gaze bore into Lachlan's face with something akin to disgust. "He came here to prove himself worthy of Town Blair."

Marcas's wide shoulders rose and fell in silence. "He didna come seeking aid from the Blairs; Thomas Annesley's mother was from the Carsons. 'Twas Carson Town he sought."

"That's shite," Lachlan scoffed. "Are you all so gullible that—"

"It's nae shite, lad," Harrell said. "'Twas I who found him that night on the old bridge. He'd come upon us at the salmon run and spilled his guts; who he was, where he was goin'. Boastin' he was a laird. We took him back with us, so he wouldna tell his kin we were poaching the salmon. 'Twas before the treaty. And besides, Carson Town was already burnin'."

Lachlan turned his gaze back to Marcas while the fire between them danced and popped. It was the only sound in the dark longhouse while the seemingly impossible implications wheedled their way into his brain.

Thomas Annesley, Englishman. Murderer. *Carson*.

Lachlan's blood was the same as some of the men who'd only just left this house; blood of the clan he held in contempt.

"I doona see how this changes anything," Lachlan said abruptly. "Tommy was dead to us yesterday, he's just as dead today. I'm still the Blair's grandson, and when I become chief—"

"Nay," Archibald rasped. The old man's body, face, were as still as the granite cliffs; only his thin, pale lips moved. "Edna put herself on that maggot when he was my prisoner. When he died..." The old man paused, and hatred flared in his eyes. "When Edna tol' me she was with child, I tol' the town they'd married in secret. To save her honor, though there was little left to salvage."

Harrell smirked at him over the fire. "Annesley wasn't Edna's first, Lachlan. Hell, I coulda been your da."

"Fuck you, Harrell," Lachlan spat, and he started to rise.

Marcas's strong hand wrapped around Lachlan's arm, staying him, centering him.

"That gel was always trouble to me," Archibald continued on a wheeze. "That's why I gave ye over to Marcas and his wife. I wanted a proper heir at last. One with some sense. Some dignity."

The damning remarks about his mother struck Lachlan like fists. "I'm still your heir."

"Yer nae grandson o' mine," the Blair lisped, and his hollowed cheeks trembled. "I believed his death had saved us, same as everyone else. But he ran like the coward he was. And so this is how I shall pay for my lie, by at last speakin' the truth: 'Twas from a traitor's loins you sprang. Dead to me—the three of you, at last. *Dead to me.*"

Lachlan rose to his feet. "Grandfather—"

Harrell rose up and laid his palm on Archibald's pate. "That's enough, Archie. Sure, you might say something you later wish you hadna."

"Get out," Archibald commanded hoarsely, closing his eyes. "Get out and doona return. Drive you from the town, mongrel dog."

"Grandfather!" Lachlan demanded, the first real spirals of panic beginning to twist his insides, just like when he was eight and Marcas had made him ford the falls for the first time on his own. The slippery rocks, the cold, crashing water...

And there was Marcas again, taking hold of his arm. "Come on, leave it for the night, Lach," he murmured. "Give him time."

"Get out," Archibald muttered, rocking his head on his thin pallet, his eyes still squeezed shut. "Get him away."

Lachlan was in such shock that he let his foster father move him toward the door, the other men rising and following them through the longhouse. The crisp air was no longer springlike on the green, but pushed into his nostrils with the lung-searing iciness of December, and Lachlan felt the exquisite chill as Harrell stepped through the door and faced Lachlan. He knew all the eyes in the group were on him.

Cold water rushing over his head, flooding his throat, his fingers and toes numb...

Be the Blair, Lachlan.

Lachlan squared his shoulders and looked around the group. "I wasna present for the whole of what the Englishman had to say. But the words on his fancy paper mean nothing. English law doesna rule us."

"Yours is the only English blood in the town," Harrell interjected, and his gaze was cool, level. "English, and Carson. And 'tis nae the paper that has damned you as much as the Blair himself."

Lachlan clenched his teeth together. "The chief only needs time," he ground out, clinging to the words Marcas had murmured to him. "In a few days, all will be as it was. Certainly by the wedding."

But Harrell was already shaking his head. "I'll nae be shackling my daughter to a Carson's bastard."

Lachlan lunged for the man without thought, and it took both Marcas and brawny Cordon Blair to hold him back.

"Mind what you say to me, Harrell. I'm the same man I was when you promised Searrach to me. She's to be my *wife*."

"I'll say what I've a mind to, pup, and naught a word less. I could have truly been yer da but for the chief's stubbornness, and we'd be havin' none o' this now. Shame." Harrell turned back to the Blair's door. "I'll watch over him through the night, lest he take another turn." And he disappeared inside.

Lachlan shook off the hands that held him, his vision throbbing with the rage that pushed blood against his eardrums.

Cordon placed his hand on Lachlan's shoulder. "Doona worry yourself. It will all be as it should. We will raise a cup together, you and I, when you are chief, Lach."

Lachlan nodded, but he could not answer his friend.

The rest of the fine turned toward their own homes singly and in pairs, with no farewells, no calls of good night or further encouraging words for Lachlan. In a moment, only he and Marcas and Dand were left on the green before the Blair's house.

Marcas spoke first. "We'll give the Blair the night. Sure, Archibald's had a shock. I ken you're angry, Lach, and Harrell had no leave to so offend you. But we canna risk further division in the clan now that old troubles with the Carsons have risen."

"*I* canna risk, you mean?" Lachlan demanded. "That's why they came, is it nae? Whatever it was the Englishman told them, they carried grievance for it to the fine."

It was clear that Marcas was carefully weighing his response. "Aye. In part. It concerns the treaty."

"I want that message," Lachlan said, and he held out his hand. "I have a right to read with my own eyes that which has damned me."

Marcas reached into his shirt at once and withdrew the sheets of paper. But before he handed them over, he held Lachlan's gaze. "What happened all those years ago—you are to blame for none of it. I know you're a good man, Lachlan." The words sounded like a warning.

Lachlan pulled the papers from Marcas's grasp. "I'm the man you raised me to be. The man this clan raised me to be." He turned and began walking back across the green.

Dand's footfalls quickly caught up with his. "Da'll talk sense to him, you'll see. Sure, tomorrow the Blair will have thought things through differently."

But what if he doesn't think things through differently? The words ran unbidden through Lachlan's mind, and the memory of the old man's condemnation rose up before him like a specter.

Yer nae grandson o' mine...Dead to me.

Lachlan didn't know what Marcas could say that would change the Blair's sudden hatefulness toward him, even considering that Marcas was the chief's cousin.

Lachlan stopped in his tracks as the implications of the thought blossomed. If not for Lachlan, Marcas—and then Dand—would have been in line to lead Clan Blair.

"What is it, Lach?" Dand asked, looking up at Lachlan eagerly.

Does he even realize? Lachlan wondered.

"Nothing. I'll be at the store," Lachlan said. "I need to be alone for a bit."

Dand seemed to hesitate for a blink, but then nodded. "Sure. I'll see that Mam keeps some supper for you."

He doesn't realize he could be chief because he doesn't care.

Lachlan couldn't reply past the constriction in his throat, so he turned away and pushed into the storehouse, closing the door behind him. He waited there in the dark until he heard Dand's strides growing faint, and then Lachlan unlatched the clasp that held the upper and lower halves of the storehouse door together. He swung open the top half and hooked it to the wall so that it remained open, and then he turned to find the lamp on the post.

The low flame gave just enough light to illuminate the luxurious piles of fragrant hay and barrels of oats in the generous space. Lachlan moved the lantern to a post nearer a tall stack of dried grass opposite the door and then collapsed back onto it, the papers still gripped in his hand across his chest. He let his gaze go through the doorway, across the green, where the standing torches were dying, the Blair's house only the faintest suggestion of gray roofline in a blacker night.

What could these pages say that could possibly give his grandfather cause to hate him?

Icy water holding him down, his foot slipping from the rock so that he fell deeper into the churning maelstrom. He couldn't get a grip. Where was Marcas...?

Lachlan's shudder jarred him back to the warm glow of the storehouse: quiet, fragrant, safe. He carefully unfolded the pages and began to read.

13 February 1458

To Edna Blair, or if deceased, the fine of Clan Blair, especially Archibald Blair:

Dearest Edna,
I will tell straightaway that which is of dire importance: if you bore my child these score and ten years ago, you and that child—anyone of my blood—are in grave danger. Gather your things at once and leave Town Blair and tell no one where you go.
'Twas not the Carsons who attacked Town Blair...

Thomas pressed his back into the smooth bark of the tree, the dawn light illuminating the cold mist swirling along the forest floor. All around him in the thick and smoky air were the sounds of active battle: swords clanging, shouts of attack and surprise, the screams and groans of the dying. He stood in the forest between Loch Acras and the sea draped in a Blair shawl, watching for more dark shapes of men through the trees. If he removed the shawl, any Blair who happened to see him would cut him down; if he left it on, it marked him as an enemy to the Carsons. He had no friends here.

He closed his eyes for a moment and forced himself to swallow, take a deep breath. He must only think of surviving this battle, staying hidden and alive long enough to smuggle Edna and Geordie from the dying, starving town without any more bloodshed. Edna, with her dark eyes and impossibly long, brown curls; Archibald Blair's defiant daughter, who had cared for him in his captivity.

You must take me with you, *she'd panted into his ear, her small, upturned breasts like pears, her body frantic atop him while he lay chained in the* storehouse. I would take my own life rather than starve or lie beneath Harrell. Men like me. You like me. You must...

There was no help, no kin to be had for him here in the midst of these warring, bitter strangers. Edinburgh, then. The king of Scotland was his only hope.

"Thomas!"

He froze, hoping, praying that it was no more than his terrified mind playing tricks on him. No one save a handful of Blairs knew his name. "Thom...Thomas," a man gasped again. "Thomas Annesley! Please, God, help me!" he sobbed.

Thomas stepped from behind the tree and was confronted by the sight of a young man staggering up the hill toward him. His hair frizzed from his head as if he had just come from his childhood bed, the gray light of dawn rinsing it colorless. He seemed like a religious icon from the East come to life, with his pale skin and upturned gaze, petitioning the heavens for the man he sought. But it could be no angel but a martyr who searched the woods for him, for Thomas saw the lad's charred arm pressed against his flank, the wash of black blood that drenched his right side to his boots.

"Thom...as," the young man wheezed.

"Here," Thomas called. "I'm here."

The man halted, bringing his gaze slowly forward but obviously struggling to focus on Thomas's face. He wobbled on his feet and then dropped to his knees. Thomas rushed to meet him on the ground, grabbing the man by his shoulders while his head lolled.

"I am Thomas Annesley," he said. "Who are you? Where are your kin?"

"No kin here," the lad whispered, looking up at last into Thomas's face. A chill raced up Thomas's spine at the phrase he himself had thought only a moment ago. "Vaughn...Hargrave."

Thomas's blood froze. "What?"

"Came by the bay." The lad's breath clicked in his throat, and he clutched at Thomas's shirt. His mouth gaped, gasping with the effort to form words, and Thomas remembered the ball through his own lung, and how each inhalation had been all but worthless as his chest sucked air and filled with blood with each wheeze. "Looking for you. Kill everyone 'til he finds you. Kill us all. Heard him. Ships...gone."

"Why are you telling me this?" Thomas asked, forcing the words through his throat while the woods seemed to burst with sunlight. Dawn, dawn was here, and there were footfalls in the leaves.

"Thomas...Annesley," the lad whispered, and his fingers tightened on Thomas's shirt, pulling him closer. "You're...Carson. Kin." The young man gave a stifled sob. "Run. Run." The word was little more than formed air, and in the dawn light, Thomas could see the speckles of blood on the

man's gray lips. And then his eyes went vacant, still, in the morning mist, and his solid frame sagged in Thomas's arms.

Thomas laid the lad in the cold, wet leaves, staring at his face as if he could decipher some relation in the features. Kin. He turned his head to peer through the trees in the shadows that still swirled along the bottom of the hill. Vaughn Hargrave had found him again. How? Did that mean he'd also found Harriet? Meg? Was Roscraig still standing? What of his friend, Iain Douglas?

Kill everyone 'til he finds you. Kill us all.

Thomas heard the footfalls coming closer, caught the English accents on the air. If there had been any hope left in him that this was nothing more than a feuding raid between clans, the man's body before him was bitter evidence. And if what the dead man had said—and what Thomas knew of Hargrave—was true, everyone between Loch Acras and the sea was damned because of him. Thomas looked back at the young Carson, wondering that he could have been his family, could have come to know him, talk with him. They even shared similar coloring...

Kill everyone 'til he finds you.

Thomas moved without allowing himself to think of what he was doing, jerking out of the Blair shawl around his head and shoulders, lifting the young man's body to place it gently around him and tuck it into his bloodied belts. Then Thomas reached behind him to rock a stone free from the mire at the base of the tree. It was bigger than it had looked when half-buried, and heavy. He raised it above his head.

"Forgive me," *he whispered.*

He brought the rock down in the center of the man's face as hard as he could, trying to block the crunch of flesh and bone from his ears. Again he struck, and again. Until his last spare glance confirmed that there were no discernible features among the blood and bits of flayed skin and muscle. Only blond hair and a Blair shawl.

Thomas staggered to his feet, the sudden chill cutting him to the bone. He heaved the rock to the south, where it crashed down the hill.

"Up there! I heard something!"

Thomas took the lad's finely made, short sword from the leaves at his side and replaced it with the dagger given to him by his father, only returned to his possession last night by a frightened Archibald Blair. There was no other made like it, of that he was certain. And then Thomas ran north, perpendicular to the hill's rise with the coast, away from Edna Blair and Geordie-boy, away from the Carsons, away from Vaughn Hargrave.

He ran and ran and ran.

Chapter 4

Finley sat at the table near the kitchen cupboard, her elbows on the wood, her chin in her hands, staring out the open doorway toward the center of town. The sun poured down on the rounded, thatched roofs and adorned each ripple of the bay beyond with blinding white jewels, and the warm breeze swirled the dirt and straw on the floor into tiny tempests. Finley could hear the buzz of the hungry bees from her seat. The path that led up the hill to their house remained irritatingly empty. She sighed.

"D'ye want a corner?"

She started and turned her head toward the fire; she'd nearly forgotten her mother was in the room. Ina sat in a low chair near the central hearth, a long piece of fabric in her lap, the end stretched tight in her hoop. She gestured with it toward Finley. "Come busy your hands."

Finley sighed again and turned her gaze back to the door. "You'd just pick out all my stitches."

"Maybe nae." Finley could hear the smile in her mother's voice. It was no secret that Finley didn't share Ina's talent for embroidery. "I doona mind. And sure, you'll drive yourself mad going on like that. He'll be back when he's back."

"I should have been allowed," Finley grumbled. "It's me they're talking about."

"Full of yourself, are ye nae?" Ina smirked. "They've been at it all night—'tis the treaty they're discussing. They've been to the Town Blair twice in as many days. That's two times more than they've been in ten years."

"If it's only the treaty, why wouldn't Da take me?"

"Perhaps because you're nae longer six, riding his shoulders in your plaits?" Ina suggested. Then she, too, sighed and dropped her stitchery to her lap. "Finley—"

"I don't care who they choose," she interrupted. "I willna have him. I don't need a man coming in to our home and behaving as if it all belongs to him."

"But it will belong to him."

"Nay," Finley shot back. "And I am not a head of stock to be negotiated away with it."

"That's not how it is, and well you know it," her mother chastised. "You had your choice of any of the men in the town."

"Aye, all three and a half of them," Finley muttered.

"Cheek. *Your choice.* Any one of them would make a fine husband and father." She paused. "Save perhaps for Eachann Todde, but I'd hoped that'd scare some sense into you, to be threatened with one so aged."

"Well, it didn't work," Finley mumbled.

"Apparently," her mother said in an exasperated tone. "The town needs bairns if we are to survive; there arena enough young folk the way it is, as you so cleverly pointed out. You'll just have to trust your da and the fine to choose the best match for you, and do your best to be a good wife." She was quiet for a beat of time while Finley stewed at the injustice of it all. "I didna choose my first husband."

Finley looked out the corner of her eye at her mother but didn't say anything. It was rare that Ina spoke of the time before Finley was born, and she didn't want to interrupt.

"And I didna want to marry Andrew either," Ina said in a low, careful voice, her gaze going to the fabric in her lap. "He was too bold, too hottempered for the likes of me. Made me nervous," she said with a smile in her voice.

"Did you love him?" Finley asked, fascinated by the change in her mother's face, how the lines around her eyes and mouth softened as if only speaking of that time, so long ago, caused the years to melt away. She had been young once, too.

Ina nodded slowly. "Oh, sure I would have. I couldna've helped it. He made me jump whenever he walked into a room. Always had some grand idea he was thinking on. His eye on the old house. Only we called it the grand house then."

Finley felt her brows raise as the image of the blackened ruin behind the town came to her mind. "He wanted to be chief?"

"Would have," Ina said. "It was in his blood."

A movement from the corner of her eye drew Finley's attention to the doorway, shoving aside all thoughts of dead young men and ruined old houses. "Da!" She lunged from her chair and dashed through the doorway, her bare feet skimming over the cool dirt of the path.

Rory caught her beneath one arm and Finley turned to walk once more toward the house with him.

"Did you talk of the treaty?" she asked straightaway, her nerves making her breathless.

"Good day to you, too, Finley."

She grinned and reached up at the top of her next stride to kiss Rory's whiskery cheek. "Hello, Da. I've kept the cakes warm for you." He squeezed her hand. She couldn't help herself, though. "*Did* you talk of the treaty?"

"Aye. We did."

Finley sighed to herself in relief. "Nothing about me, then."

"Aye. We did."

Finley's feet dragged to a halt. "Da?"

"It's been decided, Fin," he said, and it was only then she noticed her father's haggard expression, beyond fatigue from being kept at council all night, the hardness in his normally gentle eyes. "You may well be pleased. I am pleased."

"You don't look pleased," Finley argued as fear bloomed in her stomach. "Who is it?"

Rory dropped his head and turned toward the house, his arm pulling behind him, still in Finley's grasp. "Come inside. There's much to tell, and I'd have your mother know before I return to the storehouse for our share."

"Our share of what?" Finely demanded. "Da!"

But he pulled free of her fingertips without looking at her again, and Finley was left standing on the path alone while her father's stooped form disappeared into the darkness of the house. Her eyes were drawn up over the rooftop to the crumbling stone of the old house, carved from the steep cliff that sheltered their bay. The afternoon sunlight poured into its roofless depths, casting sawtoothed shadows through blackened, empty windows.

He could have been chief. Mam's husband could have been the Carson, if the Blairs hadn't killed him. Mam could, right now, be living in the old house.

Nay, the grand house, Finley corrected herself. It was grand once. Their town had been grand once, too.

For some reason, memory of the Blair who had been spying on the English knight near the bridge came to her mind, and she wondered if he was proud of what his clan had done—felt pride at that terrible massacre.

He was older than Finley, but still too young to have lived through that bloody time.

She shrugged it off. It did no good to be bitter. Finley hadn't ever known Carson Town to be anything other than what it was. And she didn't expect it to ever change. Even if her own life was about to.

She took a deep breath, squared her shoulders, and walked into the house.

* * * *

Lachlan came awake with a start, his breath hanging around him in a cloud. It was just morning, the light through the storehouse door faint and gray, the green sparkling black and frosty white. The lamp had gone out , and although Lachlan was sunk into the pile of hay that had been his bed through the night, the tip of his nose and his feet felt frozen through.

The air was silent, crystalline, like the skin of ice on the loch in first winter. What had woken him so abruptly?

He sat up fully and blinked in the shadows, the pages of Thomas Annesley's confession sliding to the floor. Then he noticed that something was different across the green: The Blair's door was open, the interior still dark.

But there—there was a wash of orange light, like a torch being swung. There it was again, only steady now, and growing larger. A man walked out: Harrell, carrying a lamp. And another man, with white hair. Archibald, so soon recovered?

Nay, 'twas Marcas, a bundle clutched in his hand. Harrell turned toward the Blair's house and held the lamp higher while Marcas strode to the wall. Lachlan saw the hammering motions before he heard the ricocheting barks across the green. In a moment, Marcas stepped away from the longhouse, and let what appeared to be some sort of banner or cloth hang free where it was suspended.

Archibald's shawl.

Lachlan gathered the fallen papers into his fist, then pushed himself to his feet and walked toward the half-open storehouse door as if in a dream. He struggled blindly with the latch, not daring to take his eyes from the dingy fabric fluttering in the weak dawn light, then emerged onto the green just as Harrell and Marcas turned. Lachlan strode forward in starts and jerks, and all around him the sounds of doors scraping open echoed over the green. He walked on toward that thin length of shawl as if entranced.

Yer nae grandson o' mine...
From a traitor's loins you sprang...
Dead to me...

He passed between Marcas and Harrell to stand before the Blair's shawl, and he stared at it as if he'd never seen the thing before, instead of having set eyes upon it every day of his living memory.

The Blair was dead.

Movement to his right drew his attention, and a line of townswomen were filing solemnly through the Blair's door, one of them his own foster mother, carrying lengths of cloth.

The winding sheets. Because the Blair was dead. Lachlan's grandfather was dead.

Yer nae grandson o' mine...

His breath caught painfully in his throat.

Neither of the men behind him broke the silence, and Lachlan knew why: There was naught they could say. Archibald Blair was dead, and he had disowned his only grandson before the entire fine just before he'd died. There would be no reconciliation, no time to think things through differently. His damnation of Lachlan was eternal.

A rumbling sound, like many hooves, vibrated in the air, and Lachlan turned in the same moment as Marcas and Harrell to behold the group of riders just coming onto the green. They stopped at the far side of the pitch, the mist from the forest seeming to have followed them through the wood to swirl around the feet of their mounts.

Carsons. And they were armed.

The red-bearded man Lachlan had confronted just last night urged his mount forward. "We've come to collect our due."

Lachlan swung his gaze to Marcas, whose expression was stony as, behind them both, Harrell addressed the man. "The Blair is dead, Murdoch. You'll have to wait."

"We have waited long enough!" Murdoch Carson bellowed. His words echoed in the valley, and birds were stirred from their treetop nests. The green was now crowded with townsfolk, wide-eyed and pale, watching the Carson chief with wariness, but the man kept his own gaze locked on Lachlan's foster father. "I demand a council. Now," Murdoch said. "This will be settled before my men depart, lest you wish more Blair lives lost this day beyond that of your thieving chief."

Lachlan and Harrell both drew their daggers at once, and the ringing of steel echoed on the green as the riders followed suit, with sword and dagger of their own.

"We'll fall upon ye like rats," Harrell warned. "Nary one o' ye left in whole-piece before my eyes can blink."

Marcas stepped between them all, his arms outstretched, turning in a slow circle. "Nay!" he shouted. "There will be no bloodshed this day. God damn whoever dares it!" He flung his arm toward Archibald's shawl, fluttering like a rag on the wall, and looked back to Murdoch. "We can call no fine until the new chief is named."

"Then name him and be done with it," Murdoch said, and to Lachlan's ears it sounded almost like a challenge. "Is it such a mystery? Everyone along the western coast knows the Blair's heir is his grandson. You will have no quarter from me for your games."

Marcas turned his head to look into Lachlan's eyes, and hope rose inside him. Lachlan stepped toward his foster father, his words coming out low and rushed.

"He's right, Marcas. I have always been the heir. I—"

Harrell thrust into the conversation. "He disowned ye, lad. Everyone heard it. And there was nae repentance from him in the night, of that I can attest."

"And I'm to take your word, am I? He wasn't in his right mind," Lachlan argued. "That English bastard, Montague—"

"Had naught to do with what yer father did thirty years ago," Harrell interrupted. "Ye hold the proof of it in yer own hand." He looked to Marcas. "The fine willna stand for it, Marcas. Ye know what has to be done, well as I."

Lachlan locked eyes with his foster father, feeling the morning air cut through his shirt like the icy waters of the Keltie, the pendulous weight of his future pulling him down just as surely as water over the falls. He could still see his grandfather's shawl on the side of the house from the corner of his eye. All he needed do was pull it down and claim it.

Marcas must have read his thoughts. "Lachlan—"

"*It's mine,*" Lachlan ground out.

Murdoch's voice rang out over the green. "As chief of the Carsons, I demand council with the Blair!" His gaze was a weighty thing on Lachlan, taunting him.

The tension between Lachlan and Marcas vibrated, and as Lachlan glanced again at the fluttering scrap of fabric, Harrell called out his own warning. "Marcas…"

Lachlan and his foster father turned toward the house in the same moment, and in hindsight, Lachlan knew he could have reached the plaid before Marcas, could even have taken it from the older man by force if he'd so chosen; fought him for it and bested him. But there had been a part of him that had thought—had hoped—that Marcas was only taking hold of the shawl in order to hand it to Lachlan with his blessing. The fine would listen to Marcas.

But the gray-haired man, the only father Lachlan had ever known, yanked the long sheet from the wall, ripping the corners from the nails and whipping it through the air. He held it in his right fist, the ragged ends now dragging in the mud as he met Lachlan's gaze.

"Marcas," Lachlan whispered to him, a quiet plea.

Marcas drew the shawl through his fists, length by length, until it dangled evenly between his two hands. Then he raised it slowly, dropping it over his own left shoulder, tucking both ends over his right hip beneath his belt.

"It's the law, Lachlan," Marcas said.

No blade delivered to Lachlan's heart could have wounded him more, and he felt the physical shudder in his chest.

It was over now. Marcas had sealed his fate.

Lachlan's foster father turned back to the group of Carsons, who weren't bothering to hide their surprised and intrigued expressions.

"The council between the clans shall gather in peace at my own house while the old chief is prepared for the funeral," Marcas called out for the benefit of the entire green, including the townspeople, who seemed frozen into place with wide eyes. He turned his head slightly over his shoulder to address Lachlan but didn't quite meet his eyes.

"Dand needs be told. I didna wish to rouse him until I knew for certain the Blair was dead. I'll meet you both there."

Each pounding beat of Lachlan's heart was like a blow. Now he was Marcas's runner? And Dand's, too, he reckoned. The chief, and the chief's heir.

It was Harrell who objected, though. "Lachlan's nae right to be present, and ye know he'll nae leave once he's there." Harrell tossed him a spiteful look. "Want to be sure of hearing everything that doesna concern him."

"Lachlan is welcome to stay," Marcas said. "It is my house and it is still his home."

"He canna address the fine," Harrell argued.

"I will decide who will and willna speak, Harrell," Marcas said, and although his voice was low and even, it was very clear that Marcas had had enough of Harrell's interference. "You demanded law, and so you shall have it. I am the law." He dropped his eyes to near Lachlan's boots again. "Will you go or nay?"

Lachlan wanted to refuse. But he could think of no other way in the moment to escape the hundreds of Blair eyes still watching him, the scrutiny of the Carsons. He buffeted through both Harrell and Marcas, striding across the green, careful to keep his eyes forward.

He pushed open the door of Marcas's house—the house he had grown up in—and was surprised to find Searrach sitting at the table. She rose immediately, and her brown eyes were startled, wary.

"Lachlan," she said, a quaver in her voice. "Is it true? Da would tell me nothing."

He took a brief moment to observe her—her dark hair, her rounded, womanly shape. Normally, the sight of Searrach could cause Lachlan to forget all thoughts besides taking her to bed. But in that moment, it was as if all desire for her had vanished; what need had he for physical distraction when his soul lay dead on the green?

"Aye," Lachlan said with a nod. "Archibald is dead. You have to go. There is to be a council with the Carsons. Here. Now."

"Oh, thank God." Searrach placed a hand on the tabletop and seemed to sag there for a moment in a strange show of relief. Then she rushed across the floor to throw herself into Lachlan's hesitant embrace. "Last night Da said you would never be chief. I'm so glad that—"

"It's Marcas," Lachlan interrupted, staring over her head at the wall.

He sensed her raising her face to look at him, and he could hear the confusion in her voice. "What?"

Lachlan's jaw felt made of granite. "Marcas is chief now. I've only come to rouse Dand."

Searrach stepped away from him abruptly, her features pulled together to the center of her face in confusion.

"You should go," Lachlan said, and turned away to walk to the door set in the partition wall. "I'm sure your father wouldna want you here alone with me." He pushed open the door and stepped inside the sleeping chamber, shutting out the woman still standing in the main room.

Dand was sprawled on his back on the wooden bed, his unruly hair standing from his head like a thistle bloom. The room was dim, owing to the small, high set windows. Lachlan walked to the side of the bed and stood for a moment, looking down at his younger brother. The heaviness of the moment fell upon him; just as with Marcas, with Searrach, nothing would ever be the same between him and Dand as soon as his brother awoke.

Lachlan's breath caught painfully in his throat for the second time that young day. He wanted to sit on the edge of the matching bedstead and put his head in his hands. Instead, he kicked the rail at Dand's feet.

"Huh?" Dand raised up his head and blinked at Lachlan, then promptly rolled to face the wall, pulling the blanket over him completely as he curled up in a ball.

"Get up," Lachlan said. "Marcas wants you."

Dand mumbled and squirmed beneath the covers.

"Archibald's dead," Lachlan said abruptly. "The Carsons are here, demanding council."

The tumbling beneath the blankets ceased, and then the coverings were thrown off as Dand sat up. "Do we fight?" he asked, wincing at the dim light. Lachlan started to shake his head, but then stopped. "I don't know. Not yet."

It only took the young man moments to dress, but they both heard the commotion in the next room well before they opened the door again. The house was packed with men, many wearing red, bushy beards. They sat on the low chairs, on the floor, at the table near where Marcas and Harrell stood; they lined the walls. There were even Carsons half in, half out of the doorway. Dand walked through first, and all eyes in the room went to him, and then over his shoulder to where Lachlan stood. The silence was loud.

Searrach had not heeded Lachlan's directive to leave, and his heart gave a hopeful twitch as she now weaved her wide hips through the tight crowd toward where Lachlan stood, bearing a mug and plate of food in her hands. At least someone was still on his side.

"Good morning," she said with a bright smile and handed the mug and plate to Dand. Her words seemed clear enough to be heard all the way to Glasgow. "I've kept you a place at the table next to your father."

Dand took the offered sustenance and glanced over his shoulder at Lachlan, who only stared straight ahead, willing himself to show no reaction.

"Let's get down to it, then," Marcas called out, at last drawing the attention away from Lachlan. "Murdoch, what is it you have so rudely come demanding on the day our clan has lost its leader?"

"So rudely come, have we?" the red-haired Carson queried. "I've never had use for Archibald Blair the whole of my life, and I've no shame in saying 'tis glad I am that he's at last dead. Rotting in hell is my hope."

The room erupted in shouts, some of the men rising and facing their clan's enemies, shoving, stumbling.

"That's enough!" Marcas shouted. "I'll nae ask you again, Murdoch."

"Verra well," the Carson man acquiesced. "We've come to dissolve the old treaty. There will be no more trespass on Carson lands—west of the falls and bridge—ever again. Guards have been set, with orders to cut down any Blair who comes in sight."

The room was tomb silent again.

"Our town depends on the river, Murdoch," Marcas said levelly. "There's a reason the waters here are named Starving Lake."

"Aye, and it's starving you were before your clan stole everything the Carsons had, tricked us into giving you rights to our bounty." Murdoch rose. "It was we who used to have the plenty. We who prospered. We havena had fodder enough to keep our sheep alive for years!" His men sounded their agreement.

"You cheated us," Murdoch continued. "Archibald Blair cheated us. And now that he's dead and we know the truth, it is up to you, *Blair*, to set things right." Murdoch paused. "We Carsons arena unreasonable people. Unmerciful people. We only want back what we have lost. And once we have gained that, we are willing to grant Town Blair two days of the run."

"Two days to harvest salmon enough to last all the year?" Harrell exclaimed. "That's nae en—"

"Two days, or none at all," Murdoch pressed.

Marcas stared at the man without expression. "What else?"

Murdoch set his mouth. "Half your stores now, and half your grazing in all the green months." He sat down while, again, the room erupted.

After Harrell had succeeded in calling everyone to order, Marcas challenged quietly, "And if we do not agree?"

Murdoch shrugged. "War, again."

Harrell laughed and looked about the room. "With this spindly lot of a dozen? I fear they might faint just from smelling my fair Searrach's cakes."

Murdoch Carson's mouth quirked. "Spindly we may be at the moment. But it's nae only a dozen of us come. I left a score of our men in the wood just at the edge of town. By now they've surrounded the Blair's house and the store as well. With torches. Should they see signs from our man over there"—here, Murdoch nodded toward the Carson standing in the doorway—"we'll fire the lot of them. Burn your town to the ground, just as ours was burned."

"Our wives are in the Blair's house, preparing him for burial," Marcas growled.

Murdoch nodded. "And I thank you for that added leverage, Marcas."

There was dark murder in Marcas's glare. "Should we agree to your demands today, you simply go away?"

"Nay," Murdoch said. "It's a new treaty I'm proposing. Our clans will at last live in peace together. Fairly. We share the resources, after we have recovered what belongs to us." He turned in his chair to look over his shoulder at Lachlan, and all eyes fell on him once more.

"*Everything* that belongs to us, I'm thinking."

Chapter 5

Finley sat uneasy in her saddle; the roar of the falls, while easily drowning out the raucous springtime calls from the birds, did nothing to quiet the revelry of the wedding party surrounding her. There were at least one hundred Carsons—most of the town—clogging the path after the bridge. Only Finley, her mother and father, and the clan elders had the privilege of riding. And, of course, Finley's maid of honor, Kirsten.

All the unmarried lasses in Carson Town had begun vying for the coveted spot at Finley's side when she married almost in the same moment that Finley herself had learned she would wed. Everyone had heard tales of the fearless, bonny Lachlan Blair, and all the little Carson girls had for years admired his escapades and fantasized about his daring and appearance beyond earshot of their parents. So Finley had no shortage of volunteers—even those with whom she shared a mutual dislike were eager to ingratiate themselves to be chosen. The feud was over, after all, and there were men at the Town Blair.

Finley had chosen meek, diminutive, blonde Kirsten Carson not only because she was the least obnoxious of the lot of them, but because Kirsten was really the only girl who'd cared to be friends with Finley since they'd both been small. And Kirsten seemed genuinely happy for Finley that she would marry, even if Finley herself was not so sure.

Lachlan Blair, the man who was once a daring legend slated to become a chief, was now nothing more than a disgraced, half-English bastard being sacrificed by his own people, if the rumors Finley had heard were true. But if the rumors were indeed true, Lachlan Blair also somehow had Carson blood in his veins.

She wondered how eager he was to marry her, what he looked like. Her thoughts went again to the Blair clansman she'd met in almost this very spot; no giant, as Lachlan Blair was rumored to be, but he'd been strong. Handsome in a gruff, careless way. He'd had a finely shaped mouth, a quick laugh, and a spark in his eye.

The crash of hooves sounded from up the hill, and a rider emerged at the crest of the path: a Carson man who had gone ahead to witness the burial of Archibald Blair, dead now these past seven days. Only once the funeral had concluded and all the trappings were hidden away in the Town Blair could the wedding party proceed. The man raised an arm high and gave a broad wave, and the townspeople answered with a cheer.

There would be a wedding.

Finley's father reached across and took hold of her horse's reins, prompting the mount to move forward over the bridge. Her mother was on Finley's left, the bride cake carefully wrapped in cloth and held at the front of her saddle. Ina looked over at Finley with a proud smile as they traveled slowly up the hill, and Finley thought she must be admiring the pale gown she and the other Carson mothers had worked on so diligently, day and night, for seven days.

"You look beautiful, lass," she said.

Finley knew she had never been a beautiful lass. A capable lass, a strong-willed lass, a lass with a quick tongue and a penchant for rows. But never beautiful like fair Kirsten, even in such a fine gown as she had ever worn, with her red curls piled up twice as high as her own head, sprigs of new, woody heather studding the twists.

She felt her cheeks heat and muttered, "I think I need a wee."

Ina laughed. "It's only nerves."

"It's the mug of cider I drank," Finley argued. *Two mugs*, she silently amended.

"We'll be there soon."

Soon was relative, for it took the better part of an hour for the procession to scale the wooded slope. The singing continued until Rory Carson led his family beyond the fringe of the wood to stop at Murdoch's side, where the path wound on through the furthermost dwellings of Town Blair. Rory paused there, still holding the reins of Finley's horse. A young lad of perhaps eight years, barefoot and curly haired, was stationed at the rear wall of the cottage nearest the path, and upon catching sight of the Carson party, he sprinted up the path toward the center of town.

Without command, the Carson fine rose up through the crowd to flank the wedding party on either side. The revelers grew suddenly solemn, and Finley realized in that moment that this journey—this ceremony—was a bigger risk than anyone had dared admit aloud to this moment. Once the procession entered the town, they would all be vulnerable to attack.

She could be dead before she ever laid eyes on the mythical Lachlan Blair. But Murdoch nodded to Finley's father, and Rory clucked to his horse, moving himself and Finley to the fore of the group, the Carson warriors escorting them.

Finley was soon distracted from her ominous misgivings as they entered the town proper; the longhouses here were wide, their thick walls cracked from the long winter, but none crumbled. The roofs were so well rounded with thatch that each one appeared a little hillock in and of itself, smoke curling luxuriously from their centers. Shutters were straight and in good repair; implements and tools hung along wooden braces, gleaming and sharp; dooryards were swept clean around sturdy benches and troughs; posts held torches or little pots of new, trailing vines. A cow lowed from somewhere beyond the rooftops and was answered in kind from the other direction. Softly clucking chickens; pigs and cats and goats with fresh, spindly kids roamed the alleys, bright and sleek and completely unconcerned with the large party stirring up dust as they moved along toward the center of their town.

Finley realized she was frowning at the clear signs of prosperity around her, so at odds with the state of her own home just beyond the falls. It was like being in a foreign land.

The maze of longhouses opened up at last to a wide green in the center of the town. To the right was a long structure studded with half doors, golden hay spilling out of the farthest openings; the fabled Blair storehouse, rumored to hold enough grain to last three towns five years. To the left lay the largest longhouse Finley had ever seen, but unlike the others she'd passed, this one was shuttered tight, with no potted herbs, no torch at the post poised for lighting. It was a dark, startling shape in the otherwise verdant tableau, like the space from a knocked-out tooth in a pretty girl's smiling mouth.

Archibald Blair's house, she guessed. As dark as any grave he now lay in.

Directly across the green from where the wedding party approached was a small, square structure, built not in the old Highland fashion, but of bright, new wood and stone above the ground, with a stone roof and a timbered cross at its peak. Town Blair even had a proper chapel. And it was before this holy, set-apart building that the unsmiling population of Town Blair was gathered, in stark contrast to the lively Carson group that had departed from the falls bridge.

The wedding party paused at the edge of the green, staring across the quietly grazing sheep, the wide, stone well. The sea breeze was only hinted at here, but the gulls wheeled overhead, their mournful calls sounding as if they were still under the impression that the crowd below was in attendance of a funeral. Beyond the seabirds' haunting cries, though, the green of Town Blair was absolutely quiet.

The crowd before the chapel parted as if made of two waves, drawing back to reveal a set of shallow stone steps leading up to the closed door. Before those steps stood a quintet of people: four men and a woman. One of them, Finley knew, must be Lachlan Blair. Her horse moved forward suddenly, causing her to grab at the front of the saddle. Finley studied the faces as she drew near: the friar in his long, brown robe—no, that wasn't him. The older man with his handsome gray plait—that was Marcas Blair, the new chief. The woman—long and angular and gray—must be the Blair's wife. A younger man with wild red hair, his sweetly solemn face coming into focus. She supposed it could be him. But—

Finley felt her mouth drop open as the final man in the group became clear, his rich brown hair, which had been pulled into a queue beneath his shawl a week ago now flowed around his shoulders, his short beard neatly groomed around his full mouth, which she knew housed straight, white teeth when he grinned. His brown eyes, stern in one moment, sparking with mirth the next, were fixed somewhere over the crowd.

Good luck to your future husband...

Her horse came to a halt, and the pinch-faced Blair woman stepped forward, her hands clasped stingily at her waist as she approached Ina's horse.

"Welcome to you, Ina Carson," the woman said, although her monotone belied the sentiment.

"God's blessing upon you, Mother Blair," Ina replied, her voice soft and conveying a genuineness of sentiment behind her words. She handed down the cloth-wrapped bride cake, clasped reverently in both hands. "May the years bring much prosperity to both our beloved children, with the joy of many bairns to add to our shared wealth."

The woman took the bread and did not return Ina's smile. "He isna my child." She gave a stiff nod and returned to her place before the chapel.

Finley's gaze went once more to the steps as the gray-haired man stepped forward. Murdoch dismounted, and the two clan chiefs met with a loud clasp of hands. They stared into each other's faces for what seemed to Finley to be half an eternity.

Marcas Blair spoke first. "Peace, Carson."

"Aye," Murdoch answered. "Peace. Today shall see a final end to our feud."

The Blair nodded. "End to it. I welcome you and your people." The chiefs parted, and Finley's stomach did a neat flip as Marcas Blair turned his steely eyes up to her father. "Rory Carson, we are well met."

Rory nodded. "Blair, I give my daughter in good faith."

"And you shall take the one as much son to me as my other, and your people shall welcome him?"

Rory nodded. "Aye." He reached up to the folds in his shawl and unclasped one of his brooches and then at last turned to Finley, offering it to her in his palm.

She looked from the silver brooch to her father's eyes, noticing the different air about him. Today, he was not just her father, stooped, aging; he was a Carson elder, negotiating an historic treaty to a generations-old war.

"We'll be back at home soon, lass," he whispered. There he was—her father again. He gestured with his hand. "Take it."

Finley took the warmed metal into her fist and turned in time to see Marcas Blair removing a brooch from his own, worn shawl. Finley held her breath as he walked toward the pair of young men.

"Lachlan," he said in a soft voice. "You have the blessing of your clan on this happy day, with wishes of a long and fruitful union with your wife."

Finley's stomach clenched as the man from the forest snatched the brooch from Marcas Blair. It was *him*. Her skin prickled, her stomach fluttered.

"Which clan would that be, Marcas?" Lachlan Blair said in a low voice through clenched teeth.

Then Rory was at her knee. Finley hadn't noticed him dismounting, so entranced had she been by Lachlan Blair. Her father helped her slide from the horse and then held her hand as he escorted her to the steps of the chapel where Kirsten was somehow already waiting. The friar had ascended to the threshold, and Lachlan Blair now stood on the topmost step. He stared over the green once again, refusing to meet anyone's eyes, including Finley's.

If he recognized her from their meeting at the bridge, he certainly wasn't letting on.

Finley swallowed as her father leaned in to press a kiss to her cheek, and then pulled his fingers from her tight grasp. She must walk to him on her own, a willing bride. But even knowing her future husband had turned out to be the man from the forest—fancied in her thoughts many times over since their strange encounter—did not make the journey easier. Finley now stood alone at the foot of the steps, the edge of the brooch digging into her palm. It took every ounce of her pride, her strong will, to command her legs to mount the steps.

At last she stood before Lachlan Blair and, setting her jaw, she raised her eyes to look up into his face.

He looked at her coolly for a moment, and then his brows rose slightly.

"It's you," he said.

An oddly pleasant wave of gooseflesh rushed over Finley's arms. He simply hadn't recognized her. "Surprised?"

"Aye." Lachlan huffed a laugh and raised his face to the sky for a moment. "I should have known."

Finley felt an unexpected grin tugging at her mouth. Maybe—just maybe—today wouldn't be the worst day of her life after all. She heard Kirsten give a dreamy sigh behind her.

Lachlan dropped his gaze back to hers. "Of course they shackle me to the only woman in Carson Town no one else wanted." He chuckled again, but there was no mirth in his tone.

The flesh of her face seemed to freeze, humiliation rising up in her like nausea. She forced it down her throat by swallowing hard. "I would have looked kindlier upon Eachann Todde had I known the alternative I would soon face."

The smile dropped from his full mouth. "More winsome is your poet, now?"

"Winsome? Nay. But he's nae half-English bastard being turned out for a disgrace."

Lachlan's face darkened, his shoulders stiffened.

Finley lifted her chin.

The friar cleared his throat. "Shall we begin?"

"Hellion," Lachlan growled.

Finley narrowed her eyes at him. "Fraud."

"Lachlan Blair," the friar called out cheerfully, "do you swear to take this woman, Finley Carson, as your wife?"

He turned to the holy man. "Nay."

The friar stuttered and harrumphed as a murmur of confusion and alarm swept over the crowd gathered on the green. Clomping footfalls heralded Marcas Blair's arrival on the chapel's threshold, and he pulled Lachlan back roughly.

Finley felt as though her very head would burst into flames at any moment. Kirsten reached out to squeeze Finley's arm reassuringly, but Finley shook her off. She had never felt such shame in her life—not even when, at ten and two, she had slipped from the roof peak of the storehouse and been caught on the hoist upside down, her skirts around her head. It had taken the better part of an hour to get her safely down, but it seemed as if she'd been standing before the chapel doors for days.

The two Blair men were arguing in hushed tones—at least, Marcas Blair's tone was hushed.

"I willna," Lachlan said, shaking his head at the older man, who was clearly attempting to persuade him. Then Lachlan leaned his nose close to the Blair's. *"Turn me out, then.* I'd rather die alone in the wood than be shackled to her. She'll likely kill me in my sleep, any matter."

The murmurings in the crowd exploded into contentious rumbles, and Finley turned on her heel and swept down the steps, swerving around her father at the bottom.

He caught her arms, preventing her from reaching her horse. "Finley, wait," Rory pleaded in a low tone. "'Tis a difficult thing for the both of you."

"I'll not be spoken of in such a manner," Finely said. "On my wedding day. *By the man who is to be my husband.* He clearly doesna want me."

"Do you want him?"

"Of course not!"

"Then you are well matched," Rory said with a stern look.

"He refused me, Da," she said through clenched teeth. "I'll not stand up there like a dog begging for his scraps when I never wanted this at the very first. You heard him—he'd rather die in the wood than be married to me."

Marcas Blair's voice rang out. "He didna mean that."

Finley looked over her shoulder toward the chapel door. Lachlan Blair was glaring at her.

"Did you mean it?" she challenged.

"Every word," he said.

Finley whipped her head around to regard her father. But before he could say anything, Murdoch Carson stepped forward once more.

"Marcas," he called out in a voice full of warning. "Have you summoned us here only to tempt our charity? I'll nae have this good family further insulted. If its injury you wish to bring upon us this day, you shall have it returned to you in kind."

"Forgive my son, Murdoch," the Blair said calmly. "He is only overcome by nerves at Miss Carson's gentle beauty."

Lachlan barked a laugh. "'Tis the Blairs you insult with this viper. I watched her throw a man from the bridge! I'd sooner bed a hornet's nest."

Finley looked accusingly at her father and muttered through her clenched teeth, "Did someone tell him about the hornet's nest I put in Dove Douglas's bed? Because, otherwise, I'm insulted."

Her father leaned in to hiss, "Why on God's earth would we want anyone else to know of that?" He looked to the Carson chief. "Murdoch?" he said pointedly.

But all eyes went back to the chapel steps, where the young redheaded man had pulled away from a voluptuous brunette woman and was striding toward the doors. Lachlan at first shook off the lad, much as Finley had done with Kirsten, but the interloper was relentless, putting himself nose to nose with the larger man, speaking quickly. He finished whatever he had to say with a punch to Lachlan's sternum.

The green was silent with expectation while Lachlan turned furious, resentful eyes to Finley. "I. *Apologize*," he ground out.

Her father was shepherding her to the steps once more. "See there? All better. Now, go," he whispered. "For the clan, Fin."

Finley jerked her arm away from her father, stinging tears welling up in her eyes. She didn't know what the red-haired man had said to Lachlan Blair, but it had obviously made an impact.

"Doona touch me," she warned Kirsten as she reached the threshold once more. Kirsten reclasped her hands meekly at her waist.

There was no pretense between them now as Finley once more stood facing Lachlan. Her teeth hurt at being ground together so firmly, and her stomach was a hot knot of fury.

The red-cheeked friar cleared his throat again and shone forth a ridiculous smile. "Now, then. As I said, Lachlan Blair, do you swear to take this woman, Finley Carson, as your wife?"

He glared at her for an interminable moment, and Finley thought she understood the true reason her father had been so insistent that she not wear her dagger at her waist.

"Aye," he snapped.

The friar squirmed. "You must say, 'I swe—'"

"I swear," Lachlan amended.

"Very good," the friar said with a sigh and a nervous chuckle. He cleared his throat again and turned, and Finley saw his enthusiastic smile from the corner of her eye as she matched Lachlan Blair's glare with one of her own. "Finley Carson, do you swear to take this man, Lachlan Blair, as your husband?"

Her jaws felt frozen shut. No matter that she commanded them to open, they would not.

Lachlan Blair's glower increased and his lips barely moved when he spoke. "If you say nay just to spite me, I'll—"

"Touch me and I'll turn your cock into crab bait," Finley said through her own teeth. Her eyes never left his face as she said louder. "*I swear.*" And she raised her eyebrows at him.

"Very good," the priest said on another sigh. "Your pledges?"

Lachlan stepped forward, producing the brooch given him by Marcas Blair. He pinned it to Finley's shawl with such a light touch that, had she not been watching his every move with her own eyes, she might not have known he'd left it.

Then Finley took her father's clasp and affixed it to Lachlan Blair's costume. She considered for a moment running the long, sharp pin into his chest, and perhaps Lachlan had expected it, for his shoulders relaxed as she stepped away from him.

"Lachlan and Finley," the friar said, and then drew a deep breath. "In-so-much-that-you-have-given-yourselves-to-each-other-and-to-your-clans-I-proclaim-that-you-are-now-wed-and-all-shall-acknowledge-you-as-husband-and-wife-from-this-day-forward." The friar gasped a breath and then paused, looking over the crowd with an expression akin to surprised jubilation. He held up his hands. "The clans are joined!"

There was a hesitant pause, and then shouts rang out over the green, and Finley turned to see Blairs and Carsons greeting each other cautiously, some shaking hands. The gravity of what had happened—and her role in it—began to dawn on her.

The clans were joined.

"Now," the friar said more quietly, leaning toward Finley and Lachlan, "we shall go in and bless this union before God in the taking of the Eucharist. And there shall be no violence from either of you. And no cursing," he added quickly. "I am more than ready, God willing, to depart from this place before there are any more funerals to keep me here. Follow me." He turned and opened the door, disappearing inside the darkened chapel.

Finley looked up at Lachlan, her whole being still filled with resentment for how he had humiliated her. But now he was watching her with a curious expression.

"This was not the wedding day I expected," he said. "And I feel that there is aught left woefully unsaid."

She wanted to believe he was remorseful, but there was a glint in his eyes that made her uneasy. And so she only nodded.

His white teeth flashed in his beard. "*Your hair is like the dawn; your eyes, a gentle fawn's...*"

"I hate you," she muttered, and made sure to tread on his foot as she turned and marched into the darkness of the chapel as if entering into a great battle. She was not heartened by the dark laugh he gave as he pursued her.

Chapter 6

The green was once more ringed with torchlight, but this time the wide circle contained a sphere of merriment and celebration as the two clans drank and danced and sang late into the night. Lachlan sat alone at the bridal table at the head of the inner circle, his elbows on the planks, a tankard in his hands that seemed to magically fill each time he emptied it. Well, he was alone save for the redheaded shrew on his left, to whom he paid no heed, choosing instead to watch the revelers twirl and spin across the green, appearing to possess a happiness Lachlan himself feared he would never again come close to. Thankfully, his new bride had just as much to say to Lachlan as he had to her.

He caught sight of Dand across the way, particularly immersed in quiet conversation with the diminutive blonde Carson woman, much to the apparent chagrin of Searrach, who also sat alone at a nearby table and glared at the pair. Apparently, Searrach's loyalty was to the future chief of the Blair clan only. Lachlan's insides burned, both with envy and resentment.

Sudden movement on his left reluctantly drew his attention, and he turned his head to look up at Finley Carson, now standing.

"I'm going home," she said. There were little shadows under her eyes, and her fairy face was pale and small with sadness.

"Follow along after you like a pup, shall I?" Lachlan shot at her, a little surprised at the comfortable slur in his words. He'd gotten properly drunk and hadn't even realized it. "Or maybe you're just eager for the wedding night, eh? Hoping I'll get a babe on you before you bite my head off and eat me." He purposefully let his gaze rove over her body.

Her expression didn't change and she said nothing, only turned from the table and disappeared into the darkness beyond the green.

But others must have been watching for her to leave, for now raucous masculine shouts echoed up into the sky, and before Lachlan could think of defending himself, he was seized by no fewer than four men, Cordon Blair leading the charge, and carried into the darkness. Their calls and songs were good-natured, but even so far into his cups, Lachlan could hear the roughness behind their meaning and felt little friendship in their jests when they flung him across the saddle of his waiting horse and slapped its rear, sending the mount charging into the darkness with a startled whinny before Lachlan could struggle aright in his seat.

He galloped past another on the path, the crown of his head just grazing some part of horse or rider, and he strained to pull himself aright. But the horse stiffened its forelegs and skidded sideways, throwing Lachlan head over heels against the wall of a longhouse before bolting back toward the faint glow of the town green.

He groaned as he turned himself over to sit on his proper end, then leaned his back against the dwelling. His stomach churned and his head throbbed and he wondered if he was going to vomit. Hoof falls came from the darkness, and when he looked up, there was Finley Carson, astride, holding the reins to his runaway horse.

Of course.

He shifted his eyes from her as he staggered to his feet and took the leather leads. The fall had done much to clear his head, though, so that he only had one false start in pulling himself up into the saddle. She was already riding into the edge of the wood when Lachlan gained her side.

"No one's following us," he said, immediately regretting the imbecilic phrase. He was truly drunk.

"Sure, they wished to give the happy couple privacy," Finley quipped. And then, "They'll be along in the morning, with the rest of the supplies."

"Ah, aye—the supplies," Lachlan said, unable to keep the sneer from his tone. "The spoils from Carson Town's victory."

Only the soft, warm spring darkness answered his words, studded with the peeping of frogs and night insects. She was ignoring him.

She was ignoring *him*.

"So, how many suitors *did* you have?" Lachlan pressed, unable to stop himself from goading her.

Finley Carson kicked at her horse's sides and left Lachlan riding alone in the darkness. He didn't bother chasing her.

He didn't see her again until the woods opened up near the bridge, and the space in the canopy above allowed the moonlight to shine through as if reflected from a lamp. He saw her gallop across in the white mist of the falls and lean into the curve of the trail, disappearing once more. He slowed his horse as it clomped onto the wooden planks, feeling the loneliness of his surroundings, both literal and figurative, press around him. He was truly between clans, belonging to both of them and neither, if what rumor and Lucan Montague said was true.

What awaited him at Carson Town?

Probably Finley Carson with a great sword, he thought darkly to himself. He paused, checking his belt for his own blade before continuing on the path.

The trail emerged from the wood above the bay, and Lachlan was struck by the beauty of the scene, the moonlight rippling on the sea like the iridescent scales of a fish, the dark shadows of the dwellings below snuggling together like newborn pups. He turned to his right, toward the cliff face to which the town backed up, and saw right angles of constructed openings illuminated by the moonlight—a tall, stone house of some sort, lording over the lower structures. He wondered if it was Murdoch Carson's house.

It was only by luck that the moonlight caught the shadow of Finley Carson galloping up a rise on the far side of the town, and Lachlan waited a while for a lighted square to shine, indicating that she had entered into the house that was to be their own. Only then did he carry on through the dark town, riding straight to her door. He sent his horse into a stall of the small animal shelter, already outfitted with the treat of oats in a bucket, and then went through the yard to the house, looking around him as he walked at the shadowed rooflines and dark shelves of pen walls in the night. It was a small stead, but a fitting gift for a couple just married.

He pushed open the door and was surprised at the comfortable interior, the selection of cooking pots and dishes, the soft welcome of stitched textiles and well-worn chairs and tables, polished to a gleaming sheen. The furnishings were old but plentiful, and the room smelled of warmed beeswax and fresh baking, so that Lachlan had to blink against sudden drowsiness.

Finley Carson was moving through the room toward a door along the left wall, her discarded cloak over one arm. He couldn't help but acknowledge how beautiful she had looked today, in the fine gown and with her fiery hair piled atop her head like a fae queen. Her rib cage narrowed to an impossibly tiny waist, and Lachlan knew from the time he'd held her against him in the wood that she possessed enough softness in the right places.

He remembered curvaceous Searrach at the wedding fete, and how she'd pouted jealously at Dand when only a fortnight ago she was pleasuring Lachlan with that same mouth. He shook the image from his mind and followed Finley Carson through the doorway, stopping short at the threshold as she spun on him.

"What do you want?" she demanded.

But Lachlan was taking in the small chamber lit by a single lamp, casting jolly waves of light over the walls, and the pair of bedsteads pushed against opposite sides of the room. Pegs and hooks ringed the walls, displaying a selection of aprons and gowns, worn trousers and bonnets. A thin curtain hung from the center of the ceiling.

Lachlan finally looked at her. "Who sleeps here?"

Her expression was unamused. "I do."

"Who else?" he pressed. "There are two beds."

"My first husband, God rest his soul," she said. And then rolled her eyes and turned away from him to hang her cloak on an empty peg. "My parents."

"Your parents live here?"

"It's their house; where else would they live?" she asked in exasperation, and then turned around to face him. "I told you they would stay in Town Blair until morning, but you…" Her eyes widened a bit, and a smile that Lachlan felt he would come to dread came over her face. "You thought this house was yours. Didn't Marcas tell you you'd be taking on the farm with my da?"

"Of course he did," Lachlan scoffed.

"He didna," she insisted smugly, crossing her arms over her chest. "And you assumed the lowly Carsons would surely gift such a mighty man as Lachlan Blair with one of the finest farms in the town just for the inconvenience of marrying me. I doona believe I've ever met anyone as full of himself as you."

"If this is one of the finest farms in the town, little wonder you all nearly starved," he said, his pride creaking under the strain of her correct assumption. "A strong fart would likely blow out the walls."

Her eyes narrowed. "No one'll be forcing you to sleep here. Certainly nae me."

"Fine. After all this, I'll nae be sleeping under another man's roof. I'll pay a visit to the Carson and avail of his hospitality until other arrangements can be negotiated."

"Avail of his hospitality, will you?" Finley laughed. "Murdoch has nae more room than we do here."

"He's a large man, aye, but he doesna take up the whole of that stone house."

Finley looked confused for a moment, and then that blasted grin was back. "Oh, Murdoch doesna live up on the cliff."

"Then who does?" Lachlan demanded.

"No one at all," she said airily. "It's completely empty." She began to stroll slowly toward him. "In fact, I'm sure no one would mind should you decide to move in there yourself."

Lachlan grew wary. "This is some sort of trap. Sure, I'm to be attacked as soon as I enter in."

"Nay," Finley answered straightaway, her eyes wide. "I swear it: no one lives there. It would be a perfect place for you to be alone to ruminate over that dark-haired cow who's after your brother."

Lachlan ground his teeth together. His thoughts weren't clear enough to trust his mouth to convey them, but he was so humiliated by his mistakes—and his clan's neglect—his pride wouldn't allow him to remain under this roof with the sharp-tongued lass, face of a fairy or nay.

Lachlan turned and quit the doorway, marching back through the warm, comfortable main room and sweeping his bag from the polished table.

"Good night, then," Finley called out as he opened the door.

He slammed it shut in answer.

Lachlan didn't bother retrieving his horse from the stable for the short walk through town and up the foot of the cliff. The chill sea air was good for his head and his temper. It was not difficult to find the path that led toward the rear of the town, although his resolve wavered as the condition of the trail rapidly deteriorated. He kept looking up as he strode up over slippery rocks and stumbled in washed-out ruts, the moonlight revealing his folly.

It was a ruin of a house jutting from the cliff. *A ruin.*

By the time Lachlan stood before the towering stone structure, he could make out the three distinct floors, the tall, narrow openings of shutterless windows, the pointed peaks where the roof had once been at the very height of the cliff. He looked back down at the town, and the moon-slicked bay beyond. He could once more see the square of light from Finley Carson's house. No doubt she was warm inside, smiling smugly to herself at what she had known Lachlan would encounter on the cliff. But he would not give her the satisfaction of returning to the little longhouse.

He turned to regard the grand, arched doorway standing empty before him. Likely this structure had once housed the chiefs of the Carson clan. But now, all around him, the sea wind was the only thing inhabiting the manor, swirling through the perforated stone column, playing as on a set of pipes a low, haunting song, the pitiful cry of some abandoned and betrayed thing. It raised the hair on his arms and neck, so familiar a tune was it to his heart in that moment. He'd drunk too much, aye, that was all. Lachlan hadn't wept since he was a very, very young lad—a bairn, near—and then it had been over his beautiful mother, who he'd been told was never to return to him. Standing before that burned-out disaster that represented his life, he was as close to once more weeping since that long-ago day.

Lachlan slung his bag higher on his shoulder and entered the ruin.

* * * *

Finley lay in her narrow bed, staring at the low ceiling, now draped in shadow from the nearly spent lamp. It would have been an outrageous luxury to enjoy such light after the sun had gone down, but there was plenty of oil to be had since the new treaty with the Blairs. Plenty of light to lie alone in, and relive her disastrous wedding day.

What a fool Lachlan Blair was, to think that any such habitable place in the town would be so empty without just cause. The old house was a burned-out ruin—full of ghosts, if you asked any of the old folk. She felt her mouth curve in a slight smile as the faint rumbles of thunder tickled her eardrums, but the amusement was short-lived.

What a fool *she* was. And a bigger fool she would be on the morrow, when it was learned that her new husband preferred the ghosts of his enemies over her, even when so drunk he could barely sit a horse. She heard the soft patter of the storm on the roof.

Even in the rain, she amended to herself.

"Maybe he'll catch a chill and die," she said out loud, trying to infuse some hope into the situation. But it did nothing to cheer her, and she couldn't help but imagine her da's face when he returned home on the morrow. How disappointed he would be with her. Again.

Finley blew out the lamp and turned over to face the wall in the dark, where she could neither see nor feel evidence of her tears.

* * * *

"It doesn't make good sense," Vaughn Hargrave said aloud, his words falling flat against the rough stone walls and sliding down along with the rivulets of dark water and patches of furry scum. His hands dangled between his knees, the finely turned pelican in his right hand nodding as he gestured with it. "How many times must one man die before he is actually dead?"

He turned his head to look at his companion. The man only stared back at him wordlessly, but Vaughn thought perhaps there were tears in his eyes. "Yes," Vaughn sighed with a nod and dropped his gaze back down to his stained boots. "My feelings precisely. So frustrating! Argh!" Normally he wouldn't slouch on a stool in such a common manner, especially in the presence of another person, but his exasperation was getting the better of him this evening. He needed the comfort of the vault, and he needed the company.

And besides, the servant would never say anything to betray his lord's abnormal display of melancholy.

"I thought I had dealt with him myself," Vaughn went on patiently, as if detailing the logic of it would somehow reorder the events. "Shot him through the gut. He should have died in a ditch along the road somewhere. But no! He found someone to take him in! Can you imagine?"

The servant sighed.

"Yes—who *would* do such a thing? A peasant looking for loose coins, that's who." Vaughn shook his head. "Meg found him, though—I knew she would. Even though she betrayed me in the end, I knew if anyone could find him, it was she. I am an excellent judge of people, as you know."

Vaughn Hargrave hummed to himself, his thoughts working around each other in an intricate dance in his head and he observed them, looking for the pattern, trying to predict the order of it.

"But I saw his body on that hillside," he said in a low tone. "I felt the cooling flesh with my own hand—there is no other sensation like it, of that I can attest." He perked up and looked at the servant again. "If you'd like to see, I can—no? Suit yourself. But he *was* dead. His cloak, his blade, his hair—his brains on the ground. *Dead.*"

Hargrave tapped the cool, sticky metal of the pelican against his other palm. "And dead he stayed until Lucan Montague carried him into London. Lucan Montague, of all people! That snot-nosed brat repays my kindness by *resurrecting* Thomas Annesley! The ingratitude is appalling."

He stood from the stool, his irritation provoking him to physical restlessness once more. He paced the width of the vault, the soles of his boots making delicious, gummy whispers on the soft floor.

"The king was remiss in not having him hanged straightaway, yes. His Majesty cannot escape his share of responsibility. But what can you do with royalty?" Vaughn held out his hands beseechingly. "If it soothes Henry to think Thomas Annesley jumped to his death, I shall not disabuse him of the fantasy. It only plays to my benefit as the last documents for Darlyrede are settled—a dead man can make no dispute. But after the debacle at the shit pile that is Roscraig, you and I both know that Thomas Annesley is *not* dead, and that I simply cannot abide. I can't, and I won't."

Vaughn stopped his pacing to stare at the dark, stony wall, marbled with moss and mineral-striped water, old crusts of matter too diverse to ever know their sources.

"I think Lucan Montague might have believed him," Hargrave mused aloud. "And since Montague first alerted Tavish Cameron of his inheritance, it stands to reason that the pious whelp's next destination could only be Carson Town. If only he had stayed in France."

He turned from the wall and walked toward the servant. The man seemed to squirm excitedly, but Hargrave would not reward impatience.

"If the emerging pattern I'm detecting is consistent, Thomas Annesley will surely follow the very man who apprehended him into the wilds of the Highlands. I will not make the mistake of leaving *anyone* on that godforsaken mountain alive this time, I assure you." He reached out and stroked the man's wet head above the cage around his face and then raised the pelican in his hand and clicked the metal arms together gaily as he peered in the man's held-open mouth.

"Ah, only twelve more to go," he said, gesturing toward the small pile of teeth lying in the metal bowl near the man's head.

The servant gave an odd, gurgling cry in the back of his throat.

"All right, then. If you can wait no longer," Hargrave said with an indulgent smile.

Chapter 7

Finley heard Lachlan Blair's return to the farm early the next morning, but she sat at the table in the main room for the better part of an hour, staring at the plate of oatcakes she'd made, waiting for him to knock at the door so that she could bid him to enter with a smug look firmly in place. He'd been miserable all night, she just knew it.

But the knock never came. And by the time the dawn had grown enough to illumine the small, high-set windows, Finley knew it was only a matter of time before her parents and the rest of the town returned. She couldn't put off her chores any longer; Da would check on the animals first thing, and he would learn of Finley's failure directly from Lachlan Blair. Murdoch might be with him as well.

That is, unless Lachlan Blair had done nothing more than retrieve his horse. He may have met her kin on the road back to Town Blair.

Finley pushed back her chair with a screech and stood, snatching the plate and mug from the tabletop with a glare. She marched out the door and up the hill around the front of the longhouse, along the stone wall and toward the barn, where she heard the rhythmic ring of a hammer on metal. She paused in her march, blowing out a shallow breath of relief; at least she wouldn't be humiliated by her family encountering her new husband as he fled from her. But now she seriously considered assisting him in wearing the breakfast she carried. Finley charged forward, her spirit renewed.

She found him in the narrow center aisle of the barn, his feet braced apart as he lifted the hammer in his right hand high above his head. In his left hand, he held a hinge against her da's old, misshapen anvil.

He was wearing no shirt, and his skin glistened from whatever efforts he'd been about that morning, his long hair pulled back once more into the queue he'd worn that day in the wood. The sight of him so scantily clothed caused Finley to rock to a halt, her skirts swinging about her ankles like a bell about the clapper of her legs.

He caught sight of her and paused his actions, standing straight and dropping his arm. "Good morning," he said in a guarded tone. "This hinge was bent. Caused the paddock gate to drag. Thought I'd knock it out."

"A ram kicked it," she offered lamely. "Da hasn't had time to take the gate apart."

He looked to the dishes in her hands. "Are those for me?"

"Aye," Finley said stiffly with a little lift of her chin. His stomach was rippled, his waist nearly as narrow as hers.

"About time," he said, tossing the hinge and the hammer atop the anvil with a clatter and moving toward her.

"You could have come inside and got them yourself."

He took the plate and mug from her and then walked to the little milking stool against the wall, where he lowered himself into a seat. "And have a cleaver thrown at my head as soon as I opened the door?" He shook his head and then took a sip of the warmed milk before nestling it into the midst of a little pile of straw and picking up a bannock and stuffing half of it into his mouth.

Finley had thought of a score of things to say to Lachlan Blair while she'd been alone this morning: rules for living at the farm, his responsibilities. How he could and could not interact with her. But she could not call one of them to mind as she watched the man sitting on her father's milking stool in his smooth skin. She'd never seen a man shaped like him before. His muscles dense and exaggerated, his chest and shoulders seeming as wide as the barn aisle itself.

He looked up at her and swallowed, licked his lips. "Did you make these?"

Finley nodded.

"They're good," he said, stuffing another into his mouth.

"You sound surprised."

"I didn't take you for a woman who cared overmuch for wifely duties, the way you shirked marriage so."

"I didn't shirk marriage," she argued.

He paused in midchew, looking up at her.

"Sure, I objected to being married off for the sake of having a hireling," she said, and couldn't help her glance over his naked torso, "but I am beginning to see how that could have its advantages."

He laughed, as if surprised, bringing the back of one wrist to his mouth to keep his breakfast contained. He swallowed, his eyes still smiling. "Is that all I need do to give you a civil tongue? Go about with me shirt off?" Finley felt a reluctant if slightly embarrassed smile play about her own mouth. "I didna want to marry you, Blair, this I canna deny. And the thought of sharing the place my da's broke his back for his entire life with someone so full of himself doesna please me. But I willna argue with you about your shirt."

His grin was back—the one she remembered so vividly, the one she'd recalled in the nights after their meeting—and it brought a measure of relief to her, like an unclenching of a fist.

She clasped her hands behind her back and strolled to a support, where she leaned her shoulder. "How did you find the old house?" she asked in a mild tone.

Lachlan nodded. "Mm. Good. You were right."

Finley felt her head draw back in surprise.

"It was wet, miserable, and freezing," he supplied. "Just what I needed to remind me where I should be."

"In a warm, dry house with a roof over your head?" Finley ventured.

"Aye, but not Rory Carson's roof," Lachlan said, brushing the crumbs from his lap and standing. He reached down and swiped his cup from the straw and drained it, stacked it on the metal plate and then walked toward Finley. "I'm meant to be chief. I was born to it. It's been stolen from me, by whatever happened between our clans these thirty years ago." He held the empty dishes toward her.

Finley glanced down at them but did not take them, looking back up into his face with a frown. "Are you blaming the Carsons for your clan rejecting you?"

"I don't know yet who to blame," Lachlan admitted. "I do doubt that the Blairs would have agreed to whatever it was that brought this town to such loss. But I have an idea that it wasn't just the Carsons who've suffered. And the proof of it might lie in what I found in the ruin."

"There's nothing in the old house," Finley objected. "I've not been inside since I was a girl, but even then—it was rubble."

He was looking at her curiously, and his intense stare coupled with the warm scent rolling off his bare skin had quite addled Finley's brains.

"What if we could make this all go away?" he asked her in a low voice.

"Make...make what go away?"

"This marriage."

"But the treaty..."

"The treaty will stand," he interjected. "I promise. You could keep your da's farm for yourself and I could go back to Town Blair and claim my rightful place."

Finley narrowed her eyes at him. "And Carson Town would still be owed its allowances."

Lachlan nodded. "I'd need your help, though."

"What would I have to do?"

"Take a walk with me later," he said, pushing the dishes into her hands just as the jingle of approaching riders filled the barn aisle. "Up to the... what did you call it?"

"The old house."

"Let me show you what I found," he said, pulling his shirt from a peg on the wall and thrusting his head through it. "You tell me what you know about it."

Finley nodded. "All right." She seemed better able to think once his chest was covered, and the ridiculousness of it made her cross. "Don't think I'll be bringing your meals to you all the time."

Lachlan walked back to the anvil and once more took up the task of straightening the hinge. He raised the hammer and glanced at her with a wink. "I prefer butter and honey with my bannocks."

* * * *

Finley followed Lachlan out the door of the longhouse after the awkward noon meal, during which Ina Carson had beamed knowingly between her daughter and new son-in-law and Rory Carson had kept his eyes fixed wordlessly on his plate.

"Do you need me, Mam?" Finley asked, fidgeting with the stack of plates on the sideboard. "Lachlan's asked me to show him about the town."

Rory Carson snatched up his faded blue bonnet and smashed it onto his head before exiting the house without comment.

Ina glanced at the door with a confounded look and then smiled at Finley. "That's a grand idea! You two go along. There will be plenty to do before supper."

They started down the dirt path away from the Carson longhouse, the tiny, early wildflowers bobbing and bowing onto the path and caressing Finley's skirts in the stiff breeze. She waited until they were over the crest of the hill and heading into the town proper to address Lachlan Blair.

"What did you do to offend my father?"

"I was going to ask you the very thing," Lachlan said. "He's barely spoken two words since he returned. He wasn't even pleased that I fixed the gate." Finley smiled to herself. "Aye, well, I think Da's realizing he's got what he's asked for these past years. He's said he wanted a son-in-law to take over the duties of the farm, but when it comes down to it, I think he doesna want anyone interfering. You probably didn't straighten the hinge to his liking."

"The gate doesna drag through the mud now, does it?"

"You could be the Christ and Da would have some advice for you on the resurrection. Nothing suits him save for what he does himself."

"You take after him, then, eh?"

Finley shrugged with a smile. "I canna deny it. That's why I had nae wish to marry, and the same reason he didn't care who I married. It didn't matter."

"No one would be good enough for either of you?"

"Something like that," Finley said, watching her slippers kick out on the road from beneath her skirts. She wouldn't tell him that every suitor she'd had had only been interested in the farm; she was an afterthought. An inconvenience.

She thought to change the focus of the conversation, if not the topic. "Who was the girl at the wedding feast?"

"The dark-haired cow, you mean?"

She tried to suppress her smile but failed, so she gave up. "Aye."

"Searrach. We were to be married," he said lightly. "Betrothed for nearly a year now. Then, I mean," he amended. "We're no longer betrothed, obviously."

"She refused you?"

"Officially it was her father who put an end to the betrothal. Harrell's never cared much for me. But Searrach didna argue. Seems she has her cap set for Dand, now that Marcas is chief."

"So I was right; she is a cow." Finley felt a tinge of outrage for the man. "Little wonder you were so pissed at the feast."

"I wasn't pissed," he scoffed.

"You fell off your horse while you were still in town."

"He threw me."

"Sure, and then the mad beast found me and led me right to you. He likely worried you'd killed yourself."

"He's a sensitive horse," Lachlan allowed.

Finley laughed out loud as they started the climb up to the old house. She felt oddly at ease with this man—officially her husband, unofficially her enemy—much as she had when they'd first met at the falls bridge. There was no pretense between them, and it was a welcome change from the interactions she'd had with the men from the town who'd come courting. The sun reflected off the sheer front of the old house with a warm blast as from a forge. Any ornamentation beyond the deepest carvings were gone—erased by wind and rain and ancient fire. The old house jutted from the cliff face with man-made angles all the way up to the top of the hill, above the wood and to the west of the Blair valley, where nothing but scrub and abandoned boulders lived to enjoy the view of the sea. A deep, rich peat bog lay between the cliff and the vale of Loch Acras, difficult to pass by foot and impossible on horseback.

"I never knew this place existed." Lachlan came to a stop on the path, his hands on his hips, looking up at the old house. "'Tis older than any Town Carson."

"The stories say that it's Norse—when they invaded and intermarried with the old tribes. Carsons used it for the chief's family, and as a storehouse for when the trading ships came into the bay. A meeting place for the fine. A stronghold in case of invasion. It was abandoned years before I was born."

"At the great battle?"

"The fire, aye." She felt his gaze on the side of her face and turned to meet his eyes.

"How old are you, then?" he asked.

"A score." Her cheeks tingled. "Come midsummer."

"Good lord," Lachlan scoffed. "Little wonder you're such a brat."

"At least I have the excuse of youth," she shot back. "You'd think someone twice my age could hold his mead and keep his seat."

"Twice your—I'm not yet a score and ten!" he argued, but Finley had started up the path once more, a smile returning to her face.

"Och, that's unfortunate, then," she lamented over her shoulder. "There's nae shame in living a hard life, Lachlan Blair. Not all of us can be plump youths."

He caught up with her in two strides. "You didn't seem to mind my dottiness in the barn this morning."

"I'm surprised you remember this morning, pap."

Now it was Lachlan Blair's turn to laugh up into the bright afternoon sunlight. He stood to the side of the dark, arched opening of the old house and swept into a bow while Finley passed with a smug smile.

* * * *

Lachlan watched Finley Carson closely as she stood in the center of the main room of the old house, probably meant as a sort of reception hall, as it contained crumbling hearth openings in opposing exterior walls. Her red hair was once more tamed into a long plait that reached even farther down her slim back as she tipped her head up to the sky and wheeling seabirds in the open ceiling, and Lachlan was reminded of how her scalp had smelled the day he'd held her against him near the bridge—like flowers washed with sea air and sunshine. She dropped her head and looked around.

She was ten and nine. Slender and blazing bright, confrontational and unapologetic. A more opposite woman from Searrach Lachlan could not even form in his mind.

"I've not been here in years," she said musingly, glancing at him as she crossed the rubble-strewn floor toward the pair of short, darkened archways in the rear of the room. She caught herself on the edges of one of the doorways and leaned in slightly, looking up and around at the interior of the cavelike storeroom that still smelled faintly of dried fish.

"As children, we would dare each other to bring back a stone or some such trophy to prove our bravery." Her words echoed slightly as she hung in the doorway, and then she pushed back, turning as a gust of wind blasted through the ruin, and the skittering sounds of pebbles tumbling down the body of the cliff punctuated her reminiscences. Small stones bounced down into the center of the room and rolled away in scattered directions, little more than tiny bits of gravel, but they hopped among evidence of much larger stony dislocations, proof that the old house was still very much in the process of decomposing around their heads.

"Seems a dangerous place for children's play."

"Aye. Many of us felt the thickness of our fathers' belts for it," she acknowledged.

"You speak from experience?"

Somehow her grins seemed that she always kept a secret. "Perhaps." She stepped through the field of rubble toward him. "What is it you wanted to show me?"

"It's up there," Lachlan said, nodding toward the stone steps carved from the cliff itself into the left-angled wall of the room.

Finley turned, and her eyes went up to the switchback staircase, each flight becoming narrower by half from the ascendant floor. Where the stairs finished at the top, they appeared to be no wider than a single foothold. She looked back to him with a wary expression.

"There's nothing up there. Literally. The floors are gone."

Lachlan walked toward the stairs. "You can't see it from down here."

"Sure," Finley called out. "Last night you couldn't stand being in the same room as me, and today you wish me to follow you to the top of a deadly precipice, under the guise of making our marriage go away. One slip and a romantic stroll becomes a tragic accident, leaving behind an eligible widower. I'm not stupid, Blair."

"You think I want to kill you?" he said on a laugh as he turned and looked back at her, standing with her hands on her hips, her head tilted distrustfully. He had to admit, were their roles reversed, Lachlan wouldn't follow her up there either.

No wonder none of the village lads dared take her on. Most men didn't want a wife who would argue with them at all, let alone be right about it when she did.

"Fine. Wait here, then," he said, and bounded up the stairs, slowing his pace as he neared the top. It would do neither clan any good if he fell to his own death.

Lachlan paused on the narrow landing before the final flight of steps, drawing his dagger from its sheath and lying flat on his stomach. He inched toward the end of the rectangular slab, reaching out across the abyss while shadows of seabirds rippled over the walls and the breeze sent sheets of pebbles and sand trickling into the void. Once his blade was loaded, he drew it back carefully and stood, supporting the blade with his left hand and retracing his steps into the main room.

Finley didn't look any more convinced the closer he got.

"Hold out your hand," he said. Once she had, Lachlan tipped the blade out into her cupped palm.

She frowned down at the orange-black, damp crumbling mass and then looked up at him. "Dirt?"

Lachlan shook his head. "Rust." He used the tip of his dagger to smooth aside the middle of the pile in her palm, uncovering a small half-moon of dark metal. He looked up to meet her gaze.

Finley's eyes narrowed, but rather than suspicion, her look conveyed curiosity. Her hand closed over the crumbly mess and she walked toward the steps. Lachlan turned to follow her progress with his eyes, but remained in the receiving room as Finley gained the topmost landing.

"There's a mound of it," she called out. "The wall's stained where it's run down." Finley looked down into the room at him. "What is it?"

"Chain mail, I think," he replied. "English armor."

"Nay," she scoffed. "How would a pile of English chain mail end up at the top of a ruined Highland house?"

"I have the beginning of a suspicion," Lachlan said. "But I'll need to talk to Murdoch about it. Perhaps your da as well."

Finley tossed the contents in her hand back at the ledge where Lachlan had retrieved them, and he couldn't help but be reminded of the way mourners dropped in handfuls of burial dirt over a grave. She brushed her hands together and started down the stairs, holding her words until she was once more facing Lachlan.

"He won't talk to you about it," she said. "Murdoch. He won't talk about this place or that time to anyone, not even Da. What I told you was true: My da whipped me fierce when I was a child for daring to come up here. But all he would say about it was that whatever was left inside the old house was dangerous."

Lachlan saw the dawning of realization in her eyes as Finley laid their discovery over her father's warnings.

"Don't you think a pile of rusting English armor could have something to do with the danger he spoke of?"

"I always assumed he meant the falling rocks." Finley turned to look about the room again, as if seeing the whole place with new eyes. "What did you want my help with?" she asked. "I know it was not only walking up here with you."

"I think we both want the same thing," Lachlan said, "and that's for me to return to Town Blair."

Finley crossed her arms over her chest and nodded. "Aye."

"I must prove that my chiefdom has been stolen from me. And in order to do that, I'll need to talk to any Carson who was alive during the time Tommy Annesley lived at Town Blair. 'Twould be fair simple, save for the fact that your people don't seem to care much for me yet."

"Nay," Finley scoffed.

Lachlan allowed himself a grin at her sarcasm. "If I can get them to see that I'm not their enemy, they might give me the proof I need to regain my clan. You can help me to do that by not showing everyone how much you hate me. Maybe even being outwardly on my side. If I'm right, the Carsons will be vindicated, once and for all."

"And if you're wrong?" she prompted with a superior air.

He shrugged. "The Blairs won't have me back anyway."

"What am I to do, go from door to door to tell everyone how lovely our wedding night was?"

"Just don't thwart my efforts," he clarified.

"Your efforts at what?"

"Now that Carson Town has the resources it needs, it's time for the people here to rebuild properly," he said. "I mean to help you do just that." Finley's expression gave nothing away, and although she didn't agree with him, neither did she argue.

"And," Lachlan continued, "speaking of our wedding night, if we are to be free of each other when this is over, it would be best if we continued to sleep apart. There can be no question that our marriage was never validated."

Her expression remained stony for a moment longer and then she shrugged and turned away. "Fine."

Lachlan frowned; it seemed as though he'd said something to anger her, but he couldn't imagine what it was.

"Fine. Good," he said. "Where are you going?"

"To help Mam with supper," she said as she exited through the doorway, leaving Lachlan standing alone amidst the rubble of the ruin.

"I'm going to find Murdoch," he called after her. He didn't hear a response, but perhaps the wind had stolen it.

He waited a moment longer, then quit the old house himself. Finley was already disappearing into the dilapidated cluster of houses in the center of town when Lachlan started down the path. He tried to shake the confused feeling she'd left him with, wondering how they could have come to the ruin in a jocular manner and then parted so stiff and cold, like some specter of gloom had descended upon their endeavor rather than the buoyancy of hope they each should have felt.

They might each get what they most wanted after all. What they deserved.

Lachlan shook his head and continued on in the opposite direction into town, in search of Murdoch Carson.

He didn't see the figure watching him from the clifftop.

Chapter 8

Finley knew before she opened her eyes the next morning that it was no longer dark in the bedchamber. It had taken hours for her to fall asleep the night before and now she had overslept, if the sunlight filtering through the sparkling air over her bed was any indication.

She swung her legs over the side of the bed and sat up, sliding her feet into her slippers and pulling her shawl from the peg. The bed was tidied in only a moment, and she set to replaiting her hair, while her eyes scanned the skirts and blouses lining the wall.

Dark gray? Light gray? Grayish-brown? Hmm. Decisions, decisions. She ignored her fine wedding costume as if it wasn't there.

Light gray, it was.

She dressed quickly and opened the door to the main room, expecting to see her mother and father—and perhaps Lachlan Blair—breaking their fast at the table after their morning chores. But although the fire in the hearth still smoldered, the room was empty.

How late had she slept?

Finley saw a towel-covered dish on the table—bannocks and butter and a cup of fresh milk. Obviously everyone else had already eaten, but where had they gone off to? She picked up a cold oatcake and took a bite, washing it down with the tepid milk. She left the cup on the table, but carried the oatcake with her out of the house.

The light outside was gray—the glowy sort of illumination where the sun is present but yet so hidden behind such a thick barrier of clouds that everything is soft and foggy. The flower heads hung low still with dew and sleep, and Finley stepped quietly on the path, her eyes searching the farm up along their stone wall, and then out over the tops of the mist-shrouded rooftops of the town. There wasn't a sound to be heard beyond the wind and the sea. Not even the bleat of a single sheep.

It was then she realized the source of the morning's odd quality: There were no animal sounds, no work sounds, echoing over the bay. It was as though everyone had vanished.

She remembered the whispered stories from the older children when she was young, about the years of silence in Town Carson after the great battle. Nearly all the men, many of the women and children, and most of the animals were dead. It had made for terrifying haunt stories when she was wee, and now the silence caused unsettling gooseflesh to rise on her arms beneath her shawl, the cool fog dampening the tendrils of hair near her temple.

What must it have been like for her young mother then, hearing the blackened town silent, her own husband gone in the fight? What terror had she felt, looking over the corpse of their town from the spared farm on the hill? What resentment, to be married straightaway to Rory Carson, a relative stranger to her, called back from Glasgow by his own mother?

Finley saw the rounded, shawl-covered head coming up the path toward her now, as if her macabre imaginings had caused Ina Carson to appear. But contrary to Finley's melancholy musings, her mother's expression was bright.

"Good morning, daughter," she called up, holding her skirts slightly away from the tall, damp grass. "Your da said to let you lie in because he and Lachlan got at the chores right off."

Finley wanted to frown at this bit of information; she had helped her father with the morning chores since she'd been a lass of eight. But she supposed that was the point of her marrying, wasn't it? Besides, if Lachlan Blair had his way, he wouldn't be here helping forever. She would be wise to enjoy what respite she had.

"Where is everyone?" Finley asked as her mother drew even with her on the path.

"Taken the animals up over the vale to graze," she said, and her eyes were almost sparkling in the foggy gloom. Finley thought that if the sun had been out properly, she couldn't have withstood her mother's gaze.

"Our animals?"

"All the animals," Ina said with a smile. "Lachlan is leading the men up to the Blair pastures we've a right to. He's showing them where the boundaries lie."

Lachlan is a harried man this morning, she thought to herself with unreasonable sourness. It wasn't as though he hadn't warned her yesterday that he would set out to gain the Carsons' trust. Finley just hadn't expected it so soon. He'd eaten supper with the family last night, and after he'd borrowed one of Mam's lamps, Finley had walked him to the path.

There he had wished her a good night and set off toward the old house, alone.

Ina Carson looped her arm through Finley's and turned them both back toward the house. "Doona worry so. I'd say it willna be too long before your husband asks the fine for permission to build a new longhouse."

Finley turned her head sharply to look at her mother.

Ina continued. "The Blair is a proud man. Your father suspected he would be when he agreed to the betrothal, and he saw that it was doubly true on your wedding day. Lachlan was to be chief of Clan Blair."

"But he's chief of nothing," Finley said sternly. "He's been sent here in disgrace."

"I suspect he belongs here just as much as he belongs at Town Blair. Sure, maybe he belongs here more," Ina said, patting Finley's arm before releasing her and disappearing through the doorway.

Finley felt confusion distort her face. "What?" she whispered to herself, and then followed her mother inside, where she appeared to be starting the stew pot.

"It's part of why your da's so out of sorts," Ina continued, hanging the large kettle on the hook and bringing the water bucket near to send ladleful's sloshing inside. "He knows he's made a good match for his daughter. To a man who wouldn't take kindly to sharing a hearth with the old folks. Lachlan was to be the chief, Fin."

"You said that already," Finley acknowledged.

"Aye, well, it's the truth, and it's now paining your da. The Blair needs his own house for him and his woman."

"He's not *the Blair*. And I'm not just his woman."

"Sure, and what are you, then? If you think we didna notice your red eyes the morning we returned, you're mistaken. You must have cried all the night, knowing he wouldn't stay. To see him go away from you to the old house."

Finley pressed her lips together for a moment. "I *sent* him to the old house, Mam."

"Ah, duck," Ina said with a sigh, rising and placing her hand along Finley's cheek. "What else could you do? It was meant for a chief." She patted her daughter's face gently and turned away, and Finley rolled her eyes toward the ceiling.

He's not a chief, she mouthed to her mother's back.

"Your da's a proud man, too, Finley," Ina said, unwrapping a hunk of hard, shriveled meat and slicing ribbons off the end over the pot, the sharp blade of the knife pressing into the fleshy part of her thumb as if it were made of supple but impenetrable leather. "He was happy to pass the farm along to whoever it was you married, but he will not let it be said that he didna give a man what deserves it his due."

"Why is Lachlan Blair different from any of the other men who asked for my hand?" Finley demanded, and then added quickly with a pointed finger, "Doona say because he was to be chief, Mam."

Ina closed her mouth in a grin. "He's different because he's ended the feud, Finley. Our animals are grazing on Blair land in this very moment! Just think of the lambing we'll have next spring!" She rewrapped the dried meat and bent to rummage in a basket for a pair of shriveled roots, muffling her words. "And it's said that he has Carson blood on his father's side."

"Is that true, though, or only something said to make us take him?"

Ina raised up with a whoosh of breath and pushed her hair off her forehead with the back of her hand. "I doona think there was ever any question of us taking him."

"Ah, I see; it was me who had to be negotiated," Finley said.

"All that matters is that you're married now. Let it go, Fin," Ina said, adding the roots to the stew with a smile. "Pray God we'll welcome more than new lambs in the spring, eh?"

Finley's sharp retort was stayed by the door flying open and the angelic-looking Kirsten bursting through. Both Ina and Finley looked at the girl with wide eyes, never having known the blond lass to have enough spirit to say good morning lest she was prompted.

"Finley, Mother Carson," Kirsten said breathlessly. "Forgive me. But the men are back. The...the Blair, and Dand is with him."

"Who?" Finley asked.

"*Dand*," Kirsten said. "The Blair's *brother.*"

Finley felt her mouth quirk and cast a knowing look at her mother before strolling to the table and taking a seat, picking up her mother's discarded knife and a bunch of the parsley from the pot of water on the table. "Oh, aye. *Dand*. What's he want?" She began stripping the leaves against the blade.

"Sure, he wishes to check on his brother's welfare," Kirsten insisted.

Finley placed a sprig of the wet herb in her mouth to chew before selecting another stem for the stew. "Making certain the crazy Carsons haven't killed him?"

"Finley," Ina chastised. "We would never do such a thing, and Marcas Blair knows it."

"Marcas Blair doesn't give a fig what happens to Lachlan now that he's not his problem," Finley said. "And just yesterday I thought of dropping a boulder on his head myself."

"Finley!" Ina exclaimed. "You did not."

"Did too. But it was only because I thought he wanted to push me down the stairs at the old house. Well, mostly because of that." Finley looked up at Kirsten, whose sweet face bore a wounded look at such violent talk. "Why did you run all the way here to tell us Lachlan Blair's foster brother has come to call?"

At this, Kirsten's face pinkened prettily. "He might stay for supper, might he nae, Mother Carson? I thought you'd want to know. In such a case."

"Och, well sure he might, and 'twould be grand if he does," Ina said with a smile, and reached once more for the hunk of meat. "You must eat with us, too, Kirsten, for your thoughtfulness."

Finley jumped at Kirsten's squeal, nearly cutting herself with the small blade. The girl rushed forward and embraced Ina.

"Thank you, Mother Carson," she gushed. "I'll get to the house straightaway and make the bread."

"You're a lamb," Ina said.

"Goodbye, Kirsten," Finley called out the door after the girl's retreating form.

Kirsten rushed back in. "I'm sorry, Finley. How are you today? Well, are you? You look well. Goodbye, then." Then she turned on her heel and dashed out the door once more.

Finley sighed. "She'll break her foolish neck getting home."

"The way Dand Blair couldn't drag himself from her at the wedding feast, there may be reason for high spirits."

"Well, I hope she's not too disappointed when she finds out someone else at Town Blair has already set her cap for the wee Brother Blair," Finley said and stood from the chair, tossing the handful of parsley in the pot and choosing a basket from a hook. "I'll go see if there's barley for the stew."

"See if there's a better attitude for you while you're there," Ina said with a roll of her eyes.

"I like my attitude just fine, Mam," Finley said with a grin and a lift of her chin and then strolled through the door.

"Sure, and you're the only one who does!" Ina called after her.

Finley kept her smile as she walked down the narrow path toward the village. She thought she could say with some certainty that Lachlan Blair didn't mind her attitude at all; he was the only one in all the town to not find her useless. But poor Kirsten was a fool if she thought Dand Blair's clan would allow him to pay any mind at all to a meek little Carson girl without two sheep to butt heads, now that Dand was in line to be chief. Finley was quite sure the Blairs would hold the opinion that they had lost just about enough of late to the little town on the bay that had caused them so much trouble.

She paused at the rise in the path as she spotted the handful of men entering the town from the direction of the bridge path. There was no way Kirsten had just happened to see them return. She'd had to follow the grazing party all the way to the Blairs' with hope of catching sight of Dand, and then run all the way back to town ahead of them. It explained why she had been so frightfully breathless.

There was her father, Rory, and Murdoch Carson; the flame-haired Dand and Lachlan. The Blair was taller and wider than his companions, his shawl hanging long and billowing behind him like some Roman conqueror of old.

He was the handsomest man Finley had seen in all her life. Even more handsome than that English knight who'd happened upon her at the bridge. Handsomer by at least half.

She shook herself with a private, outraged frown at her disloyalty. Sure he was handsome and braw; the men of Carson Town would be the same if they'd been raised with such plenty. Finley had no business admiring him for what was clearly none of his doing, and was perhaps a result of Carson misfortune. He was probably only a pretty, pampered dunderhead with delusions of being chief and he hadn't been here long enough for it to show. He'd fallen right off his own horse not even going at a trot, hadn't he? Likely his morbid suspicions were bollocks, and he'd reveal himself a lunatic creating delusions of people conspiring against him: his grandfather, his betrothed, his own brother, perhaps. Then where would Finley be when it all fell apart?

"Humiliated," she answered herself aloud. "And married to an idiot. Just as I feared."

She must help him succeed, then, and quit thinking of him in terms of "handsome" or "braw." So what that he didn't wish to remain married to her? The sooner he was gone, the better for them all.

Finley turned on her heel and strode in the opposite direction, trying to summon to her mind any image at all that wasn't Lachlan Blair without his shirt.

* * * *

Lachlan and Dand parted from the elders on the path, and Lachlan led his foster brother toward the wide, sandy delta where the Keltie slid into the bay. Dand began stooping almost at once to pick up bright shells and smooth pebbles tumbled into glassy spheres, but Lachlan didn't waste any time once they were out of earshot of anyone from the town.

"Who sent you?" he demanded of the younger man, standing on the other side of a long, twisted trunk of driftwood, letting there be a physical barrier between them to mimic the one Lachlan felt in his heart.

Dand didn't hesitate in flinging one of the rocks in his hand at Lachlan's head; it would have taken his right eye had he not dodged it.

"What are you arsing about?" he demanded. "I come all the way down here to see that the Carson lass hasna parted your big head from your shoulders and you accuse me of spying?"

Lachlan felt a twinge of remorse, but not enough to extinguish the surprising pain his brother's presence had brought to him.

"Was it Marcas? Harrell?" He raised his eyebrows pointedly. "Searrach?"

Dand's ears reddened and he turned away to look out over the rippling water, skipping the remaining stones into the breakers, one after the other. Lachlan heard the answer in the crashing waves before Dand could bring himself to reply.

"Nae one knows I've come," he said.

Lachlan, too, turned his gaze to the bay. Somehow, the idea that no one had sent Dand was worse. "I can handle Finley Carson just fine," he said. "Obviously, nobody at Town Blair would raise a finger to help me even if the Carsons decided to draw and quarter me on the green, thanks to Thomas Annesley."

"That's nae true," Dand scoffed. "The Carsons doona have a green now, do they?" Lachlan didn't take the jovial bait and so Dand continued. "Da misses you, as I do. You know he couldna go against the chief's wishes. Had you been in his place, you'd hae done the same."

Lachlan was shaking his head before Dand had finished speaking. "Nay." He turned to look at his brother. "I would never have supported stripping my son of his birthright through no fault of his own."

Dand's clear eyes held no bitterness when he answered. "I'm his son as well, Lach. Da did the best he could by you. The fine—"

"Marcas *is* the fine now." Lachlan looked back over the water. "He knew I should have taken Archibald's place the morning he died."

"If he had let you do that, the other elders would have run you out of the town, and well you know it. You would never have been allowed back. Ever. Maybe Da as well. Maybe me."

Lachlan sighed. "Damn me. Forget I said anything. None of this is your fault. I was wishing for your company just yesterday, and now here you are and I'm arsing it up, just like you said. Ow!" He flinched at the pebble that bounced off the side of his skull with a distinct *crack*. He brought up his hand to rub at his head as he looked at the grinning younger man. "That'll leave a lump."

"You'll nae be able to ken it from the others," Dand said, and Lachlan knew he was forgiven, although he still felt the idiot.

Dand then reached into the sack he was wearing against his hip. "I've brought you something, although perhaps I shouldna give it to you. I doona know if it shall please you or set you off in a rage again." He withdrew a long, slender object, wrapped up in a dingy old piece of cloth—Lachlan recognized it as one of Mother Blair's rags—and offered it to Lachlan.

Lachlan took it with a frown, and he could tell it was a blade by the feel of it even before unwinding the cloth revealed the shallowly engraved, dinged, and darkened metal sheath. Several grubby knobs of frazzled cording hung from the back edge of the sheath and at the grip, as if it at one time had been decorated with tasseled fringe. It was obviously quite old. He looked up at Dand.

"Where did you get this?"

"Archibald's house," Dand said, resting the sole of one boot on the trunk of driftwood still between them, leaning forward to cross his forearms over his thigh. "Ma's nae shut up about moving into Archibald's since he died. I was taking some things over for her last night, late, when who do I come across inside by lamplight?"

Lachlan shrugged and looked down to examine the sheath's engravings.

"Harrell," Dand said. "Near to tearing the place to splinters where the chief slept. I surprised him, coming in on him like that. He made some nonsense about losing a brooch at the funeral."

"Hmm." Lachlan ran his thumb over the swirls and angles cut into the metal and turned to sit on the driftwood facing the bay. Although he'd never laid eyes on the dagger before, the design seemed familiar.

The trunk dipped as Dand sat down next to him, facing the town. "He ran out of there like his hair was afire—you know Harrell. I saw a dark place in the wall behind a post of Archibald's bedstead; Harrell had just been shoving at the thing when I got there, and I don't think he'd seen it yet. It was a hidey-hole, and that was in it. It had to have been what he was searching for." He paused in his account. "Lach, look at your wedding brooch."

Lachlan stilled and then rested the dagger across his thigh while he reached up for the metal that fastened his shawl across his chest. He unhooked the pin and held down the sizable disc next to the sheath, then looked up at Dand.

"The pattern is the same," Lachlan said. "This is Carson steel."

Dand nodded. "So the question becomes, why would your grandda have a Carson dagger hidden in his house?"

"Sure, and why would Harrell be looking for it?" Lachlan added.

The driftwood shuddered again as Dand found his feet. "Someone here is bound to know."

Lachlan half-turned on his hip. "What did Marcas say about it?"

Dand shook his head and said quietly, "He'd have had to show it to the fine."

Lachlan realized what his brother had done for him then, and felt doubly like an ass.

"I'll be getting back," Dand said.

Lachlan, too, stood as a foreign wave of disappointment washed over him. "Stay. Come up to the cliff house with me; I'll show you what I—"

But Dand was already walking backward up the damp, brown flat, shaking his head. "I've more to do than daylight left to do it in. Harrell'll be suspicious when he discovers I've come, and Searrach'll surely tell him when she canna find me. He mustn't think I've found what he was looking for, else I'll nae be able to shut my eyes in me own bed."

"Even as his future son-in-law?" Lachlan couldn't help the barb.

Dand's face screwed into a mask of distaste. "Searrach's too eld for me. Like tonguin' Ma's sister." He gave an exaggerated shudder, then grinned. "There's nae betrothal for his dear gel now, and it's put him in a humor of sorts. He's leaving soon to take some of the sheep down the valley with the younger men to sell at market because Carsons are grazing half our pastures now. He seems eager to go, but Searrach is quite disappointed that her da's forbidding her from making the trip."

"Kirsten Carson will be sore disappointed herself that she didna get to see you today," Lachlan baited.

"Sure, she saw me," Dand called back. "And see more of me she shall, have I my way." He raised a hand, showing Lachlan a glowy pink shell before placing it carefully in the jagged end of a buried trunk sticking out of the sand. "If you should happen to see her." Then he turned away from the beach, trotting up the flat, hopping over driftwood, zigzagging around boulders on his way to the path. From Lachlan's point of view, he still appeared to be the young man just out of boyhood he'd been a moon ago.

But he was no longer a boy, and Dand's journey to Carson Town this day to give Lachlan the dagger proved it.

"Thanks, brother!" Lachlan called out, too late he knew, but Dand raised a hand in acknowledgment even if he didn't turn around again.

He had one friend yet then, at Town Blair. And one here on the edge of the sea in Finley Carson. Lachlan looked down at the dagger again.

"The truth will come," he murmured to the waves, and he didn't know if it was excitement or fear that caused the seabirds on the beach to start to the low, gray sky with shrieks.

Chapter 9

Finley didn't oversleep again, but when she joined her father and Lachlan Blair in the barn the next morning, she was promptly dismissed, by Rory Carson himself no less.

"You go on back to the house and help your mam with the meal," he ordered gruffly, barely sparing her a glance as he and Lachlan struggled with the yearling lamb. "We're nearly done here."

"But I've come to do the milk—"

"I've already done it," Lachlan said distractedly, his eyes closely watching Rory's hands at the hoof as he made sure to hold the animal perfectly still in his muscular arms. The lamb's eyes were wide and rolling, its blunt muzzle parted in its pants and frightened bleats. Finley knew all too well how deceptively strong the animals were.

"Well...the sow?" she offered, and sounded pathetic even to her own ears.

"That, too, lass," her father said on a sigh and then tossed the trimmers into a wooden tray and stood with a groan as Lachlan slowly turned his body and carefully let the animal find its feet before the gate before turning it loose in the paddock. "Eight piglets in the night. He'd most of it sorted before I was roused."

Finley looked to the large man again, trying to keep the look of resentment from her face but obviously failing if Lachlan's smug expression was an indication.

"Well, isn't he just the pet?" she said through a condescending smile. "I'd like to know what I'm to do all the morn."

Rory sighed again and looked up to the rough barn ceiling again, this time as if praying for patience.

Lachlan Blair responded instead. "Butter."

Finley was thrown off her tangent by the odd response. She frowned. "What?"

"It's the richest of cream from a milking," he said slowly, "Beaten with a paddle. I like butter with my bannocks. Be a good lass and put it on the table."

Finley glared at him, and she couldn't be certain it wasn't a sneeze, but it sounded very much like her father had muffled a laugh at her expense. He was taking to the friendly banter a bit too well, to Finley's mind.

"Sure, I will," she said sweetly. "You just be certain to eat all the sparkly bannocks. They're a special recipe I'll make just for you."

If anything, Lachlan's grin grew more sensual. "Mmm," he said with a waggle of his brows. "Butter *and* crunchy oatcakes? I'm a lucky man."

Finley could still hear her father's laughter echoing in the barn as she stalked back to the house, jerking her shawl tighter around her against the stinging chill and her throbbing pride. But she wore her own conceding grin. And she wouldn't smell like an animal at breakfast.

It wasn't an unpleasant way to start the day.

The next several days took on new routines not only for Finley and the farm, but for all of Carson Town. The first project Lachlan had proposed was the repair and expansion of the storehouse, and for the better part of a week, all the able-bodied men in the town were set to hauling rock from the north end of the beach to the center of town with one of the new Blair carts, until the man-made mountain was nearly as tall as the store roof itself, and in arguably better condition.

Sections of the existing wall were rebuilt where hastily erected stone had leaned and buckled beneath years of storms and wind and neglect. The roof was stripped entirely to its bones, many rafters replaced as a new main beam was laid above what was once the rear exterior wall, and supported with new posts dotting the shallow trench where the expanded stalls were being laid. The storehouse would be exactly twice its original size when finished, and was designed in a way that the town could use the building for several purposes. Once the thatching was in place, the women set to work sorting and organizing the bounty of provisions they'd received from the Blairs, and Finley tingled with a foreign pride as the women—both young and old—marveled not only at the windfall Finley's husband had brought to Carson Town, but at his impressive physical prowess.

More than one of the young girls blushed and giggled when Lachlan passed in the course of his labors, and Finley could hear the whispers of, "the Blair." No doubt they were retelling the same inflated escapades of Lachlan that Finley had heard as a child.

Finley found herself watching him, too, and when next he passed and caught her eye, giving her a wink, she turned away quickly while her cheeks heated and the girls giggled all the more loudly. Even Ina Carson had a secret smile on her face as she sat on a low stool, weaving wide, shallow baskets of strong, green reeds.

Their family suppers, too, were lively, salted with recounting events and progresses of the day and Lachlan and Finley's baiting of each other. By the time the storehouse was finished, a fortnight later, Finley realized the tight feeling in her chest she experienced when Lachlan took his leave from the farm every night as disappointment. She dreaded seeing his wide back pass into the darkness beyond the door, being relegated to following her parents to the rear of the house as if she were still a child while her husband escaped to the eerie peace of the old house.

But this night, Lachlan did not stand with a kind word for Ina and excuse himself for the evening. Instead, he withdrew a corked flask from inside his shawl and placed it on the table as Finley cleared the dishes.

"Sure and what have you got there, lad?" Rory queried in a high, admiring tone. "A need for the metal cups, have we?"

"Aye, and we well deserve it after the work we've done," Lachlan said with a grin, and then caught Finley staring at him and gave her another of his blasted winks.

Ina reached for the two prized, stemmed pewter cups displayed on the highest shelf and turned with a wide smile, setting the vessels on the table before wiping each in turn with a corner of her apron.

"I've nae had the mull in ever so long," she said with breathy excitement. "Sure the Blair is good to share it with us after all his labors."

But Finley knew there was more going on that *the Blair* wasn't revealing to her parents yet, and her senses were on alert as he uncorked the bottle with a surreptitious grin on his full lips set in the shadow of his stubbled jaw. He poured a splash into each cup and then picked them both up, handing one to Rory and then gestured toward the old man with his own.

"May the road rise up to meet ye," he said with a sparkle in his eye.

Rory's face brightened with hesitant surprise. He raised his cup a mite higher toward Lachlan. "May the wind allus be at yer back."

The two men drank, and then Finley's father set down his pewter cup on the wooden table with a bang and a gasp. "By God, it's Irish!" he said in a hoarse voice.

Lachlan's grin was pushing the wince from his face as he leaned up, already pouring another glug each into the cups. He handed his to Finley. "You might want some water with that, lass."

Finley gave him a skeptical look. "I've had my own share of drink, Blair, even if it weren't Irish. I'm nae child." She raised the cup and pulled a face, noting absently that her mother held her cup poised still, watching Finley. The stuff smelled odd; Finley could only describe it as hot, with a whiff of strong anise. She took the drink in a single gulp, and it seemed that her ability to breathe vanished.

When she could finally draw a searing gasp, her eyes streamed tears and the group around the table was chuckling with laughter.

"That's nae mull," she whispered.

Rory Carson slapped the tabletop with his hand as Ina gave a happy little whoop, then tossed back her drink neatly without so much as a grimace. "I'm proud of you, lass. You just had your first taste of Irish waters. A gift from God I've nae had the pleasure of in many years. Where did you come by it, Blair?"

Finley handed the cup back to Lachlan, noting the warming feeling in her stomach. It was pleasant, now that her throat didn't burn quite so much.

"Now that," he said as he refilled the cups again and handed one to Rory, "is nae important. What's important is that I've the pleasure of sharing it with one who appreciates it."

"Sure, and I do," he said, giving Lachlan a toast. "*Slàinte.*"

Lachlan tipped his cup. "*Slàinte.*" After drinking, he looked to Finley with raised brows. "Another?"

It took her only a moment to shake her head no, but in that moment it seemed as if Finley debated with herself for a month of days. She could just picture in her mind what could happen if she allowed herself a little too much to drink, and followed Lachlan through the door and up through the darkness into the old house; she could help him out of his shirt, rub his muscles, which surely must be sore...

"Nay," she said with a renewed flush blooming on her cheeks.

Lachlan nodded with an air of understanding and recorked the bottle. Finley caught her father's glimpse of disappointment turning to delight as Lachlan slid the ancient-looking flask across the table toward the old man. "For you and Mother Carson," he said, pushing back his chair as he stood. Rory was already uncorking the bottle again while Ina commandeered both cups. Lachlan held out his hand toward Finley.

"Fancy a walk?"

For a heartbeat of time, the only sounds in the Carson house was that of the sizzling fire, and if Rory and Ina Carson thought their furtive glances at each other discreet, they were mistaken. It only caused Finley's blush to deepen, which was uncomfortable enough; she wasn't used to feeling self-conscious, but it often seemed she felt nothing but that while in the presence of Lachlan Blair.

"I canna be running off as I fancy," she tried to say breezily. "Mam needs my help with the—"

"Och, doona even think it, lass," Ina said loudly with an enthusiastic wave of her hand. "I'll have this cleared in a thrice. Enjoying me taste with your da first, I think."

Rory Carson reached out a slender arm around Ina's thick middle and pulled her close against his ribs. "That's the word," he agreed with a nod, and there was a merry flush to his usually pale face.

Finley looked back to Lachlan, who was watching her parents with something akin to a wistful expression. He turned his gaze to her once more, glanced down at his offered palm.

Finley frowned and swept past him, pulling her cloak from the peg before yanking open the door and stepping into the brisk night breeze to escape the suddenly uncomfortable familiarity. She heard the door shut behind her but didn't turn, her eyes drawn to the ripening white slice of moon hanging over the inky sea like a broken pearl. The gusting wind swept up the hill, cold and clammy and washing Finley's skin in gooseflesh beneath her clothes, although with the warm whisky in her belly and her tingling cheeks, the contrast was not entirely unpleasant.

Perhaps he shall kiss me beneath the moon tonight, she found herself thinking, and rather than push such a traitorous idea from her mind at once, as she normally would, she let it stay this time, wandering around inside her head and brushing up against the prickly parts of her mind until the sharpness was all but rubbed away.

He walked past her, tossing his head toward the path as he did, grinning that terrible, secret, dangerous grin. She noticed he had taken a lit oil lamp from her mother's bench.

Finley followed and caught up with him. "Where are we going?"

"I want to show you something," he said.

"Och. What is it this time? Hoping to lure me to the river and drown me?"

Lachlan laughed right away. "And why would I want to do that to such a pretty lass, and my wife, no less?"

Finley's stomach did a sweet, wheeling flip. "Nae your wife for long though, eh?"

"Aye, probably nae for long," he agreed mildly. "You are a pretty lass, though." They walked on several more paces, through the cusp of the quiet little collection of dwellings that comprised the edge of the town while

Finley's heart pounded strangely in her chest. She fancied she could even hear it's loud thrumming.

Lachlan didn't speak again until they were on the path up to the old house. "I want to show you where I found the Irish."

"Found it?" Finley said. "I thought you'd brought it with you from Town Blair."

The moon outlined his queued hair in silver as he shook his head. "Archibald would have choked his mother to get his hands on some, I'd wager, but no Irish trader's been through with such a thing in years."

The crunching gravel under their feet was loud, and she lost her footing for a moment as a larger stone turned under her sole. Lachlan's fingers wrapped around her upper arm before she could stagger properly, and the touch of him seemed to burn through the layers of her woolen clothing, caused her thrashing heartbeat to skip clumsily.

"Perhaps you could have brought me up here when it was still light?" she grumbled, seeking to distract herself from the embarrassment of her own awareness of him, but she forgot that her sharpness had dulled and so the thrust was nothing but a feint.

He turned her loose and continued on. "I'd rather there be no chance of us being seen for now."

"Anyone at all could look out their door and see us."

"Which doesnae concern me—you are my wife after all. They're welcome to see where we're going," said he, "just nae where we end up."

Finley's eyes narrowed.

But then they had arrived at the old house, and were ducking into the central room. The skittering sounds of the pebbles, like the patter of rain, made Finley a different—unpleasant—sort of nervous. Whenever the seasons changed, the cliff showered its loosening stones more frequently. Finley feared they may not hear the next chunk of cliff to fall as it hurtled toward them, and they certainly wouldn't see it, but she thought perhaps that was just as well.

She felt her hand being pried away from the death grip she had on the front of her shawl, and Lachlan wrapped his fingers around hers.

"Let's go quickly," he said.

She jerked her hand free. "If you think I'm going up those stairs with you, you're mad."

He reclaimed her hand. "Not the stairs—the storeroom. I cleared a path earlier, and I pray God it's still that way."

"Oh well, aye, let's just leave it to God," she quipped with a roll of her eyes in the dark. "He obviously favors the Carsons above all others."

She thought she felt his fingers tighten for an instant before he nearly pulled her arm from her shoulder, dragging her through the room in a trot. Finley hunched down and brought her left hand up to cover her head, much protection as it would be. But in only a few moments, she felt the air go close around her ears, sensed the darkness deepening, and Lachlan stopped so suddenly in front of her that she ran into his wide back and bounced off. She would have fallen on her bottom if he hadn't been holding on to her still.

His hand slid from hers after she was steady on her feet, and in the next moment the weak light from the dampered lamp bloomed before Lachlan's face, washing the little cave room with warm, yellow light and Finley blinked against the glare.

He'd made a comfortable-looking pallet up off the floor against the back wall, and there was a collection of the few personal effects he'd brought with him from Town Blair on their wedding night.

"It's smaller than I remembered," she said, looking up and around at the sharply sloping ceiling that disappeared in shadows on one side. "Odd that it's so small, really. For a storehouse."

"That's what I grew to think, too. Here," he said, lightly touching her elbow and stepping forward, herding her toward the low bed. "Sit down." He set the lantern on the ground near her feet.

Finley did as he suggested without comment, her skin once more awash in gooseflesh at the intimacy implied by their location. She watched him walk back to the opening of the storeroom and crouch down before a small fire ring he'd made to one side of the doorway. He reached toward a little pile of dried peat while he talked.

"I put the fire here so as to warm the room without suffocating," he explained, and Finley thought it a rather obvious choice; the small room would easily catch the heat of the flames like the backside of a fireplace while the smoke traveled out into the cavernous opening of the main room. Did he think her so stupid?

But as Lachlan fanned the coals to glowing, throbbing red beneath the blanket of dried vegetation, Finley saw the thick cloud of smoke billow up and then into the storeroom as if a tempest was behind it. She raised her shawl over the bottom part of her face and readied herself to rise and step from the room before her lungs were choked, but to her surprise, the smoke swirled up to the ceiling and away into the deepest shadows as the fire flickered to life beneath the little sticks of driftwood Lachlan was steepling over the pit.

Finley rose to her feet, her face turned up as she walked toward the corner of the room, and Lachlan met her there.

"Do you see it?" he asked quietly, seemingly right into her ear.

Finley nodded as the bottom edge of the cut in the cliff flickered in the glow of the lamp. She turned her head to look at him and he was indeed right behind her. "Is it another storeroom?"

He shook his head. "Not quite."

She didn't hesitate to step up when Lachlan bent and cupped his hands into a stirrup. He boosted her as he straightened and then turned his hands, pushing her up as she grabbed at the edge of the opening. Finley hooked her elbows over, then one knee, and a moment later she was crawling into the cold darkness of yet another cave room. But Lachlan was right: it wasn't quite a storeroom. It wasn't really a room at all.

"My God," she breathed, gaining her feet and looking up. There was no sloped ceiling here: the space was a dark, rectangular shaft, soaring open perhaps fifty feet to a tiny sliver of night sky above.

The walls danced with upward light. "Finley."

She turned and braced her hand against the side of the opening, looking down to see Lachlan holding the lamp aloft. She crouched and reached down to take it.

"Back up," he commanded, and Finley stepped away, her slippers crunching over large pieces of detritus. She looked around the floor, holding the lamp aloft, realizing that she had stepped on long, deadly-looking slivers of dry, rotted wood planks, and her eyes went up again, seeking the sky.

She heard Lachlan's huff and grunt as he jumped and scrabbled up beside her. The towering void above seemed to start to spin, and so Finley dropped her gaze to the man flickering with shadows, but very clear to her senses.

"Do you have any idea what this place is?" he asked. "Stories you've been told...anything?"

"Nay," Finley said, and her words were hushed, as though she was afraid of being overheard even when they could not have been more alone. "None of us children were ever brave enough to stay in the storerooms for long. It's where the ghost was said to live." She looked down at the out-of-place wooden planks, and saw that some were still strapped together in broken pairs and trios, chunks of wreckage from what once must have been a construct of men's hands; there were metal nail heads and bands, rusted to black now, the stain weeping out into the murky grain of the woods like macabre tears.

It called to Finley's mind the pile of rust at the top of the stairs. *English armor...*

"Perhaps you were right to fear a ghost," he said, and she turned quickly to look at him. He pointed to the top of the shaft, so high above their heads as to be barely discernible in the gloom. "There are pulleys and stops all along the wall, all the way to the top, is my guess," he said. "Although I haven't found evidence of a winding drum, I think we're standing on what's left of a hoist that met a bad end."

Finley squinted up. "But how...?"

He took her hand again, steadying her across the debris to the corner of the room against the cliff. Once there, he slapped his left palm against the wall, his fingers disappearing into a deep, rounded indent. He withdrew and moved his hand up in a zigzagging pattern, three, four times and then stepped back, looking up and then pointing again.

"It's a ladder. To the very top."

Finley felt her eyes widen. "Did you go up?"

"Only half." He paused, his hands on his hips, and Finley could sense that he was preparing to deliver the prize. He looked at her. "It's where I found yet another chamber carved into the wall—just tall enough for a man to stand in, and filled with all manner of old things, including the Irish. A cache."

She stared at him for a long moment. "A cache. You mean the sort that smugglers would use."

His mouth turned down thoughtfully and he nodded. "Aye."

Finley shoved him. "You two-faced lout!" Lachlan rocked on his feet against her slight onslaught but stood his ground. "How dare you accuse my people of...of—"she sputtered, shook her head—"*piracy*?"

"I didna accuse anyone of anything," he clarified. "It could be from trade. I was only describing—"

"Is there anything else in it?" she interrupted, setting down the lamp. "Or just whisky?"

Lachlan stopped and pressed his lips together, watching her closely as she unclasped her weighty cloak and flung it aside. The corners of his eyes were slightly upturned.

Finley could wait no longer for his answer. She spun to face the wall and hitched up her skirts until her slipper found the first foothold.

"You're going up there?" He half-laughed.

"Well, sure; I'd see for myself," she said, looking up and then reaching with her left arm for the tread.

"Finley, wait," he said, and she felt his hands on her calves through her skirts. "It's more dangerous that it looks. If you slip..."

"You're the one who brought me up here, Lachlan Blair," she snapped at him, twisting around to give him a saucy glare. "Did you think I was the sort of woman before whom you could dangle words like 'smuggling' and 'Irish' and I'd not wish to see it with my own eyes?"

His laugh echoed up toward the tiny opening so far above the floor, and Finley started up, even as he called after her, "And you were so certain it was me trying to lure you to your death!"

She smiled smugly to the wall before her face and kept climbing. "I like to do things myself, is all."

All jest was gone from her a moment later, though, as Finley concentrated on maintaining firm hold on the sandy rock. It seemed as though her bottom became heavier, the wall slanted outward and at a gradual cantilever the higher she went, and it caused her to curl into the cliff with fingertips and toes and even her pelvis. She couldn't see the opening Lachlan had spoken of from her position pressed up against the cliff, but she didn't dare lean away from the wall to look up properly. Beads of perspiration broke out along her upper lip and hairline, trickled in itchy rivulets down her back.

She froze when she realized she'd have to eventually come back down, which would likely prove to be an even more treacherous journey.

"Finley?"

She forced herself to swallow, and her fingers and toes tightened even further, the little pieces of grit beneath her fingertips seeming to roll like marbles.

"I'm not afraid," she gritted through her teeth.

"I know you're not," Lachlan called up quickly. "You're only five handholds from the cache." He paused. "Take a deep breath."

She did, but even her lungs quivered.

"Step up with your left foot," Lachlan directed. "There you are. Right hand now. Almost there."

"Almost there," she repeated to herself in a whisper, and her movements became surer, a little smoother and faster.

And then suddenly she saw the edge of what had appeared to be a jutting place in the rock, but was actually the lip to an opening in the wall, just to the right of the stone ladder. Three more hand holds and she would be high enough to crawl in; one more and she would be able to peer inside.

Her fear vanished like the smoke in the storeroom below, and her quivering lips curved slightly. Kirsten Carson would never do something so daring.

Finley pulled up another length and held her breath as her eyes came above the level of the rock edge, ready to behold any number of ancient and stolen goods. What she saw was a monster.

Wild, yellow eyes protruded from a sunken and elongated skull; cracked, red lips stretched around a gaping mouth with a few yellow, broken teeth. He was squatting on his haunches facing the opening as if to pounce on her, his fists clenched.

Finley flinched, slipped, and screamed as her hands slid away from the rock.

Chapter 10

Finley had just reached the opening to the cache when she gave a short, hoarse scream and her hands slipped from their holds.

"Finley!" Lachlan shouted and braced himself. Even if it killed him, he would not let her body touch the stone floor.

But before her skirts could billow, before her arms stretched out in flight, a thin appendage, like a tree branch, shot from the opening of the cache and seized Finley by some upper part of her and snatched her into the side of the cliff as quickly and efficiently as a spider drawing its prey into the cage of its body. The stone shaft was tomb silent for a heartbeat of time, and then a hellish yowling filled the channel, bouncing from the rock, swelling with echoes, raising the hair on Lachlan's neck.

He leaped onto the stone ladder three handholds up and ascended as if it was of no more effort than walking down a cobbled lane. He was level with the cache in a moment, and yet the screaming did not cease even for an instant. He didn't know of a creature that could hold its breath for so long.

At least if it was screaming, it wasn't eating Finley.

Lachlan threw himself onto the stone ledge, already shouting her name. "Finley! Finley! Fin—"

He understood at once why the screaming had gone on and on—it wasn't only the creature vocalizing fear and outrage, but Finley, too, was shouting, each one leaving it to the other to carry on while they drew renewed breath. Little wonder the result was so piercing and discordant; it sounded like two cats lashed together inside a kettle.

"Stop! Stop!" Lachlan shouted, scrambling to his feet to step to the center of the small chamber between where Finley and the—man?—were crouched, each with their back to a wall of stone or piled goods, each staring across the stone floor as if looking upon a demon from the very depths of hell itself.

"*Stop!*" Lachlan roared. His own chest still heaved within the uneasy silence buffeted by gasps and sniffles. He looked to Finley. "Are you hurt?" She wouldn't take her eyes from the man, but she shook her head.

Lachlan turned at last toward the person crouched to his right and had to steel himself against an exclamation of shock. It was a man, or perhaps at one time had been a man. Only a score of thin, greasy black strands crossed the top of his head, and his long, thin, knobby fingers, like fat buds on winter-emaciated twigs in spring curled up over his temples and the blackened ovals of his fingernails pressed into the skin at his crown. His eyes bulged like eggs in his face, his lips and cheeks billowing in and out like sails with the effort of his breaths. He was dressed in an ancient tunic, impossibly long and impossibly dirty, and for an instant Lachlan's mind went to the image he held of his grandfather, Archibald Blair. The tunic sagged between the man's knees to the floor between his raw skin boots, and his knees were like skulls themselves, disproportionately large in comparison with his skeletal legs, the creases and follicles stained by what was perhaps peat.

"Finley, do you know this man?" Lachlan glanced at her only long enough to see her head shake slightly again. "All right, friend," Lachlan said softly. "We're nae going to harm you. I'm in your debt for saving—"he paused for half a heartbeat; my wife? my woman?—"my lass, here."

The man's eyes watched Lachlan while he spoke, narrowing more and more until they were barely slits in his leathery face. Then they opened so wide, Lachlan wondered that they didn't come free from his face altogether.

"Tommy?" he whispered. "Tommy, 's'it you?"

Lachlan froze. The only Tommy he knew was—

"Do you mean...Thomas Annesley?"

The man dipped his head, like a seabird swallowing a fish. "Have I changed so much that you doona recognize me?" He edged up to a crouch on his feet and then hesitantly stood straighter, although he didn't entirely rid himself of his stooped posture, and Lachlan didn't know if the affectation was physical or mental.

"You seem to barely have aged, Tommy," the man whispered, sidling nearer, reaching up a hand hesitantly and then drawing it back. "I thought you...I thought..." He reached out again, and this time touched the very upper part of Lachlan's temple; he only felt the brush of it on his hair. "I thought you was dead. But you doona bear even a scar. Where've ye been, Tommy?"

"I'm not Tommy," Lachlan said, and his voice sounded queer to his own ears. Did he look so much like the man who sired him? No one had ever mentioned such a thing to him. "My name is Lachlan Blair."

The man cried out and fell backward, as if he'd been shot, skittering away from Lachlan until he crashed into a wall of piled crates and stacks of unknown composition, causing some of them to topple and slide and tumble over the edge. Splintering and breaking sounds echoed up from below.

"You're a *Blair*?" the man said in a horrified whisper and glanced at the edge of the cache as if considering following the detritus over the side.

"Finley?" Lachlan called out.

"What do you expect me to do?" Finley edged into his line of vision, holding her slight, white hand out toward the man. "It's all right, it's all right," she encouraged. "He'll nae harm you, even if he is a stinking Blair." She glanced up at Lachlan, and then turned her full attention once more to the man clutching at the crates at his back, seemingly preparing to climb through the chamber's stone ceiling at any moment.

"I'm Finley. *Carson*. Me da's Rory Carson, an elder in the town. Do you know him? Are you Carson?"

The man didn't reply, but at least he had ceased destroying the ancient stacks behind him.

"Good," Lachlan said. "Keep talking."

Finley inched closer. "Have you been staying here? In the cliff? It must be cold in the nights."

He shook his head hesitantly and then glanced toward the corner, where black remains were piled. "I've a fire. No one sees the smoke."

"Well, that's good," Finley said, and lowered herself to a cross-legged seat, pulling her skirts down over her knees. "What's your name?"

The man looked back at Lachlan, and the terror in his big eyes was very clear. "He'll tell," he rasped. "He's a Blair and he'll *tell* them. He'll tell the chief I've been hiding all these years."

"He willna," Finley rushed, leaning slightly to put herself into his range of vision and gain his attention once more. "He is a Blair, but he and I are married. He lives in Carson Town now."

The man glanced accusingly at Lachlan again. "*He* lives *here*."

"He sleeps here, aye," Finley allowed. "But he willna tell anyone anything you doona wish him to." She looked up at Lachlan again. "Will you, Lachlan?"

"You've my word," Lachlan said at once.

The man looked between them anxiously, and it was clear he wasn't yet convinced of his safety. And so Lachlan made a fast decision—the only thing he could think of that might possibly instill some trust in him from the man.

"I couldn't tell Archibald anything even if I wished to; he's dead. And while I am called Lachlan Blair, Thomas Annesley was my father."

"The chief is dead?" The man stilled and brought both filthy, thin palms up to cover his mouth and squeezed his eyes shut. He rocked himself slightly and took a long, jagged inhalation through his nose. Then, in a blink, he had crawled across the floor of the stone chamber and wrapped his arms around Lachlan's legs, sobbing, "Edna's son, Edna's son."

Lachlan looked down at Finley and tossed his head pointedly at the man who had attached himself to him. She threw out her hands in exasperation and then, with a roll of her eyes, turned on her hip, scooting closer to the man, and hesitantly lying her hand on the bony prominence of his shoulder.

"Shh," she said. "It's going to be all right." She patted him until he had quieted and turned his head against Lachlan's knees to face her. "There you are. Hello. Can you tell us your name now?"

He gave a noisy sniff and then swallowed before speaking in a hoarse voice. "Geordie," the old man said. "I'm Geordie Blair."

* * * *

Geordie sat in the brush of the wood, the skirt of his old tunic stretched across his knees and filled with the roasted nuts he'd brought with him into his hiding place. He'd stopped crying at last, he knew, because he could clearly see the nutmeats as the shells cracked open against the hilt, and then the broken tip of his knife, and also because his cheeks had the stretched-tight feeling left by a wash of salty tears now dried up.

They'd taken so many of his friends. Would have taken Edna, too. Thanks be to God he still had her in the town, even if she was cross and shouting at everyone most of the time. She never shouted at Geordie. Edna was very sad now, just like him, and Geordie reckoned they both would be sad for a good long while.

He bit down on the walnut flesh, soft and bitter and still slightly green-tasting, and chewed it to a pulp. He didn't understand why his friends had wanted to go with the Englishman and be servants in his house, any matter. Northumberland—he didn't even know where that was. It couldn't be so nice as here, with the mountain and the loch and the wood and all their family. But Harrell had said there would be more food for them in Northumberland, and more food to go around in the town now, too. Lots more.

Blairs is poor, Geordie-boy; you know that. Poor and starving. Acras.

Geordie didn't care; he would have shared his part with them all if they'd just stayed. He'd thought perhaps Tommy Annesley would have been his best friend of all, the way he'd listened to Geordie and not shushed him or called him "daft bugger" or "runt" or "fool." Edna liked Tommy very much, too. But Tommy didn't choose to leave, so it weren't his fault, Geordie reckoned. Tommy was dead, his skull bashed in on the hillside by them mean, greedy Carsons.

His chin flinched and his vision grew watery at the remembrance of it, and he would have descended into weeping again had it not been for the crashing sounds of someone approaching in the underbrush. Geordie turned his head and listened, and the sound grew louder and closer, the arrhythmic crunching hinting that there was more than one person sharing this corner of the wood with Geordie.

"It must be tonight." Harrell's voice; Geordie recognized.

"Good God, Harrell, they're still buryin' their dead." That was Archibald. "Give the bastards at least the night."

"Sure, give them the courtesy they've nae shown us," Harrell taunted, and his voice was rough, not the way he usually spoke to the chief. It made Geordie feel sick in his belly. "They torched the boats with our own aboard."

Geordie's mouth fell open and his temples ached at trying to make sense of what Harrell was saying. Did he mean the Englishman's boats? The boats his friends had gone on?

"And you would have had Edna going with them!" Archibald accused.

"Hargrave would have made it worth yer while—he said as much. Look here."

Geordie leaned down to peek through the brown and red dying leaves to see Harrell handing a sack to the chief.

Archibald took it. "What's this?"

"Yer share. Payment for us finding Hargrave such fine servants."

Archibald was quiet for a long moment. "You...sold them, Harrell?"

"They went willingly, did they nae?" Harrell argued. "They was lookin' for a better life than what they'd had. They chose to leave, Archibald. They get what they deserve, if ye was to ask me."

Geordie didn't see Archibald's hand striking Harrell's face, but he well recognized the sharp crack of skin on skin.

"You're a disgrace to this clan," Archibald gasped.

In a moment, Harrell had seized the chief by his tunic and jerked him up close to his face. "Am I, Archie? Am I?" He shook Archibald, but Geordie didn't think of going to the chief's rescue; he could call to mind too many times when Archibald himself had laid hands upon Geordie, usually as a result of things that were none of his own doing.

"Seems to me it's yer precious Edna that's played ye false. I only tried to turn it to our advantage. For the clan." He shook him again, then Harrell shoved the chief away so roughly that Archibald fell to the leaves on his arsey-parsey, as Edna always called it.

"We have but one chance to take the upper hand with the Carsons," Harrell continued, coming to stand over the half-reclined chief. "We gather the fine and ride in an hour, and we tell them we're willing to make a treaty so that Vaughn Hargrave willna return. We take the river, the salmon. We take the wood. We take whatever else we want in the whole of that town, and then we tell them that if they take on cargo from another merchant ship in the bay, Hargrave will hear about it. It's time the Blairs prospered, and I mean to see ye stand up to it, Archibald."

"They'll never agree," Archibald rasped.

"Sure, they will," Harrell said. "I might have been rough on ye tonight, Archie, but ye'll soon see that I've done it for yer own good. For the good of us all. And when the treaty's agreed to, and all's quieted, ye'll consider me for your Edna."

"I canna do that, Harrell. She knew Tommy. She told me they—"

Harrell leaned down and picked up the sack Archibald had dropped and tossed it to the man's chest, where it landed with a tinkle.

"I'll nae be needing any dowry, then."

Geordie's rage threatened to deafen him, his thoughts buzzing so loudly in his head. He shot to his feet, the nut shells falling to the ground, and he burst from the brush toward the two men.

"Nay! Nay!" he shouted, swinging his arms in great circles, hoping he could get close enough for just one blow before Harrell stopped him with a fist. "You canna have Edna! You've done enough! Yer bad, Harrell! Yer bad!"

He expected the clout to land at any moment, but Harrell only grabbed hold of his wrists, jerking him to a stop, and struggling to hold him at arm's length while Archibald scrambled to his feet.

"Now hold on there, Geordie-boy," Harrell grunted while he struggled. "Hold on there. What are ye on about? Ye must have misheard."

"I didna mishear nothin', Harrell Blair," Geordie shouted. "You sold my friends to...you sold them for coin! That English coin! An'...an'..." He jerked himself free at last and stumbled back a pair of steps. "Now they're

dead! Dead o' fire! Just like all them Carsons—dead o' fire! Dead like my friend Tommy! And you got coin for them!"

He turned his eyes to Archibald. *"Say you willna let him have Edna, Chief. You canna. Nay. I'll tell her."* He swung his glare back to Harrell. *"I'll tell Edna what you done, and then she'll never want you. Never-never!"*

"Och, Geordie-boy, calm yourself," Archibald said in a shaky voice, running his fingers back through his graying hair. *"There's naught to tell anyone. You didna hear right, is all."*

"I did hear right," he said, stumbling backward. *"I'm not a fool and I did hear right!"*

Harrell and Archibald shared a glance, and Geordie knew all too well the meaning of it. He turned and ran, intending to gain the town and shout for Edna's help, but the town was on the other side of Harrell Blair, and Geordie found himself running down, downhill through the wood, leaping over logs, sliding through the leaves, blocking Harrell's shouts from his pounding ears.

He ran and ran, until at last the rickety old bridge to Carson Town was in sight, and the roar of the falls pushed the air around him like invisible waves. He could still smell the smoke on the air from the smoldering town, and occasionally little flakes of ash swirled in the air like dry, dirty snow. Geordie dashed onto the treacherous bridge and froze in the middle, clinging to the rope as Harrell heaved to a stop on the end.

He stepped carefully onto the bridge. *"Now, Geordie-boy, doona be running off like that. If ye'd have waited, I could have told ye it was all right. Yer right."*

"I'm right."

"Aye." Harrell moved closer. *"I willna take Edna from ye. And I'll tell the town all that was done. They'll understand. Ye'll see. We'll all share the coin."* He was standing next to Geordie now. *"Come back with me, Geordie-boy."*

Geordie looked down at his offered hand, the wide-gapped teeth of the bridge planks burring in and out of focus beneath his palm. The water from the loud, loud falls misted around them, the ash whirled on the soot-scented wind.

Geordie had first laid eyes on Tommy on this very bridge.

"I doona trust you, Harrell."

"Och, now." Harrell Blair smiled. *"Maybe yer nae so dumb after all."*

And then Geordie was falling through the mist, turning, turning. The water was cold, but only for an instant, and then the top of his head was very hot. But it didn't matter that he was wet because he was going to sleep.

* * * *

Neither Finley nor Lachlan said anything as they made their way to the lower chamber of the old house's storeroom. Lachlan descended first and then reached up to take the lamp and her cloak, and then guided Finley down as she slid over the rounded, sandy lip on her stomach. She couldn't help the awareness of his strong fingers pressing into her waist in the moment before he released her and turned away to resurrect the fire.

Finley sat on the edge of Lachlan's pallet in the flickering shadows of the lamp and pulled her cloak up over her legs and to her chin, watching him stoke the blaze. Her mind whirled with the disjointed bits Geordie Blair had just told them. If any of it was even partly true...

The fire grew taller, warming the small storeroom and giving it a cozy glow that Finley very much needed. Lachlan turned on one knee and then sat back on his foot, resting an arm across his stomach. He was staring through the flames, but Finley didn't think he really saw her. He was lost in thoughts, perhaps of the past. Perhaps of the future.

And Finley reckoned she didn't play into either one of those circumstances. For Lachlan, Finley was only his inconvenient present.

She pushed herself farther back on the pallet and pulled up her feet beneath the cloak. It was surprisingly pleasant to lean against the cliff wall and watch Lachlan watching the fire with his furrowed brow, his smell wafting up from his blankets all around her, like the fragrance of summer from warm sand. Her muscles were already stiffening from the climb and the shock of nearly falling to her death, and the sight of him with the glow of the fire flickering over the planes and angles of his handsome face soothed her, pushed the troublesome worries of her own future from her mind.

There were two other people in the old house this night who had burdens far heavier than hers.

"I have to take him back," Lachlan half-muttered.

"*Geordie?*" Finley whispered, and then glanced up at the passageway to the upper chamber as if he might overhear their conversation. "He's frightened to death of Harrell, Lachlan. He'll nae go. Or worse, he'll run off, and then where would you be? I canna believe he survived the falls in the first place, never mind all these years alone on his own. What that must do to a person..."

Lachlan's generous mouth pressed into a line. "There's no one else who knows what he does. No one else who can confront Harrell before the fine with the truth."

"Do you think it will matter if he does?" Finley pressed, even as an uncomfortable feeling sank into her middle. "The man's clearly...I mean, he's been alone for such a long time. Perhaps it's affected his thinking—his memories, even."

"Perhaps it has," Lachlan agreed. "I've heard Geordie's name mentioned, although it's been years now. But never by Harrell or my grandfather. Everyone at Town Blair has thought him dead, all these years." He stared at the fire again. "I've got to find someone to corroborate his tale, and Murdoch's been avoiding me." His brows lowered even further.

"Aye, Murdoch does tend to disappear now and again. There's my father, though he didn't return to Carson Town until—" Finley broke off as Lachlan bolted to his feet and rushed toward the pallet, plunging his hands beneath the makeshift mattress and causing Finley to skitter back against the cliff wall.

"What are you doing?" she demanded.

"Not some*one* to corroborate the tale," he muttered as he rummaged beneath the lumpy cushion. "Some*thing*." He withdrew his arm, and there was a long, cloth-wrapped object in his hand. Lachlan got to his feet only long enough to turn and perch on the edge of the pallet, and Finley pulled herself next to him as he unwrapped the mysterious item.

"What is it?" she asked as the dull metal of a sheath was revealed.

Lachlan tossed the cloth aside and held the dagger point up across his chest. "Carson steel," he said, and then reached up with his right forefinger and tapped the brooch on his shawl.

Finley leaned forward to examine both pieces and gasped as she recognized the identical pattern. Then she reached up and slid the dagger from his hand. Lachlan let it go easily, and this time it was he who moved closer to look over her shoulder as Finley settled back on her hip and turned over the sheath in her hand.

"Did it come from the cache?" she asked.

"Nay; Dand brought it to me the first day we took the sheep up to graze," Lachlan answered, and his breath was warm on her neck, his low voice tickling her eardrum with its deep resonance. "He came upon Harrell tearing apart Archibald's house, searching for something. Dand later found this, hidden in a wall."

Finley turned her head and was nearly nose to nose with Lachlan. "Thomas Annesley's, you think."

"Possibly. Where did my brooch come from?"

Finley felt her brows raise in surprise. "It was my mother's, of course. Received on her own wedding day. But neither she nor my da's ever said anything about it having a twin in a dagger."

"Hmm." He was lost in thought again, and Finley could see every pore and line and dark hair on his face. Such a combination of rough and smooth. She wondered what it would be like to slide her hand along his jaw...

"I'll show it to Murdoch tomorrow," he muttered. "If I can find him. He must know something." Then he blinked, bringing his thoughts back to the present and meeting Finley's gaze once more.

"But you won't tell him about Geordie, will you?" Finley pressed. "Lachlan, you gave your word."

"I won't," he promised, seeming to search her eyes for something he expected her to be or say or do. Finley wished she knew what it was he wanted. "I'm glad you came with me tonight," he said. "We're friends now, are we nae?"

Finley barely nodded. "How can we nae be?" She felt an inexorable pulling sensation in her middle, as if some magnetic force was drawing her closer to Lachlan Blair, a force she couldn't resist.

Now he was closer to her, too, so perhaps this force was pulling him as well. Or pushing him. But when he closed the distance between their mouths, pressing her lips with his, bringing his hand up to cradle the back of her head and deepen the kiss while the Carson dagger rested between their hearts, Finley realized that Lachlan himself was the force.

Finley felt every bone, every muscle in her body with exquisite detail, heard the rushing of her blood in her veins, pulsing like the roar of the falls above the bridge. It was a new world spread before her to discover; it was an ancient secret, her palm brushing away the centuries in a sparkling cloud to understand the very meaning of her existence. It was magical and mundane; made law by their marriage vows and also forbidden by their own agreement with each other.

Finley's world changed with the mingling of their breath.

Lachlan pulled away and yet stayed near, his thumb stroking her hair back and forth.

"Do friends kiss like that?" she whispered.

"Probably not," he admitted with his wry grin. His hand fell away from her scalp, and the chill rushed in maliciously to replace his warmth as he rose from the pallet. "I'll sleep on the floor."

"Nay," she said, her head swimming with confusion and excitement and sadness, and she gained her feet. "I'll go." He started to protest, but she cut him off. "I'd not have my parents searching for me in the morning and take the chance of Geordie being discovered."

"He's managed to stay hidden for thirty years," Lachlan argued, his hands on his hips causing him to look oddly unsure of himself. "Are you afraid I'll kiss you again?"

"I'm not afraid of anything," she said and stood before him, presenting the dagger to him across her palms. She looked up into his face, and perhaps now she understood what he had been looking for in her eyes.

Who was Lachlan Blair to her? Who would he be to her in the future? Did he care? Should she?

"I'll see you in the morning," she said.

Lachlan wrapped his fingers around the sheath and took it, not meeting her eyes. "I'm sorry. I shouldn't have—let me walk you back."

She shook her head and then did what she'd been longing to all evening: She reached up and placed her hand along his jaw, her skin breaking out in gooseflesh again at the warm, prickly feel of him against her palm. She smiled at him.

"You didn't take advantage of me, Lachlan," she said. "And even if you had…we are married."

His eyes smoldered. "Stop."

Her smile grew, triumphant that she had gained the upper hand at last. "Good night," she said pointedly. She turned and ducked out of the storeroom, running lightly through the cavernous hall until she burst through the wide, arched entrance of the old house, beneath the sky pricked with countless blazing stars.

The village below was dark. Everyone was asleep, oblivious to the secret Finley had discovered tonight and was walking away from, back to the old farm.

Not Geordie Blair; no, no.

Finley Carson was in love with Lachlan Blair.

Chapter 11

Lachlan met Finley coming out of the door of her house, a plate of bannocks and a mug of milk in her hands.

He noticed at once that her hair was different that morning: plaited along each side of her head and coiled neatly at her neck. The effect was pretty and showed off the creamy, pale skin along her cheekbones.

"What are you about so early in the day?" she demanded, stepping outside after Lachlan had relieved her of her burden. She pulled the door shut after her and wrapped her shawl tighter, her breath misting in the heavy, cool air. "Da's not roused himself yet."

"He might be in no hurry; the first work is done. I've a mind to speak to as many of the townsfolk as I can," he said, pausing to take a bite of an oatcake, chew, and swallow, not bothering to tell her that he'd finished with the chores hours ago by lamplight before the sleepy, blinking animals in the darkness, trying to push the memory of Finley's kiss from his mind and failing. "I reckon the next step to earning their trust is to lend my help."

Her spare eyebrows rose. "You mean to help everyone in town with all their chores?"

He nodded while he chewed another mouthful. "As many as I can. Your da's got the largest stake besides Eachann Todde."

"And he's over the mountain with the sheep," Finley said. She paused, her lips pressed together. "Can I come?"

"Aye." His answer was out of his mouth almost before she'd finished asking the question.

"If I'm with you—" She stopped, as if just realizing he'd already said yes. She smiled at him. Lord, she was enchanting.

Lachlan smiled back.

* * * *

By the time the sun was high, Lachlan had tended no fewer than one hundred animals. He'd mended two gates, sewn thatch into three roofs, and held one infant while Finley helped a woman hang out her washing. The infant was, by far, the most difficult chore of the day—like holding a very short, thick eel. An eel that wanted to pull your hair and stick its slippery, wet fingers in your facial orifices and shriek when it was disallowed. Lachlan resorted to placing the child in a tall basket for a time, swinging it by one handle when the creature became restless.

He was thankful when they were on the path to the next longhouse, and he recognized the familiar blond head of Kirsten Carson, scattering grain for the ducks gathered around her in the dooryard. The young woman glanced up and immediately blushed, dumping out her apron and brushing her hands over the fabric before clasping them behind her back.

"Good day, Kirsten," Finley called out.

"Good day, Finley," the blonde replied, and then gave Lachlan the briefest of glances. "Blair."

"Miss Kirsten," Lachlan said with a slight bow, knowing it would cause the shy girl's cheeks to flush even deeper.

Finley gave him an exasperated glance before addressing her friend once more. "The old folks about?"

"They're bringing in nets," Kirsten said.

"Would you know of any work about the place your father would welcome help with?" Lachlan asked, and held up the box with Rory Carson's tools. "I've little knowledge of fishing, else I'd head to the beach to lend a hand."

Kirsten's eyes widened slightly, and she glanced at Finley as if to gauge the sincerity of his offer. "I don't suppose it takes much learning to haul in nets, now does it? Only a strong back. Seems an odd thing, though, for the Blair to be hiring himself out," she hedged.

Finley's sigh was audible. "He's nae the Blair."

"Not hiring out," Lachlan corrected, ignoring Finley's comment. "Just offering help as a gesture of goodwill from a Blair to the Carson Town." He remembered the item in his pouch and set down the box, finding the shell quickly and holding it toward Kirsten. "Speaking of goodwill from Blair to Carson, this is for you. From Dand."

Kirsten's eyes widened again, but it was only for a moment, and then her pretty, pleasant face went blank and she raised her gaze to Lachlan.

"Forgive me, Blair, but I canna accept a gift from a man promised to another."

Lachlan cocked his head. "Dand's nae promised to anyone."

Kirsten sniffed. "I've heard otherwise."

"How could you have?" Finley said.

"I've heard it," Kirsten insisted. "And I've seen proof of it with my own eyes. It's that...*Searrach*." She said the name as if she was spitting poison from her mouth, and then she looked at Lachlan again. "Weren't she to marry you, Blair?"

Finley gasped. "Kirsten Carson, have you been to Town Blair on your own again?"

Lachlan looked between the two women. "Wait—what?"

"You just mind your own business, Finley," Kirsten said with a lift of her chin and a final brush of her skirts. "You forget that while you might be fortunate enough to have a husband, there are others who've not yet had one placed on their very doorstep. *And* who wouldn't be so very ungrateful as you have been to have it happen. So you just mind your own business and let me mind mine." She frowned at Lachlan, and he could see the glisten of tears in her eyes. "Good day, Blair." She stalked through the open doorway of her family's longhouse and closed the door firmly behind her.

Lachlan looked down at Finley in the same moment that she lifted her eyes to him, and Lachlan suspected they were wearing similar expressions of surprise. From what Lachlan had seen of the blond Kirsten, she was gentle and friendly by nature, so this change in attitude had to have been brought on by something significant.

"She knows something," Finley said, echoing his thoughts. "Or at least she thinks she does. Have you any word from Dand?"

"Not since the day he gave me the dagger. And this," he said, gesturing with the shell still in his hand. "I'd be told if my brother was to wed."

"Maybe she's mistaken," Finley offered. "Kirsten's feelings can be a bit exaggerated at times, and she has been daft over your brother since she first caught sight of him."

"Perhaps," Lachlan acceded. But to himself, he thought it was more likely that Dand had been prevented from making the journey to Carson Town. "Dand's already said he wouldn't have Searrach. For Kirsten to be so convinced that they're to wed..."

Finley held out her hand. "Give me the shell."

"What, you're going to chuck it through her window?"

She wiggled her fingers and thrust her palm forward. "I'm going to go inside and find out what's wrong while you go speak to Murdoch, who's just coming up from the beach there."

Lachlan turned to look behind him and felt the shell snatched from his hand. When he looked again, Finley was already marching to the closed door. She raised her fist and rapped.

"Kirsten? Open the door."

"Go away," came the wailed response.

Finley rolled her eyes and then reached up to pull the rope hanging along the doorframe, disengaging the latch on the other side.

"I'll meet you back at the house," she instructed over her shoulder and then disappeared inside.

Lachlan stood nonplussed in the sunshine for a moment. He'd wanted Finley Carson along this morning for what he thought were his own reasons, and yet she had succeeded in a way that far surpassed any usefulness Lachlan had hoped for, and it caused him to frown.

Why had he been so stupid as to have kissed her last night in the old house? Sure, it had addled his wits. She wasn't sweet, like Ina; she wasn't gentle, like Kirsten; she didn't love him, and she certainly didn't want to be married to him, like Searrach had.

So why did that make Lachlan want her with him more and more?

He shook his head and picked up Rory Carson's crate and turned toward the path, walking to meet Murdoch Carson, who had spotted his approach and didn't look the happier for it.

It was time to talk of daggers and battles, of people long dead, of smuggling and of feasts.

* * * *

"I said, go away," Kirsten sobbed as Finley entered the house and closed the door. Her friend was seated at a table, her face buried in the nest made by her arms.

"Kirsten?" She slid into the chair next to Kirsten and hesitantly reached out a hand to touch her shoulder. She had played the comforter twice in as many days now, and it was an odd role for her.

Kirsten didn't flinch away, but it was obvious her anger was still present, along with her sadness. "You doona understand, Finley. You've got your husband—and it's the Blair."

"He's nae the—"

She raised her tear-streaked face. "I'm already ten and eight! Who am I to marry in Carson Town? Hairy old *Eachann Todde?*"

Finley drew her head back. "Weren't it you who encouraged me to consider Eachann Todde not so long ago?"

"Well, aye," Kirsten said with a sniff and a roll of her eyes. "He's got all those nice sheep, Fin, and you're forever going on about the farm. And you *are* older than me."

"By a year!"

Kirsten winced. "Almost two."

Finley pressed her lips together and looked down at the tabletop with a slow intake of breath. "Kirsten, what makes you so sure of Dand Blair being matched?"

"They're going to make him marry that *woman*...that...that..." Kirsten, who'd never had a bad thing to say about anyone, seemed to be struggling to find the right word.

"Coo?" Finley offered, thinking it should be strong enough of an insult.

"Aye," Kirsten said with a scowl. "Aye, that *coo*, Searrach. Slutty pile o' tits."

Finley pressed her palm over her mouth and bit the inside of her cheek to keep from bursting with laughter. She blew out a short breath through pursed lips. "How do you know Dand is going to marry Searrach?"

"How do you think, Finley Carson?" she demanded. "I saw them. Searrach and her father."

Finley gave her a sideways look and waited.

"Sure, I went to Town Blair," she admitted in exasperation. "Harrell had just come back from away. I heard them talking about it. Are you happy now?"

"Kirsten," Finley gasped and laughed at the same time. "You know we aren't to go past the bridge. I would never have thought you so bold as to go all that way alone. *Again*," she added.

"No one thinks me so bold," Kirsten said, wiping at her eyes and sniffing. "That's how I can go and not be missed. Besides, since the treaty, we doona have to keep to this side of the bridge now, do we?" She paused, glancing at Finley. "That was the third time I've gone the whole way to the town."

"You sly lass," Finley said, hearing the admiration in her voice.

"Oh, doona say it like that," Kirsten wailed. "I didna do it to be sly, or just to see what mischief I could get away with, like you would, Finley."

"Och!"

"I love him," Kirsten went on plaintively. "I *love* him and I…I think he might love me, too, given the chance. So it's nae fair!" She lay her head back down in her arms and sobbed.

"There, there," Finley said, patting Kirsten's back awkwardly. "Oh, would you stop? Squalling won't solve anything, and you're making my head ache."

"You're a terrible friend." The lament was muffled by her arms.

"Just finding that out, are you?" Finley kept patting. "I'll tell Lachlan what you saw. Maybe he'll know what's at the bottom of it; he's a knack for finding out things that were meant to be hidden."

Kirsten raised her head. "Really? What things?"

"I'd be here all day if I told you," Finley said, and then stood up from the chair. She set the pretty, pink shell on the tabletop, and Kirsten stared at it with a pout. "Dand wanted you to have this. If you love him so, I think you'd wish to keep it."

Kirsten reached out and took the shell in one hand, then ran the fingers of her other along its ruffled edge. "Perhaps if I do wish upon it every night, he'll be mine."

Finley rolled her eyes but didn't disabuse her friend of her fanciful notions. "I'll let you know if I find out anything." She turned to go but stopped abruptly. "And Kirsten, stay away from Town Blair unless someone is with you, whether the old boundary applies or nay."

Kirsten might think herself brave enough to traipse through the woods, but coming face-to-face with real danger would be an entirely different matter. Finley suspected anyplace housing a man such as Harrell Blair was decidedly dangerous.

"I'll nae promise you anything, Finley Carson. Although I doona truly think you a terrible friend, you know," Kirsten said in an airy voice, worshipping the pink shell in her palm with her eyes. "Just in case you thought you could be rid of me. We're friends for life, you and I."

Finley sighed as she opened the door. "Sure, until I murder you."

Kirsten gave her an indulgent smile. "I love you, too."

* * * *

"Murdoch," Lachlan called out as the older man plodded up the path, his head down, his breeches darkened with water to his knees. "I'd speak to you a moment, if you have the time. I've sought you the past several days, but you were nowhere to be found."

He didn't look up as he neared. "I was hunting, if it's aught for you to know. Building another storehouse, are ye?"

Lachlan ignored the taunt and fell in step alongside the Carson chief as Murdoch continued on through the town. "I have questions about the great battle."

Murdoch gave a dark chuckle. "The great battle, eh? Everyone has questions about the great battle. Yer nae special."

"Have I offended you?" Lachlan frowned and stopped in the street. "For as much as you argued to gain me for the clan, you seem to resent me being here."

Murdoch halted and stood a moment facing away from Lachlan. Then he turned and began walking back toward him.

"Aye, *some of us* do resent you being here," he said. "You wedding Rory's lass has brought us food and grazing and things we can hold in our hand, but it can never bring back what this town lost all those years ago. Seeing you every day is only a reminder." He stopped nose to nose with Lachlan. "For some of us."

"That's what I want to ask y—"

"Who the hell do you think you are, up in the old house, shaming Finley like that? Still fancy yourself chief, do ye, Blair? Living in town nae good enough for you?"

Lachlan huffed a laugh and shook his head. This was not going the way he'd imagined, and he was trying to keep hold of his temper. "I'm shaming Finley? Who thought it was a good idea to have a newlywed couple sharing a bedchamber with the old folks?" Lachlan held up a hand. "Never mind. I've no desire to quarrel with you, Mur—"

"Well, beg yer pardon for nae building you a manor to suit, Blair," Murdoch sneered. "In case you hadn't noticed, there are a score of empty cottages you could have taken for your use." He leaned even closer. "Empty for years, because so many of our clan were killed, and most of the ones that survived chose to leave rather than starve to death."

"You didn't leave," Lachlan shot back.

"*Because I couldn't,*" he said, and his entire body seemed to tremble with frustrated rage. "They became my responsibility when my father and brother died. This is my home, my clan. Or what's left of them all now. You were a necessary evil to try to get back some of what we lost. Doesna mean I have to like you."

"Fair enough." Lachlan reached into his pouch and withdrew the dagger. He thrust it flat against Murdoch's chest, causing the older man to take a step back.

Murdoch reached up and took hold of the sheath before the heavy piece could tumble to the road. "What's this?"

"Recognize it?" Lachlan asked.

Murdoch's brow furrowed. "Where did you get it?"

"Do you recognize it or nae?"

The older man held his gaze for a moment and then thrust it back toward Lachlan. "Nay."

"You're lying."

"The design on it is Carson, aye. But I've nae seen it before in my life. Now leave me be." He turned to walk back up the path once more.

"You're angry about me staying up at the old house because you're afraid I'll ask about the smuggling, aren't you?"

Murdoch froze in his step again, but didn't turn as he called out, "I doona ken what you're yammering about, boy."

"The smuggling the Carsons were part of before the war," Lachlan called out, even louder this time. "Or perhaps it was simple trade? Did you try to strike it back up again and fail? Is that the real reason Carson Town was starving? Why everyone left—"

This time Murdoch didn't stop at being nose to nose with Lachlan, but barreled into him, taking him by surprise and causing him to stumble on his feet. From the corner of his eye, Lachlan could see the group of villagers coming up from the beach carrying heavy, dripping nets and baskets of bounty between them.

"You doona know *anything,*" Murdoch warned in a low voice, pointing his finger in Lachlan's face.

The murmur of conversation from the group stopped, and everyone stared at the two men in the street.

One of the townsmen called out, "Aught amiss, Murdoch?"

The Carson chief's glare never left Lachlan's face. "Not a mite, Dove. The Blair and I are just having a wee discussion. Innit, Blair?"

"Aye," Lachlan agreed. "Fine as fallow."

The crowd moved on through the town, but they were casting wary glances behind them.

"I want to understand what happened," Lachlan said evenly.

"Understand? Understand this: You are a Blair. You'll always be a Blair. An outsider here."

"I know that," Lachlan said, ignoring the twisting in his gut at the words. "I need to prove to Marcas and the fine that Town Blair is where I belong. Someone is lying about what happened those terrible days when Carson

Town was attacked. And those lies have cost me my own people—all but my life, Murdoch. I want them back."

Murdoch's frown lessened for a moment in surprise, but then it lowered nearly to the bridge of his nose. "What about Finley? You'd just abandon her, making it so that she can never marry again?"

"Finley doesn't want me any more than I want her. She wishes me gone so that she can do what she likes, when she likes, without any husband to rein her in. You know that as well as I do, else she would have been wed long before I came around. Instead you used her to punish me."

"Doona be so full o' yerself. 'Twas a bit o' punishment for her as well, I admit." The Carson chief's mouth quirked despite himself. "But she's a bonny lass. You seem to be coming out no worse for the wear."

"It's because I'm sleeping somewhere else!" Lachlan defended himself.

At this, Murdoch almost chuckled. "Well, aye. Wise, that." He looked at Lachlan from the corner of his eye. "Sure, you heard about the hornets."

Lachlan raised an eyebrow. "I pretend I havena."

Murdoch's faint grin faded and he sighed. "What is it you want from me, Blair?"

"I want to know exactly what happened the night Carson Town was attacked," Lachlan said. "I want to know who was here; in town, on the beach, in the old house. I want to know how the old treaty was struck after the fighting stopped."

"The treaty was struck how it had to be," Murdoch rushed in in a low voice, and Lachlan could tell that even the mention of that night placed a pall over the robust man, darkening the hollows around his eyes, graying his complexion, rounding his shoulders. "I wasna myself. My wife..." He broke off and made a quarter turn away from Lachlan, as if he were looking over the rooftops toward the bay, searching the horizon with his eyes for the shape of the thing that haunted him.

"My wife and daughter," he continued, "they had taken shelter in the old house when the town was attacked and were trapped in the fire. They... well, they both died, is all. After some days. Her and the bairn. By that time it was already decided. By the whole of the fine, nae just me." He paused a moment, and Lachlan saw his shoulders heave in a silent sigh. "I've naught else to say about it. Some of it I canna even recall anymore."

Lachlan thought his answer odd, but let it pass. "There are others in the town, though, who might remember more," he hedged.

Murdoch shrugged and turned back to him at last. "Perhaps. Most of the old ones are dead. Thirty years is a long time."

"There will be tales."

"Aye, and that's all you can take them for," Murdoch cautioned, and the stern look had returned to his face. Lachlan was glad in a way to no longer be made witness to the man's agonizing grief. "Tales. Stories none should believe. You know what use gossip is good for."

"It's all I have."

Murdoch paused. "Sure, and that reasoning right there is enough to convince me you doona ken yer arse from a knothole, lad. Is that what you're about this day, with Finley's pappy's tools? Rapping at doors and listening for bits of gossip?"

Lachlan's pride smoldered.

Murdoch flapped a hand at him, then started up the street once more. "Bah. Isnae one'll tell you anything, any matter. Outsider, like I said."

"That's why I want Carson Town to hold *Lá Bealltainn*," Lachlan called after him. "If any town needs a feast and a fresh start, it's this one. And I say you should have it. *We* should have it," he corrected. "Finley says there's never been a May feast that she remembers."

The chief kept walking, so Lachlan made the final move in his strategy.

"I've come upon a goodly amount of Irish to contribute. Along with whatever work needs to be done to make the town ready."

Murdoch Carson stopped in his tracks, but didn't turn around.

"We still have a week to prepare," Lachlan called out.

"That's not enough time to ready a proper *Lá Bealltainn*," Murdoch said loudly, apparently to the empty street before him.

"I can do it," Lachlan said. "We can do it together—the fires, the sport, the food. I know we can. It will do the town good. It will do you good, Murdoch Carson. Another step toward reclaiming your town."

"That does sound fine to my ears," he said quietly. The chief was silent for a long moment. And then he called out, "I still say a week is nae long enough. So I reckon you'd best get to work, if you're to prove me wrong."

Even though Lachlan had hoped for this answer, he was still surprised. "I have your blessing?"

"Nay," Murdoch said, looking over his left shoulder. "But you do have my leave, and you can tell aught who asks that you have it." He turned his head a little further. "And Blair?"

"Aye?"

"While you're still playing at tinker, there's yet nets to be hauled in."

Chapter 12

It seemed to Finley that she had just closed her eyes when she felt her shoulder being gently shaken and the stir of Ina's breath in her ear. Finley rolled over partway and squinted in the dark room at the darker shape of her mother.

"What is it?" Finley whispered.

"Shh." It was barely a sound as Ina motioned her from the bed.

Finley swung her legs over the side of the mattress and was searching the floor with her toes for her slippers when she was pulled away from the task.

"Leave them," Ina breathed, and even in the whisper Finley could hear the thread of girlish excitement.

The main room of the house was clammy and cold; the fire was gone. Finley didn't think she could ever remember another time in her life when there hadn't been at least coals hidden beneath a fluffy pile of ash. But there was no time to wonder about the fire as Ina was pulling her through the doorway onto the path.

The sky was tall and wide and gray, freckled with the last straggling stars, and Finley's breath was thick in the humid air. She heard sounds of people approaching and turned; there, coming up over the hill on the path, were other women and girls from the town, all still in their nightdresses, all without their slippers.

"They remembered," Ina breathed.

There was a low buzz of whispered excitement flavored with giggles from the very young, and any thought Finley had of their farm being the destination was quickly forgotten as the women glided around and past her and Ina and headed to the small, sloped pastures beyond.

"Come," Ina said, just as the sun began to peek over the ben, the strip of sky above the cliff and trees going white, then butter yellow. Her mother's eyes sparkled like a girl's as she pulled Finley along into the feminine current.

"What are we doing?" Finely laughed as the sounds of the women's chatter grew higher with the rising of the sun.

"*Lá Bealltainn!*" Ina called up to the sky.

They reached the pasture, the grass longer than Finley had ever seen it now that Carson animals had infinitely larger and better meadows to feed on, and plunged into the sea of greensward. Ina pulled Finley around in a half circle until they were facing each other, and then released her. All around them, the older women, even to the eldest widow, were bending their stiff knees, crouching with spread arms and then sweeping their hands over the heads of the grasses and wildflowers, scooping their palms toward their faces and leaving their cheeks and foreheads, eyes and décolletages shining with dew, their sleeves clinging wet and transparent to their skin.

The littlest girls squealed and giggled as understanding dawned on them. Finley looked again at her mother, now participating in this slow, graceful dance, her smile as radiant as the beams of morning that shot over the cliff and set the pasture to sparkling with dew and femininity. She swooped down and swept her hands toward herself, daubing her face with the cool, lubricous dew that still smelled like night and also green, still-tight buds ready to burst forth with life. Finley laughed and laughed as she, too, washed her face with summer's arrived ripeness, while the youngest Carson daughters raced around the pasture with their palms skimming the grass like swallows.

Lá Bealltainn.

Then the women began picking the flowers—yellow and orange and all shades of lilac—until their arms were laden. The young girls made beautiful crowns of blooms for them all, ropes and necklaces and waist garters, all frilled with soft, fragrant petals. Back down the hill they went, looping the wreaths and circlets onto low-hanging branches along the path, on doors and windows, overhangs and well handles.

Finley and Ina diverted through their own barn, laughing and skipping as they christened the tired old building with the bright gaiety of summer. Lachlan and Rory were in the aisle about their chores and stopped to lean on their fork handles as the women swept toward them. The old milk cow won a crown hung over one sweet ear; her calf received the treat of a thistle flower to crunch.

Ina draped a necklace over Rory's head, who grinned proudly and pulled his wife to him for a peck on her cheek. Finley was caught up in the moment as she skipped up to Lachlan and tucked a bell heather behind his ear. She rose up on her toes without thinking as he leaned forward to grant her her kiss, and Finley didn't turn her head. Lachlan's hand came up to cup her jaw as their mouths met, and when Finley pulled away, his fingers lingered on her skin as he looked into her eyes with a faint, bewildered smile.

"Dew suits you," he said.

Finley felt warm to her very toes, and rather than ruin the moment by saying something ridiculous and clumsy, she skipped away from him and out of the barn, her spontaneous laugh the only betrayer of her ecstasy.

The entire town was soon bedecked in bright blooms and then, as if prearranged, the menfolk emerged onto the streets, the elders of the town, the young men and boys afoot with rowdy shrieks. The feminine and masculine halves of Carson Town melded as streams converging into a river. And that river wound its way up the main street to the expanse of rolling hill before the old house, where the evidence of the long hours scouring the bay for driftwood was piled.

A cassock stuffed with heather lay on the ground near the base of the mountain of fuel wood, a bow and cord and dry, fluffy tinder at the ready. Murdoch stood patiently by the quiet pile until everyone from the town had arrived and was attending him with great anticipation. Just as he opened his mouth, Finley felt a warm hand slide along the small of her back. She looked up to see Lachlan at her side, and although he didn't look at her, his hand remained resting on her waist.

As if he had truly come to meet her.

As if she was truly his woman, his wife.

As if he cared not who saw him touch her and the conclusions they would draw from it.

"*Lá Bealltainn*, Carsons!" Murdoch bellowed, startling Finley back to the present. The gathering returned the greeting to their chief with whooping cries of revelry.

"It has been many a long year since our town has celebrated. Many a long year since we've had aught to celebrate," Murdoch allowed more solemnly. "But let today mark the beginning of nae only a fruitful growing season for our crops and our animals, but a future of abundance for all our folk." He paused, seeming to struggle with a bit of emotion, and the sight of it brought a prickle to Finley's eyes. "Never again, God willing, shall our people suffer from such want as we have endured. With this need-fire, we kindle renewed wills—the very thing that makes us Carsons. Never a stronger clan was there, and never a stronger clan shall there be!"

The crowd cheered, and Finley noticed that Lachlan's shout was one of the loudest, and her heart squeezed painfully, wonderfully.

"Now, as I'm sure yer all in want of a hot meal," Murdoch went on to the laughter of the crowd. He bent and picked up the corded bow and spindle, held them in his hands for a moment, looking at them in a most melancholy way before raising his gaze once more to find Finley's father nearby in the crowd.

"The need-fire must be struck by a married man of the town." He bundled the tools together in one hand and held them out. "Rory Carson, you gave up the life you were making to return to us when you were needed. You've done everything you could to see that your kin in blood and in name survived. You have proved a friend to me. To us all."

Finley's father stepped forward and took the tools with a humble nod of acknowledgment, and then he turned away, looking over the sea of faces before him. "I did return to Carson Town. But it was nae unselfish, as I wouldna've had my good Ina, nor my sweet, gentle, meek, wee lass."

At this, the crowd broke out in good-natured laughter, and Finley felt a creeping blush steal over her face even as she sent her father a mock scowl.

Lachlan squeezed her tighter to his side for the briefest moment, as if he was proud to be standing with her. Finley didn't think anyone had ever been proud of such a thing in her whole life.

Rory continued. "But I am an old man now. And I am not so proud as not to know that the burden of Carson Town's success rests on the shoulders of the young. And I hope you will agree with me, Murdoch—that all of you will agree—that there is one here who has done much that was unexpected of him for our good." He paused, and Finley held her breath. "My gel's husband, Lachlan Blair."

Rory extended the corded bow and spindle into the empty space at the center of the crowd. "You are well met to us, Lachlan Blair. *Lá Bealltainn* is your doing. Would that you kindle the need-fire."

Finley couldn't help the gasp that escaped her, and she felt Lachlan stiffen at her shoulder. This was a clear olive branch from the town, delivered through her own father, even if Murdoch could not bring himself to extend it. It was a laying to rest of the past, and the grudges held against Lachlan for the sins of his clan. All those gathered watched him with anxious, hopeful expressions. There was no animosity here for the man at her side, not any longer. Lachlan had worked every day to win over the town as he had set out to do, and Finley could think of no stronger evidence to prove that he had succeeded.

He pulled away from her gently, taking care to press her shoulders with his palms and look into her eyes before he turned to the center of the crowd and stepped toward her father. He held out his hand.

"You do me a great honor, Father Carson," he said.

Rory placed the bow and cording into Lachlan's palm with both hands, reverently, ceremonially. Finley's throat constricted.

Lachlan went to the cassock and knelt. He squared the thin pine board outfitted with a divot between his knees, and then set the spindle. He laid the cord over the spindle, twisted the bow to form a loop, and began to work.

Lachlan was sweating within minutes, and the longer he worked, the closer the crowd drew to him. Tiny tendrils of smoke began curling from beneath the blackening spindle, and a circular ridge of brown dust rose up from the divot. More smoke, and now a whiff of burning wood on the air.

"Almost there, lad," Rory said in a soft voice.

The encouragement seemed to give Lachlan renewed strength, and the bow was a blur as he sawed at the wood. And then, suddenly, his actions stopped and he reached for a pinch of the fluffy tinder. He laid it on the smoking pine board and leaned down, blowing gently, gently. Smoke rolled, and then a small lick of flame flickered up from the center. Lachlan added more tinder, tucked it in, prodded the flames, and then carefully picked up the hearth board.

He rose up on his knees and turned toward the base of the smaller fire that had been laid, nestling the hearth board in the pile of kindling, feeding the baby flames thin strips of bark, wood shavings, then twigs and shards of light, percussive driftwood.

A teasing crackle of proper wood, and then the flames grew tall, spread. The crowd gathered around the fire erupted in a cheer.

Lachlan Blair had brought life back to the town.

* * * *

Every female in Carson Town kissed Lachlan that morning.

As they came up by family to collect their bit of need-fire to carry back to their own hearths, they pecked his cheek, squeezed his hand, gifted him with warm smiles of welcome and thanks. Genuine welcome. Oddly, it was Kirsten Carson who had been the most reserved.

"Doona forget, Blair," she whispered in his ear.

Her reminder sobered him. In the busy days leading up to this morning, Lachlan had indeed almost forgotten about the valley of Starving Lake beyond the edge of the cliff, about the family he'd left behind there. *Nay, nae left behind,* a dark voice argued. *Forced to leave.*

It was like another lifetime.

Thoughts of his brother brought to mind the idea that Town Blair was also celebrating *Lá Bealltainn* at this very moment, Marcas likely lighting the need-fire with Dand at his side. There would be roast lamb on the green, and the unmarried women and girls would dance around the well. He knew they were carrying on without him, and it caused a darkness to dampen his spirits, much like a lone, laden cloud passing menacingly before the warm sun. Perhaps it would pour out its rain and ruin a pleasant day, or perhaps it would drift by still laden, leaving behind only a brief chill and a thankfulness for the light.

Ina Carson was the last of the townswomen to come forward after everyone else had dispersed to their homes for a hasty breaking of their fasts. Her gentle smile had grown familiar to him, her way of looking out for him as a mother would, and yet still always granting him respect as a grown man. He'd never really had a mother.

"You did so well, Lachlan," she said, pulling him into her embrace and patting his back. She leaned away to beam up into his face. "So well. We're all proud as can be."

Lachlan's throat constricted.

"Naw, doona embarrass the man, Mam," Rory interjected gruffly as he steered his wife toward the path. But he gave Lachlan a wink and a nod before he turned away, and there was a sparkle in the old man's eye that meant just as much to Lachlan as Ina's maternal praise.

"Good morning."

He turned back his head, and there was Finley. He'd thought she'd gone ahead, but he was inordinately pleased that she'd waited for him. Her red locks were tamed into two long braids that hung over her shoulders, a score of bright, tiny blooms woven in among the strands. She still wore her flower crown, and her wide, blue eyes seemed to reflect the smile on her pink mouth.

"Good morning," Lachlan replied.

"Care to walk me back to the house?"

"Will you feed me bannocks?"

Finley nodded.

Murdoch was at his side then, taking the narrow spade from Lachlan's hand. "Go on, lad. I planned on tending the fire 'til the games begin, any matter. Brought meself some good eld victuals." He patted the pouch on his belt.

It seemed the most natural thing in the world to Lachlan that he drop his arm across Finley's shoulders as they walked down the path, and for the briefest moment, he allowed himself to again pretend that it would always be this way. That Finley would give him smiles and kisses, and walk home with him.

They were friends, were they not?

But the pretend was becoming more challenging of late to reconcile with the real, and it was difficult for Lachlan to accept that he was just biding his time at Carson Town, doing what was necessary to bring about what he'd set out to do. The game he was playing could turn him into a helpless pawn, he warned himself. And Lachlan dreaded the time drawing near when Finley would not smile at him, would reject his kisses.

But then he squeezed Finley to him for a moment as they approached Rory and Ina's longhouse. It was just today. Just today. And it was *Lá Bealltainn*. Nothing so drastic was going to happen today to prevent him from enjoying this town, this woman, on such a special day.

Today, he belonged.

* * * *

Murdoch sighed and sat down on the rock rolled near to the fire. He tucked the handle of the spade behind his arm, and reached into his pouch for the skin, but rather than opening it at once, he rested it across his thigh and stared out over the low rooftops of the town toward the sparkling blue bay and the wide, seemingly endless sea beyond. No ships. No ships for years.

He'd kept his word.

If he hadn't been listening for them, the need fire would have surely masked the hesitant, shuffling footsteps behind him.

Murdoch retrieved one of the cold oatcakes from his pouch and then unstoppered the flask and took a mouthful of the whisky. Then he reseated the cork and rose slightly to place the flask and the oatcake on the sandy, rocky ground away from where he sat. Murdoch took the spade from beneath his arm and stepped to the fire to herd the spreading flames. He couldn't hear the footsteps so near the roar, but he knew they were still there.

"You are welcome at my fire, Geordie Blair," Murdoch called out.

* * * *

The leftover food from their morning meal was packed into the baskets, along with the dishes made the day before, and Finley and her mother looped the handles over their arms as they preceded the men from the house and toward the beach. A few townsfolk had carried tables and benches out onto the sand, and even now, some were busy setting up short, staked flags, placing painted targets and piling wood for smaller fires.

The wind was gentle and warm over the waves, sending the flags fluttering. Children took shifts guarding the food baskets from the excited seabirds that swooped over the beach like banners tethered long on the end of the children's sticks.

The men and older boys wandered down the beach in loose groups, their belts heavy with weaponry, and in moments, the first rounds of the games began. Axes, daggers, and freshly sharpened spears were hurled over the sand toward the targets, with shouts of triumph and cries of lament decorating the air. The girls and younger children had stick horse races, and water-carrying competitions, and there was a net-plaiting contest for the women. Ina Carson won it easily, and to the laughing encouragement of all the women gathered when she'd told them the secret was all the years she'd spent trying to get Finley to hold still long enough to have her hair tamed.

The food was brought out. Then the mead. And then the second round of men's games began. Lachlan had a good showing, and Finley wanted to think it was because he knew she was there watching him, cheering for him.

Her husband. Her husband whom she wanted to stay in Carson Town. She wanted him to stay and be her husband in truth.

And tonight, emboldened by *Lá Bealltainn,* she would tell him so.

Then all were divided into groups for the foot races. The youngest children went first, along a short course on the beach, and Finley thought no one at all won that heat, because most of them ended up on their faces and squalling because they got sand in their eyes and—soon after—their mouths. The older children were divided by age and sent into and through the town, with the victors winning special shell necklaces.

As the afternoon slid into evening, all the men thirteen and older were gathered together for the longest and most anticipated foot race: through the town, past the old house, to the falls bridge and back. A lad of ten and four easily claimed the prize of a pewter mug, and it was soon filled with rewarding mead for the victor as the sun hovered over the horizon and the beach fires were lit.

Finley found a panting and sweating Lachlan near the mead barrel and strolled up to him, her hands clasped behind her back.

"Showin' your age are you, Blair?" she taunted with a smile.

The men around the table laughed as Lachlan turned to face her. He paused a moment, taking in her appearance. She still wore her flower crown, but her hair was loosed from her plaits and flowing over the bodice of the gown she'd worn on their wedding day. Appreciation burned in his eyes.

"Och, I let the lad have it," he said. "Every boy needs a bit of encouragement now and again."

She snorted. "*I* could have bested you in that race."

Lachlan turned up his cup and drained it, set it on the table, and then reached out to snag Finley around her waist. He pulled her to him and leaned his face close to her, but just when Finley thought he would kiss her, he touched her nose with his fingertip and grinned.

"You're adorable."

He released her, and Finley tried to hold back her own smile. "Does that mean you willna accept my challenge? I understand if you're afraid."

The men ooh'ed in anticipation. A set of pipes squeezed out a few hesitant notes, and then took up a lively tune, while a pair of drummers added high and low percussion to the salty, cooling air.

Lachlan placed his hand on the tabletop and leaned his face toward hers. "A challenge, is it?"

"Aye. Down the beach to the pools."

"To what spoils go the victor?" Lachlan asked.

She shrugged, as if she hadn't thought that far ahead, as if it didn't matter. In truth, it didn't, because she hoped to gain her victory before returning to the festivities. "Boon of his or her asking."

"Lurin' ye to yer death, Blair!" one man called out in a laughing warning.

"Doona trust her comely face!"

"Aye," said another, and to Finley's chagrin, she saw it was Eachann Todde. "I'd stay far from the water's edge, were I you."

"Take a knife!"

"Take a *gun*."

The winning young lad from the foot race stepped up between them, his cheeks telltale roses from the mead he'd gulped. He hitched up his breeches and puffed out his chest.

"I'll take her on, Blair," he boasted, and the cat calls of the men only encouraged him, even if Lachlan rolled his eyes. "I like a feisty lass. Perhaps she'll give me a wee kiss if I—"

The lad was abruptly silenced as Lachlan placed his entire palm over the boy's face and shoved him backward, where he fell on his arse in the sand amidst his own self-indulgent giggles.

"All right," Lachlan said with a smile. He reached for his belt and unbuckled it.

Finley's heart stuttered in her chest.

"I accept your challenge, lass. And I'll engage in yer contest—"he dropped the belt with his dagger and hatchet still attached onto the tabletop—"unarmed."

The men ooh'ed in a humorous combination of admiration and dismay.

Finley slipped off her shoes, held them up dangling in her fingertips for a moment, and then dropped them atop Lachlan's belt.

"Goin' off into the dark with 'er!"

"Yer a dead man, Blair!"

"Good i' 'twas to know him!"

"So good!"

They collectively took up singing a mournful dirge to the tune supplied considerately by the pipe player.

Eachann Todde rose from his seat with a groan and walked around before the pair of them, holding up his hands. "I'll officiate such a serious contest, then." He took out a kerchief from the folds of his shawl and held it up while Lachlan and Finley crouched down. And then Eachann looked over his shoulder, speaking to the eager onlookers. "And as such it'll be me to be first to comfort the black widow after the Blair's funeral. I'll require a length of rope and a large sack."

Finley left her readied stance to place her hands on her hips and glare at Eachann Todde. "Are you—"

"Go!" Eachann shouted, waving the kerchief, and Lachlan was off with a spray of sand.

Finley shrieked her rage, but then dashed after him, leaving behind the howls of good-natured laughter. Even with having to hold up her skirts to her knees, Finley closed the gap between her and Lachlan in moments, and the sunset provided the perfect light to see the look of surprise on his face when he turned his head to find her gaining on him.

"Going to let me win, too, Blair?" she taunted with easy breath.

He pulled away from her, then, and at first Finley fought to keep pace with him, but his lead lengthened until he had disappeared into the gloom of the beach's end, where the grassy dunes rolled over to meet the tide pools. She lost sight of him for a moment, but kept running. She knew he would be there, waiting for her.

She saw him, then, standing facing her in the sand, and still she ran on. As she grew nearer, he held open his arms.

Finley leaped into them, and their kiss was immediate. Lachlan sank to the sand, turning Finley in his arms until she lay on the beach half-beneath him. She cradled his head in her hands, surrendering to his mouth, his hands roving her body.

"Finley," he groaned against her lips. "You torture me."

"Nae torture," she said, returning his kisses and drawing him closer with her leg. "Reward. You want me, Lachlan."

"I do," he said, trailing his mouth down her neck. "So much."

"You've already said I was your friend," she whispered. "Let us be married in truth."

He stilled against her. "Finley—"

"You belong here now," she said, and she ignored the icy tendrils of doubt that were creeping around her heart. "Carson Town will prosper again, and it is because of you. The people love you."

I love you, she wanted to say. But now the uncertainty was making her afraid. His silence was making her afraid.

"You knew when I came here that it was always my plan to go back to Town Blair," he said in a low voice. "Nothing has changed."

"They've not accepted you back," she argued.

"I don't have proof yet."

"Even if you get that proof, they still might not take you."

"They'll have no choice," Lachlan insisted. "It is my place by rights. By clan law."

Finley pushed him away and sat up. Night had taken hold fully now, and the stars pricked the sky with twinkling mirth. As if they didn't know how close Finley was to crying.

"I doona understand why it's more important to you to be the Blair than it is to be happy," she said in a low voice. "You are happy here, Lachlan."

"I am happy here," he admitted.

"Mam and Da, people in this town have accepted you as one of their own. Do you have any idea the victory that is for you? Or is your head so stuffed with thoughts of greatness that it has no room to recognize the good around you?"

"That's not it," Lachlan said, and there was a tinge of offense in his tone. "Do *you* have any idea what it will mean for the future peace of both our towns when I return to Town Blair as chief? I care for these people as my own as well, now. Never will there be another feud between the Carsons and Blairs."

"If you cared so much for the people here, you wouldn't leave, and the devil take the Blairs. They discarded you."

If you cared that much, you wouldn't leave me.

She had found his sore spot, evidenced by the way his voice hardened. "Have I not given enough?" he demanded. "What else do you want from me? To ruin you for any future chance of marriage? Is that what you want, Finley? Because, make no mistake, when Town Blair calls me back, I will go."

Finley swallowed down the bitter disappointment lodged in her throat. She could think of nothing else to say to him. He had rejected her. Had rejected her town, just as his town had rejected him. And yet they both still yearned for the thing that had spurned them.

"I do want you," he said and suddenly seized her shoulders, pulling her face close to his in the darkness, but Finley kept her eyes cast to the bay. "I shouldn't, and I never intended to want you, but I do. And it's because I care for you that I wouldna be so selfish as to act on it. I am bound to lead my clan. To clear my name, and perhaps my father's name. It is a responsibility I will not shirk. Even for you. *My friend.*"

Finley shook him off and gained her feet, walking to the sand dune and starting up awkwardly through the deep, sandy hillock. His friend. Nothing more.

"Where are you going?"

"Home," she said, allowing the tears to find their freedom on her cheeks in the night air, now that she was walking away from him. "A place you will never know."

"Finley!" he called out.

She broke into a run through the gravelly dune, the seagrass whispering against her skirts like mourners. He may as well already be gone, for in her heart, Lachlan had left her that night.

She slowed to a walk as she came into the quiet alleys, the houses all empty and dark. The dirt beneath her bare feet was still warm, even as the cooling breeze brought out tall, prickly gooseflesh on her arms and legs, and she was glad to step through the door of her own home and close out the night.

She lit the lamp and looked around the room, saw the familiar walls and furnishings, smelled the familiar smells. This house had been her home as long as she'd been alive. She'd slept in the bedchamber every night since she was born. And when her parents became tired of the festivities on the beach, they, too, would return to the house, and go to sleep in the same chamber. Just as it had always been. Just as it would always be, until the ends of their lives.

And then Finley would be alone.

That was the future she'd wanted, though, wasn't it, before she'd married Lachlan Blair? This farm, all to herself, with no husband to tell her what to do. She suddenly looked down at her hands, saw how smooth and clean they were now that she wasn't doing more than half the rough work. She glanced up and saw the small piece of embroidery around the hem of a little wool gown she'd left on the table. It wasn't art to behold, but she was getting better. And, truth be told, she was growing to enjoy it. The gown would be a fitting gift for the next woman in town to have a bairn.

Finley had briefly fancied she might be that woman.

Instead, her husband intended to disavow her and return to the people who had thrust him from his home, stripped him of the only family he had ever known, and sent him away disgraced. She ripped off her flower crown and flung it across the room. What a fool he was, she thought bitterly. Even the woman he was to have married had betrayed him.

The knock on the door startled Finley, and she spun around to stare at it, her heart pounding. Could it be Lachlan?

The rap came again, quiet but insistent. "Finley?"

She walked to the door and opened it. "Kirsten, what are you doing? Why aren't you at the beach?"

"Why aren't you?" her friend returned, pushing past her into the house.

Finley closed the door and turned to face the blonde. "I was tired."

Kirsten simply stared at her.

"Och, I doona wish to talk about it, all right?" Finley said.

"Sure. And nae talkin' about it suits me fine," Kirsten answered quickly. "Get your shoes, and hurry. Better fetch a cloak as well."

"Kirsten, I'm not going back to the beach tonight."

Finley's friend held her gaze. "Neither am I."

Finley knew in a moment what she meant to do. She held up her hands, then turned back to the door and opened it. "Good night, Kirsten."

The little blonde marched toward the door and pulled it from Finley's hand, closing it firmly. "You told me nae to go alone. I'm tired of having nae say in my own happiness, Fin. I'm tired of waiting and hoping for others to act."

Finley held her tongue. She'd had no say in marrying Lachlan Blair, and now she had no say in his leaving.

Kirsten went on. "I want to ken once and for all if that ferret-faced bitch has her claws in Dand truly, or if it's against his will. And I think there is plenty you've been askin' yerself about Lachlan's future between the towns," she said.

Just say nay, Finley told herself. But aloud, she said, "It's pitch-dark in the wood, Kirsten."

"Better to nae be seen."

"We'll get lost."

Kirsten gave an uncharacteristic snort. "*You* might get lost at night on yer own. But nae me. Nae now."

Finley thought in silence for a moment. "What happens when everyone returns to find us gone?"

Kirsten shrugged. "I already told my folks I was sleeping at yours."

"Let me guess: you told mine I was sleeping at yours."

The very faintest grin quirked a corner of her mouth. Kirsten Carson *was* sly. And she was right. Maybe this was a way to get some of her questions answered, or at least gain some insight about Town Blair's feelings toward Lachlan. Normally, sneaking through the woods to spy on the town wouldn't have the potential to be so promising, but today was *Lá Bealltainn*—all but the very oldest and youngest in the clan would revel until nearly dawn.

Finley sighed. "Fine. But if the Blairs catch us, we're both drunk and lost our way hunting fairies in the wood."

"Sure, and what will they do even if they catch us? Kill us?" Kirsten clapped her hands and bounced on the balls of her feet. "Hurry now, before your folks return—oh, I could run all the way there!"

Chapter 13

Lachlan returned to the festivities on the beach, but the celebration had lost its happiness for him. He slowly eased away from the crowds to find a spot between a bonfire and the sea where he could be alone to think. He had hurt Finley, he knew that, but he didn't understand how. They had both agreed from the beginning that he would return to Town Blair. That they had managed to become so close should have been an added boon. And yet it had caused her heartache because she had wanted him to stay.

Finley wanted him to stay.

Lachlan shook his head to clear it of the memories of holding her sweet-smelling body close on the night-soaked beach. Why had he not been content with having her not try to kill him? Why had he let himself sink into the easy friendship that had developed between them, and then developed into something more? Why had he been unable to keep her from haunting his thoughts since that evening so long ago, when he'd watched her dump Eachann Todde into the river? In truth, he could hardly imagine his future without her now, a future without the old house looming behind him as he went about his days, or the sun sinking into the blazing waters of the bay. Of early mornings in the barn with Rory Carson or sweating afternoons pulling in miles of netting, writhing and sparkling with sea life.

But he had an obligation to fulfill. He had been wronged. Robbed. Slandered. That must be remedied.

His mind went still. Why hadn't it occurred to him before? He didn't have to leave Finley. She was his wife, and if she truly wanted to be with him, she would go with him when he returned to Town Blair. She would be the chief's wife—and a more fitting station there could not be for her. She would bring the much-needed spark and brightness that Lachlan hadn't even known he'd been craving all his life. It was so obvious, so simple: Finley would go to Town Blair with him. Of course she would.

Murdoch Carson caught Lachlan's eye, then, leisurely making his way up the beach. The chief stopped to chat with this person and that while the faint notes of the pipes still floated on the air; to ruffle the fire-gilded curls of a sleepy child snuggled into his mother's arms; to share a swig of Irish with a group of men. Then he approached the leaned-together figures of Rory and Ina Carson and, after a moment, Ina bestowed a peck on Rory's cheek and allowed Murdoch to help her to her feet. They carried on up the beach together, and Lachlan's brows knit together in curiosity as they neared him.

"Blair," Murdoch said by way of greeting. "Didna expect to find you alone."

Lachlan was thinking of something to say when Ina saved him.

"Doona be very aggrieved at Finley," she said. "She's never been one for womanly companionship, and I think it well that she has a friend in Kirsten, even if all that little one will do is moon over yer own brother. She'll be home by breakfast."

Lachlan nodded, as if he knew Finley's plans all along, but inside he was relieved that she was spending the remainder of the evening with Kirsten Carson. He would seek her out on the morrow and tell her of his new plan. "I'm not aggrieved at her at all. The contrary, in fact."

"Walk with us," Ina said, and her smile was as gentle and genuine as ever, even if in the back of Lachlan's mind, warnings were sounding. "I've something to show you, and likely some answers to your questions."

Lachlan rose from the sand and took up the place on the other side of Ina as the trio made their way from the beach, Murdoch pausing to rock a lit torch free from the sand. As they neared the path that led to the Carson farm, Murdoch stepped away to the door of a cottage whose roof Lachlan had helped replace. He opened it and held it aside while Ina and Lachlan passed through.

There were coals glowing in the hearth, and a small table with two little stools. The cottage was comprised of a single room, with the bedstead snugged into one corner. The other end of the house was fitted with the partitions for the animals in winter, although now the gates were opened flat against the wall and the floor was swept clean and dry. The smell of fresh sod gave the air a heavy, wet feeling.

Murdoch gestured to one of the stools as he walked toward the hearth in the darkened room, his torch washing light across the walls. "Sit down."

Lachlan crossed his arms. "I'll stand, if it's all the same to you."

"Och, naw, doona be that way," Ina scoffed as she lowered herself onto a chair. "Sit with me, son. Let me talk to you without having to twist me old neck."

Mother Blair, Lachlan's foster mother, had never referred to him as "son" in all his life. Not once. Lachlan reluctantly pulled out the other chair and sat.

"You've been asking a lot of questions since you came to Carson Town," Ina began, and while from anyone else the declaration may have come off as sinister or accusing, her words were accompanied by her same gentle smile. "Even of my Rory."

Murdoch had added fuel to the fire and then slipped his torch into a holder on the wall. Now he leaned a shoulder against the door, his arms crossed over his chest. "I told him Rory wouldn't have the answers he sought."

"Aye," Lachlan acknowledged. "And you were right. Any who remembered the battle could only repeat what everyone else said. The attack from the sea. The fire. The Blair townsfolk who were in league with the enemy ships."

"And nae a one could tell you about Thomas Annesley, or how he was connected to the Carsons," Ina said. "Because you never asked the one person who knew."

Lachlan felt his brows lift in surprise. "Mother Carson, I—" he began.

"Did Fin tell ye about your brooch?" Ina interrupted him.

Lachlan looked down reflexively, his right hand going to the round, silver filigree on his shawl. "Aye. She said it had been yours on your wedding day."

"And that it was," Ina acknowledged. "But nae from my Rory. When his poor Mam called him back to Carson Town, he'd had yet to make a solid trade. He wasna the eldest son of his family, you see, but his brothers, his sisters, his da—all died in the fire. Their house was burned to the ground, and everything in it. All their animals, gone. The only thing he had in the world was his mother when he returned. But I…" Ina paused, and Lachlan could see that memories were clouding her aging eyes, causing them to mist over behind decades of painful loss.

"I had the farm. It was set up so high and apart from the town or the old house, most everything was saved. I was alone. Widowed. Frightened." She paused again, and then looked up to meet Lachlan's gaze with her own. "Rory married me for the good of the town. Both our resentments and mourning made us little use to each other for a good long while."

"I ken the feeling," Lachlan said.

"Nay," Ina said gently and with a little shake of her head. "Years, Lachlan. Our bedchamber has always kept two beds, if you ken."

Lachlan stilled. He could hardly imagine the loving couple he knew as Finley's parents so at odds with each other.

"So the brooch, it was my marriage gift from my first husband, and I wanted Finley to give it to you." She held out her hand. "May I?"

Lachlan undid the clasp and laid the brooch in her wrinkled palm.

Ina brought the piece close to her, stroked it with her thumb. "I never took it off. For ten years after he was dead. In my heart, I was still Andrew's wife."

Out of the corner of his eye, Lachlan saw Murdoch look away with a pained expression beneath his beard.

"Let me at last see this blade." Ina drew his attention once more, returning the brooch to him. Lachlan refastened the pledge, then reached to his belt to remove the sheath. He laid it on the wood with barely a sound and Ina leaned forward, admiring the piece, stroking it with her fingertips. "Ah, aye. It's just as he described it." She sat back in her chair. "My first husband was Andrew Carson, Murdoch's older brother. It was he—Andrew—who told me of the dagger."

Lachlan turned to the bearded man still leaning against the door. "You said you'd never seen it before."

"And I hadna," Murdoch said. "'Twas Andrew who would have been chief. Andrew what was Da's pet, the one he confided in. The man barely looked at me."

"Murdoch," Ina chastised.

"It's true, innit? The chief wasna surprised when I disgraced him by Sal falling pregnant and having to marry her. Nae that I was put out by it. Would have done it anyways."

He looked back to Lachlan. "I wasna supposed to marry before Andrew. But that's how it happened. After our bairn was born, Ina wed the future chief of Clan Carson. All stiff an' proper, the way everyone liked it."

"Murdoch," Ina said again, and this time there was a thread of warning in her tone. "I'll nae let you speak badly of it."

"The dagger belonged to Andrew?" Lachlan interjected, fearing that a row between the older people might jeopardize the entire conversation.

"Nay," Ina answered. "It belonged to Andrew's grandfather."

"Then how did it end up hidden in Archibald Blair's house?"

"They only ever called him the Old Carson," Ina said, ignoring Lachlan's question. "He had two children, a son who became chief; that was Murdoch and Andrew's father. And a daughter, Myra."

Lachlan waited, listened, the back of his neck prickling, but for what reason he could not say.

"The Carsons were always mighty, warring. Especially with the Blairs, but we've been at war with nearly all the clans along the coast at one time or another," Ina said. "And foreign enemies coming from the sea as well. We were nae without our own ships, after all. Our clan grew wealthy, and we began to command trade along the coast." She paused with a pleasant smile. "Can you imagine wealthy Highland Carsons, Lachlan? It was true for a long while, I suppose."

"We brought goods into the Highlands from the Irish," Murdoch added. "Traded with all the clans. Took their wools and their skins. Sent them to Edinburgh, Glasgow, west back to the isles. North to Skye, all along the coast south of us."

Lachlan's head spun with all the things he was learning. "But you didn't trade with the Blairs," Lachlan said. "I've heard the tales; you left them to starve."

Murdoch shook his head and met his gaze squarely. "That was an old feud and one I wasna witness to. But my understanding of it was that it was a punishment for a wrong done to my grandda's da—a Blair lad killed a Carson lad in a bit of mean play. He was just a wee boy, they say; nae old enough to join in the sport, but had gone along any matter. Just a bairn. It grieved the Carson's wife something fierce, and she swore an ancient hatred that was never to be forgiven on earth. Carson women can hold a grudge like nae other."

This information shook Lachlan, as he realized how deep the resentment of the Blairs by the Carsons went. And yet, he had kindled the need-fire today, with the Carson Town's blessing.

"Our success gained our clan powerful friends in Edinburgh," Murdoch continued. "Friends who made it possible to secure a hold on the Forth in order to continue our trade when the tolls in the city became unfair, and they thought to cheat the stupid Highlanders. But we could nae claim the keep as our own without help."

It was Ina's turn. "And so the Old Carson arranged a marriage for his Myra to a baron of the Borderlands. The keep on the firth was her dowry. And the dagger, matching the marriage brooch that would go to the Old Carson's son, and then to my husband Andrew, was her legacy." She paused. "It is likely she gave the dagger to her new husband as a wedding gift."

Lord Thomas Annesley...

"Do you mean to say," Lachlan began haltingly, "that Thomas Annesley was—"

"Myra Carson's son," Ina supplied with a gentle smile.

Lachlan went stone still for a very long moment. Then he turned his head slowly to regard Murdoch Carson. "If Thomas Annesley is my father, that means I am descended from the Old Carson. It means…it means we are blood kin, Murdoch."

"Aye," the chief agreed in a neutral tone. "Cousins, by my reckoning."

"It's why you let me kindle the need-fire," Lachlan realized. "My lineage is as much Carson as it is Blair."

"More so, I'd say," Ina interjected. "Edna and Archibald are both dead. Even if Thomas Annesley is, as well, you have us, Lachlan." She gave him an encouraging smile. "Me and Rory, we think of you as ours already. Murdoch is your blood. And sure, you've a Carson bride." She looked about the little room, quiet, warm, safe. "Do you think this place is suitable for living yet?"

"You did this for me?" Lachlan hedged, a thorny pit widening in his stomach.

Ina shook her head with a mischievous smile. "Nay. It's for myself and Rory. We want you and Fin to have the farm to yourselves."

"I've no heir, Lachlan," Murdoch said abruptly. And then he left it alone, hovering between them in this quiet place that Lachlan had unwittingly helped ready.

"Is their aught else I should know?" At their shaking heads, Lachlan stood up from the chair, his own head buzzing with confusion. "I need to be alone." He walked to the door, still blocked by Murdoch's considerable size, but then was struck by another thought.

"Did you know who I was when you bargained for me?" he demanded of the chief.

"Aye," Murdoch answered. "After the English knight came with the letter."

"And still you kept it from me. Called me an outsider, when I was your kin."

Murdoch stared at him. "You still have Blair blood in your veins. And everyone knows Blairs canna be trusted."

Lachlan shoved Murdoch away from the door and stepped toward him, daring him to retaliate. He wanted to plant his fists in the man's red-bearded face. He wanted to take his rage, his pain, out on Murdoch Carson. How dare he speak such insults against the people who had raised him? Against the people who had—

The people who had turned on him. The people who had exiled him. The people who had forgotten him.

Murdoch only stood with his hands resting at his sides and met Lachlan's gaze. "What are you goin' to do, Blair?"

Lachlan wrenched open the door and left it swinging as he exited the little cottage. He stormed up the street into the darkness, his gaze fixed on the bonfire that was still being kept before the old cliff house. The old cliff house where the Carson had lived.

Where his great-grandfather, the Carson chief, had lived.

Lachlan stopped in the street, his breath heaving in and out. He turned in a circle, looking at the quiet, peaceful town. The wood, the falls, the old house, the sea; they all seemed to be whispering his name, vying for his attention, his affection, his loyalty. He didn't know which way to turn.

Even though he now knew from where he had come, Lachlan Blair had no idea who he was, or where he belonged.

* * * *

"Shh, get down," Finley hissed, and yanked on Kirsten's arm, pulling her into the black shadows of the underbrush. Her legs were trembling and heavy from the slow, steep climb through the wood in the dark, and the thick wool of her gown was scratchy and damp with sweat. Kirsten had led them directly to Town Blair as a hound on a scent, but if Finley hadn't stopped her, she swore the idiot would have walked straight into their midst without pause.

The pair of men passed less than ten feet from them, but didn't so much as glance in their direction as they carried on with their low conversation. Finley at last let out her breath.

"That was close," Kirsten said with a giggle. Then she rose. "All right, let's go."

Finley reached up with a roll of her eyes and pulled Kirsten back down into the brush so the blonde gave a little yelp.

"Where do you think you're going to, Kirsten Carson?"

"Sure, to the green. We aren't bound to hear or see anything, hiding here behind the trees like ninnies."

Finley laughed despite herself. "We can't simply go marching into town."

"Really?" Kirsten asked, holding Finley's gaze intently. "Let's hear your plan, then, if mine is so terrible."

"That wasn't a plan," Finley muttered, putting off answering immediately. She blew her hair out of her eyes and peered toward the backs of the houses nearest the wood.

Lachlan was right; most of the town must still be about the festivities, for the air beyond the sloping roofs seemed to glow like an iridescent mushroom cap over the green. And although the town appeared brightly lit, and indeed there were faint strains of music floating on the breeze fragrant with delicious smells, there was no hushed roar of a gathering. No whooping or shouts of gamers and dancers; no bawdy songs.

It seemed odd to Finley that so large and prosperous a town should have such a solemn feast to welcome the summer when poor Carson Town had been redolent with music and laughter all the day.

Very odd.

"All right," Finley said at last. "Let's move a little closer, then. Only to the nearest house, though."

"Och, you mean we're to march into town, *closer to the green?*" Kirsten taunted. "I'd never have thought that up on me own."

"Shut up, Kirsten."

"Good thing I brought you along, Fin. Master of strategy, you are."

Finley growled a bit, but let her friend have her say. She was right, after all.

"Don't run, and don't crouch," she instructed. "That would only draw attention. We'll walk purposefully, arm in arm. If anyone happens to see us coming from the wood as if we belong to the town, they won't raise the alarm."

"Who made you the leader?"

"You did, when you asked me to come," Finley said. Then she looped her arm through Kirsten's and stood and, after taking a deep breath, the pair of Carson women stepped into Town Blair proper.

They were strolling across the short expanse between the wood and the house when they saw the same two men who had passed moments before returning in their direction.

"Oy! Oy, you women—halt!"

Halt?

"What now, leader?" Kirsten whispered.

Chapter 14

Finley fell onto her hands and knees, belting out a high-pitched shriek of laughter, and then an oof, as Kirsten fell atop her, crushing her into the soft dirt and rolling across her spine in hysterical squeals.

The footfalls of the approaching men sounded near their heads, heavy-soled shoes, the jangle of metal.

"What are the pair of you about?" one demanded in a nasally accent. "Why aren't you at the green with the others?"

Finley burst out in forced laughter again, and Kirsten howled as if it was the funniest thing she'd ever heard. "Fairies! We've found 'em at last!" And she dissolved again into convincing giggles.

They don't recognize us, Finley realized. *They think we're Blairs.*

Finley took a chance.

"Wait a minute," she slurred and turned her body onto her flank toward the men, dumping Kirsten to the dirt behind her with another yelp. "Just who are you now, to be askin' us such a thing? Yer nae Blairs."

"Aye," Kirsten added indignantly, popping up over Finley's shoulder. "We doona know you. Mind yer *o-o-own* business."

"Get 'em on their feet," the first man said and stepped forward.

Finley's struggle against the hands that gripped her upper arms painfully was real, and Kirsten gave a sharp screech.

"Sure, you'd better mind what yer grabbin', ye bastard."

"I'd nae jostle her too much," Finley warned as she was yanked about to face the man. He was wearing a strange leather vest, with plate armor draping his shoulders, and a smooth metal helm outfitted with small round rivets along the brow and nose piece.

English armor...

Finley shook herself. "I've just spent the past hour in the brush with Miss while she puked up her guts and half a barrel o' mead."

Kirsten gave a loud, dramatic *hurk* and brought her hand to her mouth. She leaned into the man holding her, her shoulders hunched.

All in all, Finley thought her show very impressive.

The man shoved Kirsten away, and Finley jerked free of her captor to go to her side. She ducked beneath her arm and pretended to support Kirsten's sagging, spasming frame.

"She just needs her bed," Finley said, sidestepping toward the house. "Beddy-bed for Miss; nae more feasting for you this night. Here we go." She turned toward the narrow space between the houses.

"Oy, where do you think you're going?"

"Good night, fairy man," Kirsten called, flopping her head back onto her shoulder.

"Just here. This is our own place, right here," Finley said, slapping the wall of the dwelling on her right as she kept walking, praying it was actually a longhouse and not one of the many animal shelters she'd seen when last she was in Town Blair. "Misses to bed."

"*Straight to bed!*" Kirsten called out in a singsong.

"Wait just a—"

"Let 'em go," the other man said. "They're too pissed to be any threat. Too stupid as well, likely. Scotch whores."

Finley stiffened.

"Shh," Kirsten warned against her neck.

"Aye," the other answered. "Not worth it. We'll be gone by morning, and they'll be just as dead on the green or in their beds."

As soon as Finley and Kirsten were around the front of the house, they came away from each other. Looking in all directions for anyone else who might raise a warning, they bolted hand in hand toward the shadows of the roof overhang. Kirsten went immediately to the door of the house.

"Nay," Finley warned in a whisper, pulling her away. "That's the first place they'll look for us if they change their minds. Come on."

They crossed the narrow street and headed northeast toward the center of town, ducked through two narrow passages, and then Finley fell upon the door of a longhouse with a back made up the outer edge of Town Blair's green. It opened easily, and the two women dashed inside, closing the door as silently as possible.

Finley and Kirsten worked together to quickly locate the bar and secure the door. Then they both stood panting, staring at the closed barrier in the dim light of the house's interior. They looked at each other in the same moment.

"What is—"

"Who were—"

Finley drew a breath and started again, in a whisper. "I think they're English soldiers."

"*English soldiers?*" Kirsten squeaked.

"Shh!"

"What are they doing at Town Blair? On *Lá Bealltainn?*"

"I don't know," Finley said, looking around the dim, unfamiliar interior. Snugged under the eaves of the rear wall was a short window, its wooden shutter propped open at the bottom with a stick so that it slanted outward. Light from the green beyond filtered through and down into the room. Finley walked toward it.

"And why did they say we'd be dead in the morning?" Kirsten whispered.

"I don't know." Finley picked up a chair to move it soundlessly beneath the window and lifted her skirts to step up to the seat in a crouch, so that her head was not above the bottom edge of the opening.

"What are we going to do, Fin?"

Finley half-turned on the chair. "Why do you keep asking me questions you know good and well I have as much answer for as you?"

"I thought you were the leader."

She sighed and turned back toward the window, gripping the ledge with her fingers and then rising up slowly, slowly, until she could see the scene beyond. Her breath froze in her chest, her fingers digging in to the hard sod window ledge.

It looked as though all the inhabitants of Town Blair were indeed gathered on the green. But rather than singing and dancing and gaming, instead of laughter and making merry, the people sat silently on their benches at the tables lined up like a battalion. The children and those for whom there was no seat were clustered on the ground, huddling together as if in fear.

Around the perimeter of the green, also nearly shoulder to shoulder, stood a ring of men dressed just as the ones who had stopped Finley and Kirsten. Most of them wielded broadswords at the ready, although some braced wicked-looking crossbows on their hips. Finley realized that if she could see a solid ring of soldiers *across* the green…

She rose up on her toes slowly, slowly, and cast down her eyes. Indeed, there was the shiny silver top of a soldier's helm just beneath the window. If he fancied to turn and raise up on his own toes, he'd be looking directly into Finley's eyes. She eased down again and stepped silently off the chair, careful not to make a sound, turning toward Kirsten and swiftly bringing her hand to cover her friend's mouth as it opened.

"Shh," Finley breathed into her ear. "The green is crawling with them—there's one standing right under the window." She leaned back to look into Kirsten's eyes, and her friend nodded her understanding.

Kirsten pulled away and moved to the chair, and Finley heard the murmur of voices coming from across the green. She watched as her friend took in the scene out the window, and Kirsten brought a hand to her mouth suddenly. She looked over her shoulder and waved Finley forward, pulling her up next to her onto the makeshift stool.

Finley at once saw the cause for Kirsten's alarm: A lone man had stepped onto a tabletop, a well-dressed man in finely cut clothes, and who was addressing the crowd. But while it was clear from his costume that he was a foreigner to this Highland town, the most startling aspect of the changed tableau was the presence of Marcas and Dand Blair, standing to the side of the table. Two soldiers aimed their crossbows at father and son.

"That's all I want," the man on the table said to the crowd, and his words were ghostly and hollow-sounding from inside the house across the green. He held his arms wide and looked around in each direction at those seated nearest him. Several of the women were weeping into their shawls, and Finley was glad that that particular sound did not carry.

"You got rid of him for reasons of your own—I'm certain you were quite justified," the man went on in a queer, almost praising tone. Finley noticed then Harrell Blair and his daughter Searrach standing at the opposite end of the table as Marcas and Dand, and although the dark-haired woman who would have been Lachlan's wife looked frightened and unsure, clinging to her father, neither of them were being held under the threat of weapons.

"But now someone will volunteer the trek to Carson Town, someone Lachlan Blair will trust, and they will bring him back to me without revealing my...occupation of your town, as it were. They will bring him, *and* Thomas Annesley."

Marcas Blair called out then. "I've told you, Hargrave: Thomas Annesley isn't here. He hasn't been here since the day thirty years ago when you made the ben run with blood."

The gray-haired man whipped around and pressed his palm to his chest. "Why, I did no such thing. I was merely seeking to apprehend a fugitive. Thomas Annesley's destination was Carson Town, so that is the town where I made my initial inquiry."

"You burned it to the ground," Marcas accused.

"And did that not work to your advantage?" Hargrave demanded in a bewildered tone. "It is my opinion that the Blairs were rewarded most generously for their aid in delivering to me what I thought was the carcass of Thomas Annesley."

"More than two score Blairs lost their lives that day."

"Through no fault of mine," Hargrave said dismissively. "You know as well as I that it was the Carsons who set my ships—as well as their own—alight. We nearly capsized with the weight of the additional men, even though they abandoned their armor on the beach."

The rusting English armor, hidden away in the old house...

"But," Hargrave continued, "it appears I was misled. The body shown to me that day in the woods was not Thomas Annesley's. I want him—and his son—delivered to me, now." He paused. "Swiftness may perhaps be rewarded with more mercy than I had originally intended."

"Thomas Annesley isn't here!" Marcas shouted.

The Englishman pointed a finger at Marcas. "Deny me again. Deny me once more and I will have your precious son shot in the head. Right here before you." He held Marcas's gaze a moment longer.

Harrell Blair drew the man's attention back to the crowd on the green. "Marcas speaks the truth, Lord Hargrave. We've nae seen hide nor hair of Annesley since the day we found him dead."

"We didn't find him dead, though, did we?" Hargrave said in a smooth, poisonous tone. "If he was *dead*, I wouldn't be in this godforsaken *bog* with muddied *boots*!" He paused, as if to compose himself. "Thomas Annesley is here, you mark my words. He knows I am coming after him through his bastard children, and he is trying to stay one step ahead of me. But that ends tonight. *Tonight*."

He surveyed the crowd. "Who will go? Who will go and fetch the men who have revisited this wrath upon you? Hmm? No one? No one at all willing save your townsfolk? Your *kin*," he sneered. His query was met with silence broken only by the cry of a babe. "Very well, then."

He looked to the soldier standing closest to him in the outer ring. "Kill one of the men. I care not which one, only do it quickly." A cry went up from the crowd, some of the folk stood, drawing the ring of soldiers close like the drawstring of a sack.

"Do it!" Hargrave shouted.

A high-pitched scream cut through the chaos, bringing silence once more before a single, long, mourning wail of horror. The crowd pulled away to reveal a woman bent over the still form of a man prone, an arrow sticking awkwardly from his head.

"Now, I'll ask again," Hargrave said with an air of patience. "Who will go?"

There was a beat of silence, and Hargrave turned once more to the soldier and opened his mouth.

"I will!" a man shouted and stood, holding his arm in the air. "Lachlan knows me well. I'll go."

Hargrave looked to Harrell, who shook his head subtly.

"Oh my, that's not good." Hargrave looked at the soldier and gestured to the volunteer. "Shoot him, as well; he cannot be trusted."

"Nae! Nae!" Harrell shouted frantically.

Finley and Kirsten clutched each other as the big man stumbled backward in vain, while the soldier stalked toward him calmly. The Englishman stopped, lowered the crossbow to step into the stirrup, and set the bolt...

The women at the window turned their heads to each other and squeezed their eyes shut as the jarring clack-swish of his weapon sounded. There were more screams.

"I didna mean for you to shoot him!" Harrell cried, his voice breaking. "I only meant he was Lachlan's mate. He might have...he might have..."

"I knew exactly what you meant, Harrell. And that is why he is dead." Hargrave seemed to consider the visibly distraught man for a moment, and then he looked directly at the raven-haired woman at Harrell's side. "How silly of me. Of course. We shall send her."

"What? Nay! She's me only—"

"Your only child, yes. And once betrothed to Lachlan Blair, wasn't she? I don't know why I didn't think of it sooner. The perfect choice."

"Nay," Searrach pleaded, grabbing her father's shawl. "Da, nay. I canna face him. I'm afraid."

"I'll go," Harrell offered. "You know you can trust me above all."

"That I can," Hargrave allowed. "You proved that by alerting me to Lucan Montague's visit to your town. But Lachlan Blair would *not* likely trust you."

"I can convince him," Harrell pleaded. "I can—"

"I've made my decision," Hargrave announced. "Your daughter will do my bidding or I shall let the soldiers take turns with her here on the green." He returned his attention to Searrach. "You have two hours to return with Lachlan Blair and Thomas Annesley and not a moment more. If you fail, I will kill everyone in town, including your father. Then I will find you. And when I do, you'll wish you had chosen the soldiers."

"Da," Searrach wept.

"It's all right," Harrell soothed, changing tactics. "A simple task. Go straight there and back. He'll be easy to find." Harrell half-carried, half-shoved her to the edge of the green, toward the house from which Finley and Kirsten watched, then pried his daughter away from him.

The women ducked down beneath the window as the townspeople turned to watch, and Harrell's last murmured instructions wafted through the opening.

"Go, me lass. Quick as ye can. Thomas Annesley willna be found, but Hargrave won't care about that if he has Lachlan."

"But what do I tell him, Da?" Searrach whined. "He knows I doona want him."

"Tell him...tell him it's his brother, then," Harrell suggested. "Tell him Dand's hurt bad. It'll like as nae be true," he added in an ominous tone.

"Da?"

"Doona worry about it, gel. Quick as ye can, now. It'll be over soon enough, and we shall have everything we want."

Finley heard footsteps walking away, but dared not look out the window just yet. It didn't really matter to her now, though, what went on on the green. She climbed down from the chair, prompting Kirsten to follow. They both paused at the door.

"What are you doing?" Kirsten breathed.

"We're going after Searrach," she said. "She canna be allowed to lure Lachlan here with lies. He must know the truth of what's happening at Town Blair."

"But...Dand," Kirsten whispered. "I canna leave when—"

"What will you do for him here, Kirsten?" Finley demanded. "Watch him be killed?"

"Fin!"

"If we can overtake Searrach and warn everyone ourselves, we might have a chance to stop this whole thing from happening. You especially know the fastest way through the woods."

"They've taken the Blairs' weapons; they'll be no aid."

Finley just stared at her. "Think you Lachlan will be frightened of that? Think you the Carsons will be either? You heard as well as I: that man—that Lord Hargrave—is the one who burned Carson Town thirty years ago. And from what we heard his guards say, I don't think there is much chance the Blairs will come out as fortunate as before. He's going to kill them all, Kirsten, not just Dand. This time, I say it should be he who is taken by surprise."

Kirsten's gentle brown eyes smoldered in the shadows for a long moment, and then she nodded. "All right. Let's go."

* * * *

By the time Lachlan returned to the old cliff house, the bonfire had been abandoned, the mountainous pile of fuel spent. A tall ring of protective rock walled in the thick bed of coals and ashes, allowing the rippling glow to do what it would. Lachlan stood on the edge of the fire he had helped kindle what seemed years ago now, soaking in the warmth pulsing from the ring.

Myra Carson...Myra Annesley. Thomas Annesley. Edna Blair.

Lachlan.

Rather than show Lachlan a clear path back to Town Blair, the information he'd learned about Thomas Annesley's connection to Carson Town had only thrust him deeper into the wilderness. He turned toward the old house, tired to his bones, unable to think any longer.

He was only halfway across the ceiling-less entry chamber when he saw the flicker of his own fire in the doorway, which caused him to stop in his tracks, the hair on his neck raising. He hadn't been back to the old house since this morning. He could feel eyes on him. Lachlan turned in a slow circle, looking up and all around him, but he could neither see nor hear anyone else. There could only be one person brave and careful enough to come into Lachlan's home.

"Edna's son," the voice called to him from the storeroom.

Lachlan crossed the floor swiftly and found the strange, shriveled man sitting on the edge of the pallet, an ancient leather skull cap covering his head. His knobby fingers were laced together on his lap atop his old, long tunic; his roeskin boots were tied around his ankles like sacks.

It was as if he had readied himself for a journey.

"Yer verra late, Edna's son," Geordie said. "I thought I'd have to find ye." He stood up, his gangly arms now hanging at his sides. "It's time for us to go now."

Lachlan stared at the man for a long moment. "Go where, Geordie?"

"Back."

"You mean Town Blair?"

Geordie nodded. "There's troubles."

Lachlan sighed and walked toward the pallet Geordie had abandoned. He sat on the edge and then turned, swinging his legs up onto the thin ticking and cocking one arm behind his head.

"Troubles at Town Blair." Lachlan stared up at the ceiling, fluttering in relaxing waves of shadows and light. "I would think you to care little for any troubles at Town Blair, even if there are any. Seems to me Town Blair has everything they want now, and nothing they don't."

"That man come back," Geordie said, looking down at Lachlan where he lay.

"What man?"

"The man with the boats. The man who wanted Tommy."

Lachlan looked at Geordie from the side of his eye. "Aye? How would you be knowing that, Geordie? You said you doona go near Town Blair."

"Murdoch told me."

Now Lachlan turned his head to look at the man properly, then he swung his legs over the side of the pallet and sat up.

"Murdoch knows you're here?"

"Murdoch's always knowed I was here. Was him let me stay."

A little shiver of cold raced up Lachlan's spine. "Did he tell you to go back, Geordie? To take me with you?"

He shook his head solemnly. "Nay. It was a warning, what only meant for me. So's I could be sure to stay away from the wood. It's the reckoning, Edna's son. When the Blairs will pay for all their wickedness."

"Then why tell me? Why do you want to go back?"

"Them fair lasses. Finley Carson. And the yellow-headed lass. They've gone up the path. They doona ken what will happen."

Lachlan felt his brows draw together and he stood slowly, slowly. Finley and Kirsten, whom Ina thought were at Kirsten's family's longhouse. What possible reason could they have for going to Town Blair?

Geordie's unsettling, queer gaze never wavered. "It's time for us to go now." He turned away, but, rather than exit into the receiving chamber of the old house, Geordie wobble-walked to the high-set opening in the storeroom that led to the soaring shaft. In a blink, he had scrambled up the rock and was gone.

Lachlan stood there for what felt like a very long time, unable to make sense out of what Geordie Blair had told him. Was he dreaming? All of it seemed impossible. Murdoch had known a Blair was living in the old house? How could the Carson chief know the same man who had ravaged Carson Town had called on Town Blair? And why would Finley, of all people, decide this night to make the long journey to the people she swore were her enemies?

Where had Geordie Blair gone?

Lachlan walked to the opening. "Geordie!"

"Hurry, Edna's son." His voice sounded somehow far away.

Lachlan scrambled up the wall and into the dark shaft, where the flickering light of the fire could not reach. His boots crunched over ancient wood as he came into the center of the shaft, squinting up into the darkness, blinking in hopes of accustoming his eyes to the gloom, the tiny square of night sky so far above him moonless, starless.

"Where are you?"

Lachlan heard a huff of breath and then a skittering of pebbles rolling, bouncing down the walls of the shaft.

"Up top," Geordie called. "Hurry now."

Geordie had already climbed all the way up and out of the shaft, to the clifftop above the town, Lachlan realized. He walked to the wall and felt along its rough surface for the indentations of the crude ladder.

"Edna's son!" Geordie chastised in an annoyed tone. "It climbs the same, all the way. You doona need your eyes."

Lachlan could not hazard a guess as to how many times Geordie Blair had made the treacherous climb to the top of the cliff in all his hermit years living in the old house. Thousands, likely. And so what Lachlan could claim over the man in youth and strength was easily eclipsed by Geordie's experience.

And he could not simply forget that he was being led to the top of a deadly precipice by a man who'd been in hiding from his people for thirty years, upon receiving information from the chief of Lachlan's enemies.

Murdoch Carson is also your cousin, he reminded himself.

And what if Geordie was right, and Finley *was* in danger? If it hadn't been for her, Lachlan never would have discovered that Geordie Blair was alive, or his own connection to the Carsons. He never would have run on the beach at sunset on *Lá Bealltainn*. He never would have known the passion possible in an innocent kiss; the sweet excitement of the unknown; the laughter of a different people.

But why had she gone to Town Blair?

Lachlan began climbing.

Geordie was right; the hand- and footholds carved out of the cliff were so evenly spaced, and it was so pitch in the shaft, that it made little difference if Lachlan's eyes were open or closed. He concentrated on the grip of his fingers, the distribution of his weight from foot to foot as he climbed for what seemed an hour.

"Almost there." Geordie's voice seemed right above him now, and Lachlan at last looked up.

He was perhaps only four feet from the opening, and the fresh air rushing over the shaft made a sad, empty sound. It pricked Lachlan's conscience to think of the man now helping to pull him over the edge and on to solid ground listening to that lonely, howling wind, alone, for years and years and years.

And Murdoch Carson had known Geordie was there.

Lachlan stood, and the wind immediately assaulted him, buffeting him with a surprising strength as he looked out over the town and the bay below. Several tiny pinpricks of light could be seen along the strip of beach: the remnants of the celebration he had taken part in. So close, and yet so far away from where he stood. From where Geordie Blair stood. Outsiders.

"Stay close to me, Edna's son," the man warned. "Sinkholes. Wet pits. Right behind me now, ken?"

Lachlan nodded. "Aye, Geordie. Lead on."

They walked a narrow path that would have been invisible even in the daylight, its solid, zigzagging trail covered over by huge tufts of heather and brush. The buzz of insects and chirping of frogs were thick in the air, and Lachlan kept his eyes on the hunched and oddly loping form of Geordie Blair as he led unhesitatingly toward the line of the wood marking the top of the ben that could be seen from Town Blair and Loch Acras. This area had always been spoken of as a dangerous wasteland, useless for game because of the bog, but Lachlan reckoned if they went down the side of the mountain from here, the distance between the two towns was likely half that of the falls path.

Again, something so far away, and yet closer than he'd ever known.

The bog narrowed into a rocky ridge that disappeared into the black night, and the men veered south toward the edge of the wood. Geordie suddenly stopped near a seemingly out-of-place pile of rock and shell, mounded up in a little hillock at the base of a tree. He dug in his crude, skin sack for what appeared to be a small stone, but then he simply stood there, staring at the thing in his hand.

"This is where I buried him," Geordie said haltingly, as if the words were difficult, or the sentiment foreign. Lachlan reckoned that the man had never thought to have to explain the location's existence to anyone.

"Who?"

Geordie turned his face toward Lachlan, his expression full of confusion. "Yer da, I thought it was." He looked back to the pile of stone. "Dragged him up here meself after everyone stopping comin' to gawp at him. They just stared and stared." His breath was coming heavier now, and Lachlan couldn't tell if it was with anger or sadness. He was a difficult man to read. "They talked over him like he was a hero. He was, to me. Edna, too. But they was so bad to him. So when they was gone, I took him. Brought him here."

Geordie straightened his shoulders as much as his bent posture would allow. "Visited him every day. I had nae tool to dig with, so I just brung him a few stones or shells or a little piece of something each time to cover him with. I thought one day, when the chief was dead, when Harrell was dead, I could bring Edna here to visit with him."

"That must have been hard," Lachlan said, a catch in his chest taking him by surprise. "Seeing your friend like that."

Geordie gave a jerky nod. "I had to run off animals sometimes. 'Til he was covered up proper. But now..." His voice trailed off.

"Now what?"

Geordie turned his bulging gaze to Lachlan once more, and the look of puzzlement was greater than ever. "It isna him."

Lachlan shook his head. "I doona think so."

"Well." Geordie gave his queer bird-head nod and then leaned over to place the small stone on the top of the pyre with the thousands of others. "He didna deserve what happened to him anyhow. And he's been company for me all these years. A thing to take care of. Like I was for yer mam. I owed it to her, I reckoned."

Lachlan suddenly didn't want to be here with Geordie Blair anymore. He didn't want to be thinking the things he was thinking, feeling the emotions flooding him; opening his mind to the sinister conclusions that were taking shape from all the little bits and pieces of the past that were rolling downhill to come to rest against his feet in the shape of something dark and ugly and unfair.

Geordie Blair turned away from the pyre and started down the hill.

"Come on, Edna's son."

Chapter 15

Finley and Kirsten didn't have to go far in the wood until they found Searrach Blair, and even if she hadn't been directly on the path so as to have stumbled over her, her wailing would have given away her location had she been underwater. As it was, she was sitting on the path with her back to a tree, legs flopped out before her, and her hands in her lap, sobbing aloud like a wee bairn just learning to walk and having fallen soundly on its bottom.

"What's she doing?" Kirsten hissed in Finley's ear. "She's just stopped!"

"I don't know," Finley muttered, wincing at the renewed wails. "But it's obvious she's not hurrying along like her da told her."

They carried on down the path and were almost on top of Searrach Blair before she noticed them approaching. She gave a sharp shriek of fright and struggled to her feet, stumbling from the path into the wood.

"Get away!" she hiccoughed. "I'm go-going! L-leave m-me alone!" She stepped on the tail of her shawl and fell heavily into the brush.

Finley loped along to reach her side, setting her foot between Searrach's shoulder blades before she could rise fully to her hands and knees. "You may stay right where you are."

Kirsten came up behind Finley and planted her own foot with some force on the Blair woman's full backside, sending Searrach face-first into the loamy forest floor with a yelp.

"Traitorous coo," Kirsten spat.

The dark-haired woman turned her face toward Finley and Kirsten, blowing the leaves and hair from her wide eyes as best she could.

"You two!" she said, her round face full of genuine surprise. She began to struggle, but for all Searrach's greater size, she had little actual strength. "Get off me, you Carson whores."

Finley leaned onto her foot more firmly, until the Blair woman began to whine. "Who's the Englishman whose dirty work you're doing?"

"Get off!" Searrach screamed again, flailing with her arms and legs. "You doona ken what you're doing! He's already killed two men!"

"We know," Kirsten said. "We saw it. And doona play at being in a hurry to warn anyone; it was clear you had nae other plans save for sitting on your arse and feeling sorry for yourself."

Searrach stilled, then. "Spies," she hissed. "You're spies! I knew it! I told my father—"

"Shut up," Finley said, pressing her heel into the woman's back. "Who is the Englishman, and what does he want with Lachlan?"

"And what have you done to poor Dand?" Kirsten demanded.

"I'm nae telling you anything," Searrach cried up at Finley. "You, who took my Lachlan. You ruined my plans! And you—"she craned her neck to glare at Kirsten—"throwin' yerself at Dand. As if he'd have a *Carson*. The new treaty means nothing to us, you ken? Nothing! You'll see!"

Kirsten made a growl deep in her throat and started toward the woman with her fists clenched, but Finley threw out an arm to stop her.

"Nay, Kirsten. It's a waste of time. She's nae going to tell us anything, are you, Searrach?"

"I can tell you what Lachlan's cock tastes like," Searrach said triumphantly.

Finley's hands went to the belt at her waist. "Sit on her."

Searrach craned her neck again. "What?"

Kirsten didn't hesitate, drawing a pained "Oof" from the prone woman.

Finley straddled Searrach's legs first, to stop their dangerous kicking, securing her ankles together with the tight cording, then drawing up her lower legs toward her buttocks. "Now that she's seen us, we can't have her running back to Town Blair and telling Hargrave we know he's there. Can you reach her arms?"

Searrach screamed.

"Thank you."

"Anything for you, Fin."

"You stupid bitches!" Searrach cried. "They'll kill all of you! You have nae idea what you're doing!"

"I've had just about enough of that," Kirsten grumbled, ripping a long, fraying strip from the edge of her shawl. She turned on her bottom on Searrach's back and looped the strip around the woman's wildly tossing head. Kirsten secured a double knot, and then a rather unnecessary bow, in Finley's opinion, and then Searrach's vitriol was reduced to muffled barks.

The two women stood up from their prey.

"We'll tell someone where you are when this is all over," Finley said.
"Probably," Kirsten added.

Searrach writhed on the forest floor, her rage muffled and impotent.

"But if ye ever think to go near Dand again," Kirsten added, "I'll be shaving yer goddamn head and usin' yer hair to wipe my—"

"Good lord, Kirsten." Finley sighed, yanking her friend back toward the path. "It's true what they say about the quiet ones, isn't it?"

* * * *

Lachlan saw the bonfire lights from Town Blair's green when they were still halfway up the mountain, north of the lake. Unlike the bay beyond the clifftop, Loch Acras seemed to suck what little light was in the new moon sky and hold it just under the surface of the water like a mottled looking glass, turning the vale into an ominous scrying tool.

Lachlan remembered so many happy nights of his childhood before Dand was born, scouring the reedy shore of the lake with Marcas for the hardy, thick-skinned frogs that hid there. He could recall with crystalline clarity still the peace and security he'd felt then, although had anyone asked him at the time, he would have been unable to define the contented feeling he carried with him; it had been nothing more than his childhood. Looking back, he could see now that it had been a heaven of immeasurable worth, now gone forever.

He had the sudden desire to run down the remainder of the hill to the shore of the brackish lake, as if he could dive headlong into his past, when he was Marcas's only son and he was loved by his grandfather, by all of Town Blair.

There was a foreign ring of lights on the road to the east of the town, and as Lachlan and Geordie traveled through the trees, Lachlan could see that it was a corral of sorts, roped and bordered with torchlight, holding what must have been fifty horses and several two-wheeled carts, mounded into black hillocks by whatever cargo they contained.

Someone had indeed come to Town Blair. A wealthy someone, with many companions. Could it truly be the Englishman, Vaughn Hargrave?

Geordie stopped suddenly, and Lachlan drew even with him, watching his old, misshapen profile, somehow already familiar to Lachlan. Geordie's bulging eyes glistened.

"Sure, it looks bigger," he said gruffly.

Lachlan turned to regard the town. "Aye. I reckon it is bigger since you left it."

"More houses."

"There's a chapel now, as well," Lachlan said. "A friar comes a few times a year."

"Aye. Uh-huh," he said with his dipping nod. "Nae matter that. Still just as black." There was bitterness in his hoarse voice.

Lachlan felt a cold emptiness in his chest that mirrored the sentiment of Geordie's callous words, and it unsettled him. "Geordie, you canna mean that. Isn't some part of you glad to see it again, being so long away from the only home you've ever known?"

Geordie Blair turned his eyes up to Lachlan's face, and the pain and sorrow there was raw. "Nay. Nae a single part of me. Sure, that isna my home. I was a score-three, reckon, when Harrell sent me into the falls. I've spent more of my life away from Town Blair than I have in it, and I can tell you now that in all them lonely, hungry years, the thing I feared most was having to return," he finished with a rasp. He blinked, and a tear rolled down his sunken cheek even as he lifted his chin.

"You remember it, Edna's son. You remember the leavin'. It stays with ye."

And, just like that, Lachlan forgot about warm summer nights on the loch with Marcas; forgot about the indulgent smiles from the town mothers, if not from Mother Blair. Instead, he remembered the look on his grandfather's face when Archibald disowned him; remembered being sent from the town the night he'd married Finley Carson, and the palpable relief emanating from his own townsfolk at the wedding feast. Aye, Lachlan's leaving had stayed with him.

Still, he prayed Geordie was wrong.

"Whoever has come to Town Blair has left their horses unguarded on the road," he said to the man at his side. "Doesn't seem like a decision made by one wishing to secure an easy escape."

"He doesna want to escape," Geordie scoffed. He walked to one of the trees on the edge of the wood and sat down against it. "I'll wait here."

"Geordie, this could be your time to be avenged," Lachlan said, striding down the hill toward the tree. "I'll stand by your side. We'll both confront Harrell, and you'll be accepted." He crouched down with one hand braced on the tree trunk above Geordie's head. "You can come home."

The old leather skullcap shook. "You're nae the chief, Edna's son. Harrell made sure of that, dinnee? Doona want any part of it. With none of 'em. You go on, if yer a'goin'." He stared ahead stubbornly. "An' ye shouldna stay. Like I told you, it isna my home. And it isna yours, neither."

"What do you mean?"

"I'll wait here," Geordie repeated. "If I spy ye comin' with any other than the lasses..." He gave his swooping nod. "Ye'll nae be seein' me agin."

Lachlan sighed and rose from his crouch. "I gave you my word. I mean to keep it." He emerged from the edge of the wood toward the lake shore, staying back from the marshy margin to approach the town from the north. He had hunted this stretch with Marcas for years; he knew each dip and washed-out gully, each bleached boulder thrusting through the thistle and briars. They caught on his breeches like little hands clutching at him.

Lachlan ignored them, thinking of the last thing Finley had said to him: *You'll never know home.*

Wasn't this it, though? This place where he was born and raised? Didn't he know each corner of every house? Didn't he recognize the silhouette of each rooftop, know who lived where as sure as he knew the pattern of his own shawl? The acrimonious thoughts made his footfalls drop harder onto the earth, cause his fists to clench as his arms swung at his sides, turning into pendulums, then pistons, as he broke into a run.

Home. This was his home, no matter what Finley, what Geordie Blair, what Marcas said. His legacy. Sure, they will have missed him. Someone... someone would be glad to see him. Even if it was only Dand.

Even if it was only Finley.

He wove his way through the maze of houses on the outer edge of the quiet town, heading relentlessly toward the blazing green. The blazing, quiet green. One more alley to traverse, and then there was a man blocking the end of the passage, facing the green, where obviously the town had been gathered for the festival, but it was quiet...so quiet.

The man ahead had a sword, Lachlan saw, almost too late.

But his brow lowered, his pace increased. No one was going to stop him from taking what was his tonight: Finley and Town Blair. No one would stop him.

Lachlan blasted into the man blocking the way, taking the stranger so off guard that he lost his feet and skidded away into the dirt as Lachlan burst into the green. His pace slowed to a trot, then a walk, and then he stopped as the hundreds of eyes beheld him with shock and horror. There was sound now, he realized: weeping, and metal on metal. He turned in a full circle slowly, saw the two long, wrapped shapes lying on the green, saw the ring of armed men who now aimed their weapons at him.

English armor...

"*I told ye!*" came the ragged crowing voice, drawing Lachlan's attention back to the center of the green, where Harrell Blair was pointing in Lachlan's direction but staring up at the lone figure of a man standing atop one of the tables. "I told ye my Searrach would bring him back!"

The stranger was tall, large, but without an abundance of spare flesh to allude to the suggestion that he was unfit. On the contrary, his fine velvet clothing fit him like a second skin, from his barreled torso to his thick arms. His graying hair and the aristocratic swoop of his jowls betrayed his age, but when he hopped down from the tabletop, it was clear that although this was a man of some years, he was in vigorous health and used to physical efforts.

He was smiling, though there was no kindness there, no welcome from this outsider in the midst of Lachlan's own town. It was a predatory grin, sly and delighted at once.

"Lachlan Blair?" the stranger queried. "Can it be?"

Lachlan caught sight of Dand behind the stranger, and next to him, Marcas. Lachlan's foster father had lost all color in his face, his long gray hair pulled from its usual tidy queue into matted strands. And unlike the Englishman, who continued to advance on Lachlan, Marcas looked old—so much older than he had when last Lachlan had seen him. Dand shook his head frantically, his eyes wide.

Lachlan looked back at the stranger, and despite Dand's silent warning, began advancing to meet him on the green. "Who are you?"

"You resemble him, you know," the man said. "Your hair is darker, but the face—yes." He came to a stop some ten feet from Lachlan and turned his head this way and that, then held up his hands for a brief, affected moment, as if to frame Lachlan's countenance. "You could be his twin. I speak of Thomas Annesley, of course. Where is he?"

Lachlan, too, stopped on the green. "I've never laid eyes on Thomas Annesley the whole of my life," he said. "I've thought he was dead all these many years. I do wish he'd had the courtesy to have stayed that way."

To Lachlan's surprise, the gray-haired man threw back his head in laughter. "Oh! Yes! I feel much the same, young man—much the same!" Like a dish falling to shatter on the hearth, the smile fell from the man's face. "But we both know that he is not, in fact, dead. And so you will tell me now where he is. Or I will have everyone in this town killed, one by one, ending with you." He paused, and his smile returned with a diabolical brilliance. "But I will start"—he turned and pointed to Marcas—"with the chief."

"Exceptin' me, Lord Hargrave," Harrell interjected, taking several hesitant steps forward. "Exceptin' me and Searrach, aye? I told ye she'd find him."

Hargrave waved a hand with an annoyed frown, but he didn't turn around to regard Harrell Blair.

"Hargrave," Lachlan said. "You're Vaughn Hargrave."

The man's smile widened, and he pressed a palm to his chest. "You've heard of me? Well, I shouldn't be surprised, I suppose, although I am flattered."

Lachlan looked to Dand. "Where's Finley and Kirsten?"

Harrell stepped closer. "What are you goin' on about, ye bastard? Where's me own gel? Where's Searrach?"

Lachlan glared at the traitor. "Searrach didn't come for me."

"Yer a liar," Harrell stammered. "She had ta. You wouldna've come, otherwise."

"It matters not," Hargrave interjected in a magnanimous tone, holding up his palms and looking around at everyone with his broad, false smile. "Thomas Annesley's son is here now. And as soon as he tells me where I can find his father, we will leave you good people to enjoy the remainder of your feast." He looked back at Lachlan again. "If he does not share the whereabouts of his murdering, lying, cowardly sire, I fear my original intentions must remain in place, with all of you dying. So—" He clapped his hands together and bent slightly forward at the waist.

"Which shall it be, Lachlan Blair? Either way, you will die this night."

* * * *

Finley's throat and lungs burned by the time she and Kirsten ran up the sloping path to the old house, although the air felt icy cold on her cheeks and in her ears. Finley dashed past the dead bonfire and into the cavernous room.

"Lachlan!" Her voice echoed in the chamber. "Lachlan!" She caught herself on the doorway of the storeroom: empty, though the fire in the small ring smoldered. She looked behind her to make sure Kirsten hadn't followed her in before moving to the opening of the shaft and calling out in a hoarse whisper.

"Geordie! Geordie Blair, it's Finley. Are you here?" But there was no answer.

Finley turned and ran back to the yard, past Kirsten, who was doubled over with one hand on a knee, the other pressed to her ribs.

"Maybe still at the beach," Finley said in explanation.

"Fin," Kirsten gasped.

Finley stopped and turned impatiently, panting.

"I canna," Kirsten gulped. "My side."

"Wait here; this is where they'll gather," Finley said, already trotting backward. "I'll meet you."

It would take several more minutes to reach the beach, and she didn't know if Lachlan or Murdoch would even be there. As long as Lachlan didn't know Town Blair—Dand and Marcas—were in danger, he was safe. Carsons must be alerted to the danger first, so that Lachlan didn't go to Town Blair alone. And so she dashed up the path around the town instead, pushing her legs as hard as she had the energy left to do so. Her da would know what to do.

The low longhouse came into shape out of the night shadows, and Finley felt a catch in her chest that had little to do with her physical exertion. Her eyes blurred with tears and her next inhalation was a sob.

"Da," she called, even before her hand was on the door latch. "Da! Mam!" She pushed inside and ran to the bedchamber door.

It opened before she could reach it, and then Ina Carson was there.

"Finley? What is it? Is Kirsten ill?"

Finley threw her arms around her mother and squeezed her tight for only a moment, but it was enough to reset her heading. "I've nae been at Kirsten's, Mam. I need Da." She left her mother in the doorway and went to her knees at the side of the bed, where her father was already leaning up on an elbow.

"Da, you must get up," Finley gasped. "Town Blair is under attack."

Ina gave a soft cry from the doorway. "What?"

Rory threw off the covers and swung his legs out of bed. "Who?"

Finley stood and moved back as her father alighted, reaching for his shawl, stepping into his unlaced boots.

"It's the Englishman who burned Carson Town."

Rory stilled and turned to face her, his expression blank in the sudden light of the lamp Ina had returned with.

"He's asking for Lachlan. And…and for Thomas Annesley," Finley said. "He's horses and soldiers, and it looked as though they've taken all the Blairs' weapons in the town. Kirsten and I saw two Blairs shot dead on the green. I…I think he's going to kill them all, Da. Lachlan, too, if he can lay hands on him."

Rory was a blur of motion once again, pulling his old blue bonnet from the hook, fastening the ends of his shawl tightly. He went to the end of the bed and reached beneath it, pulling out an old wooden trunk.

"Have you told the Blair?"

"Nay. I didna find Lachlan at the old house. I came straight here after."

Rory Carson opened the trunk and pulled out a short, wide sword in a leather sheath. He laid it aside and removed a pair of matching daggers, and began attaching them side by side on his belt.

"Ina, Fin, go on and wake everyone. Call the fine and all to the old house, with whatever weapons they can carry." Finley's mother disappeared from the doorway while Rory stood and tied on the sword. "I'll find Murdoch meself."

Finley was struck for a moment by the change that had occurred before her eyes. Her gentle, elderly father, the farmer, was gone, and in his place stood an armed Highlander, ready to go to war. He glanced up at her. "Go, Fin. Find yer husband before he can hear from somewhere else."

The quiet command broke the spell, and Finley dashed through the main room and the open door, running down the path toward the bobbing light of the lamp ahead of her.

Ina stopped at the first house and banged on the door. "The fine is being called! All men and weapons to the old house." She rapped again, harder, on the door, and then turned her face toward Finley, who was just nearing the end of the path. "Check the beach and work your way back." The door opened, and Ina repeated her message, then turned and disappeared around the corner of the house.

Finley ran. She encountered a handful of people on her way through the town and set them to task, adding, "Have you seen Lachlan?" At their quizzical looks, she clarified, "The Blair—where is the Blair?"

No one knew.

Carson Town became pricked with torchlight, and the sounds of anxious voices swelled, as did the river of bobbing light that flowed up the path to the cliff house. Finley sidled and pushed her way through the throng to reach the clearing where the bonfire had been lit, and she saw her father and the other elders with their heads bowed together.

"Da!" Finley called and grabbed at his sleeve.

Rory looked at her and then around, his expression grim. "The Blair?"

Finley shook her head, the fear catching in her chest with a sharp pain. "Da, where's Murdoch?"

* * * *

Geordie heard the unmasked crunching of the underbrush, someone approaching who cared not that their arrival was heard. But Geordie was not afraid. He was familiar with the sounds of those footsteps coming closer in the night, when guilt and drink and lonely memories demanded company.

"Murdoch," Geordie said as the big man sat at his side. "Why'd ye come?"

"Same reason you came, I reckon." There was a soft *pop*, and Geordie felt a nudge on his arm.

He looked down at the flask of fiery water Murdoch was offering him, then turned back to the view of Town Blair.

"You know I doona drink that stuff. Would have fallen to me death years ago, had I started."

Murdoch took a noisy swig and then sighed. "You had to think on it, though. At times. Would have been easy, from the top of the shaft. Never feel a thing."

"Aye. I thought on it, time to time."

"Me too." Murdoch was quiet for several moments. "You brought the Blair, didn't ye?"

"Aye."

"Godammit, Geordie. I told ye what I did for your own good. To stay away."

Geordie stiffened. "He's got family there, Murdoch. Friends. He had a right to know."

"Aye, family maybe. But doona no one got a friend in Town Blair, eh? And you've got family down there, too."

"Nae only Blairs he come for," Geordie clarified. "His lass, as well."

"Rory's gel?"

Geordie only stared at the town.

"Jesus," Murdoch whispered. "Jesus, why the—"he broke off, and the Irish in the flask sloshed again.

Geordie heard a sniffle, then a gasp, and a moment later Murdoch Carson was sobbing into his elbow. Loud, pain-filled bawling, choking.

"I just...I just want it to be over," he cried hoarsely. "I just want it to be over, Geordie."

Geordie continued to stare at the town, although from the west through the woods—along the falls path—he could hear the faint, ghostly sounds of many feet approaching, the slithering, sliding noises of metal and leather, the jingle of chained weaponry.

"I reckon it will be, soon," Geordie said.

Murdoch quieted suddenly and raised his tear-streaked face from his arms to listen. "Oh God," he breathed. "What have I done? What have I done?"

Chapter 16

Lachlan ignored the Englishman's threat, the identities of the two wrapped bodies lying on the green behind making everything else unimportant.

"Finley Carson," he said again.

"She's nae here, Lachlan," his brother answered with a worried frown. "Nor Kirsten. Why would they be?"

"Are you certain, Dand?" Lachlan pressed. "You must be certain."

Dand looked over the crowded, nervous green. "Has anyone had sign o' Lachlan's bride?"

No one answered.

Hargrave's face was darkening. "Do you think this some sort of commemoration where you are master of ceremonies?" He brought both his hands to his chest with a loud thump. "I am the master. Of ceremonies. Of this night. *Of it all*. And you are running out of time, Lachlan Blair."

Lachlan stared into the man's flat, gray gaze for a long moment, considering his options. If he turned and walked away, it was possible an arrow would find its way into his back. But if one of the bodies on the green was Finley's, if they'd killed his wife and no one here had tried to stop it, did it really matter what happened to him then?

But Lachlan didn't think Hargrave would kill him just yet. The man wanted to talk, wanted to find out any information about Thomas Annesley that Lachlan could provide. And so Lachlan turned his back on Vaughn Hargrave and began crossing the green toward the closest of the wrapped forms.

No one stopped him. No one spoke.

He knelt at the side of the body. Already he knew it was too large to be Finley or Kirsten. But blood had soaked through the wrapping. He had

to know who it was. Lachlan lifted the top edge of the sheet and pulled
it down, and his teeth clacked together as his jaw involuntarily clenched.
Cordon Blair.

We will raise a cup together, you and I, when you are chief, Lach.

Lachlan replaced the cover and took a moment, still kneeling, before
he rose. He went directly to the other body. Smaller, this one, but he didn't
think by its shape it could be Finley's. And yet his mind was so twisted with
fear and anger, he couldn't be sure. He knelt again, pulled back the cover.

Another townsman, a husband, a father. He'd never come out against
Lachlan, but neither had he spoken for him. It didn't matter now; he was
just as dead.

Lachlan returned the man to the privacy of his shroud and stood once
more, turning to face Hargrave across the green.

The man held his arms away from his sides. "Satisfied?"

"Nay." Lachlan looked around at the frightened townsfolk gathered
on the green, and it was toward them he directed his words. "How could
you allow this to happen? Again?" He swung his gaze to Marcas, and his
heart clenched with pain and bitterness. "Where is your chief? Who was it
that allowed you to be stripped of not only your weapons, but your pride?
Again," he added with a wince.

Hargrave gave a chuckle. "Methinks you are investing these simple folk
with too high ambition. All they ever wanted was a little trinket. To be
told they were mighty Highland Scots!" He shook his fists in the air and
laughed again, as if it was a great, pathetic joke. "So common. So small-
minded. They could have asked for anything. Instead, they wanted a few
baskets of fish. Some trees. A chance to trade Lowland. And several of
them even begged me to take them with me to be my servants."

"They didn't beg you to take them," Lachlan clarified, and then he
looked to Harrell Blair. "They were sold. By that man right there."

Harrell glared at him. "That's a lie."

"You convinced your own people to leave their town as this Englishman's
slaves. But it was *you* he paid for each of their heads, and then you split
the money with the chief. With my grandfather, Archibald Blair."

A murmur slithered through the crowd like an invisible snake.

Lachlan addressed the green again. "Thomas Annesley was trying
to reach Carson Town when he was captured by Harrell and taken as
prisoner by the Blair fine. He was kept against his will with the intention
of ransoming him to the Carsons. Because Thomas Annesley was the son
of Myra, daughter of the old Carson chief." He looked to Harrell, then to
Marcas. "And the Blair fine knew it."

Again shock rippled over the captive audience.

"But when Hargrave attacked Carson Town, besieged it for days and found no Thomas Annesley, he ordered his men to move up the ben toward Town Blair. Archibald freed Thomas and charged him with the task of protecting my mother from the invading horde, because he knew in his coward's heart that, despite what he'd told you all, it wasn't Carsons attacking Town Blair. It was Hargrave's hired men, looking for Thomas Annesley." Lachlan made sure his gaze bored into Marcas's. "Looking for my father."

"You are surprisingly well-informed for one who has never laid eyes on Thomas Annesley," Hargrave accused with a sly smile. "I wonder, though, how Archibald learned of my intention that night? Hmm. It's as though…I don't know…perhaps someone from Carson Town was complicit in the events of that time. And perhaps this person had an attack of conscience when it was discovered you were not only the grandson of Archibald Blair, but also descended from the Carson chief. Perhaps blood really is thicker than water."

Lachlan froze, confusion tangling his thoughts. It had been Geordie who'd told Lachlan of Harrell's evil deeds, of course, but everyone here thought Geordie Blair was dead. Who could Hargrave be speaking of?

Who was the only other Carson who had known Geordie Blair had been alive all these years, hiding in the old cliff house?

'Twas Andrew who would have been chief. Andrew what was Da's pet, the one he confided in. The man barely looked at me.

Our wealth gained our clan powerful friends in Edinburgh.

I have no heir, Lachlan.

"Murdoch," Lachlan said aloud.

"Murdoch," Hargrave repeated with a satisfied smile as he beckoned to a soldier to approach. "He was to travel back to England with me; did you know that as well? He and his woman and their brat. He didn't give a damn what happened in this hellish little shit stain on the upturned arse of Scotland. He hated them all. Not just the Blairs."

The summoned soldier approached Hargrave with a chalice and placed it in his hand, and Hargrave took a deep drink and then turned and raised his cup toward the people behind him. "Ah! This mead is quite good. Really. It simply dances on the tongue. Well done."

He looked back to Lachlan. "You must have made an impression on the bullish, bitter Murdoch, who couldn't come along after all his hard work because his stupid cow of a wife didn't have the sense to be where he'd told her to be. Then the Carson ships we confiscated got set alight, along with my own hired vessels by none other than Murdoch's *brother*. Deliciously ironic, isn't it? Was he ever found, by the way?"

Lachlan wouldn't give him the satisfaction of an answer.

"Then, lo and behold," Hargrave went on, "it was discovered that Thomas Annesley escaped death that day. You, as his son, are *banished*"—here Hargrave gestured around with his cup again—"from this lovely burg just short of seizing the mighty scepter, married off to the enemy town that is ruled by none other than the very man who no one ever suspected gave me the veritable *key* to his *city*! If it was a city. That required a key." He flapped a hand. "*Any matter*. It was Murdoch, you understand."

"And Harrell," Lachlan added, looking over at the man who appeared to have gone rather pale.

"Yes, and him, too, I suppose," Hargrave ceded. "Although he isn't really very smart, is he, so you'll understand that I think him to have a lesser part in the whole thing. I actually thought everyone would have figured it out for themselves by now, but I suppose your stupidity only worked to my advantage. So—"

He handed the chalice back to the soldier-cum-servant. "Now that everything is out in the open, and you have yet to provide me with the information I desire, I would request that my men begin forming orderly rows of the masses so that we might get on with it. I have every intention of getting a thorough night's sleep after we march on to Carson Town. Traveling tires me so and I lose that *verve* after so long in the saddle. Not good for one's humors."

He wiggled his fingers at Marcas and Dand. "Two rows; those two at the fore."

"Wait," Lachlan shouted, drawing Hargrave's attention with an exaggerated expression of curiosity.

"Yes, Lachlan?"

"I know where he is."

Hargrave's smile turned indulgent. "No. Really?"

"You'll call off your men, though. Send them from the town first."

"So you can have time to fabricate a likely sounding story? I think not. I promised myself that I would not leave anyone on this mountain alive this time, and I really must keep my word. It's a matter of self-discipline, you see."

"I'll not make anything up," Lachlan said and reached into his pouch for the now-worn, folded letter given to him by the black knight. He held it up in the air for all to see. "It's right here. In Thomas Annesley's own hand. Given to me by one Lucan Montague. Perhaps you know of him, Hargrave?"

Hargrave began marching across the green at once, all traces of joviality gone, his hand held out. "Give it to me now. *Give it to me!*"

Lachlan backed up until he was standing next to one of the balefires, and held the letter over the licking flames. All around him the creak of crossbows being drawn sounded.

"If they shoot me, the letter falls," Lachlan pointed out.

Hargrave stopped his advance and held out his hands. "Disengage your weapons! Disengage." He turned his face back to Lachlan. "I'm sure we can come to an understanding. What do you want?"

"I've already said what I want. Send your men away, and I'll give you the letter."

"And kill me straightaway afterward, no doubt," Hargrave smirked. "No, I'm afraid that won't work."

"My arm's getting tired, Hargrave."

Hargrave's face brightened. "Why don't we let the mighty chief decide? Surely he will not risk your life—the life of the foster son he's raised—over his own, isn't that right?" He turned. "Marcas? Care to contribute?"

Lachlan's foster father stepped forward, Mother Blair hanging on his arm and weeping. He shook her off roughly. His face was stony and he seemed to be staring beyond Lachlan, even beyond the ring of guards to the darkness past the green, as if he could not bear to meet his eyes.

Lachlan remembered the day at the falls after Dand was born, the water tumbling him over and over, holding him under. Marcas had not saved him then. He hadn't saved him from the fine when Archibald lay dying. He wouldn't save him now, and somehow, Hargrave knew it.

Then Marcas's eyes were boring into his, with an intensity that Lachlan could nearly feel. "Forgive me, Lachlan," Marcas began, and although Lachlan thought he could not be hurt any more deeply by this man, the only father he'd ever known, he feared he was wrong. His last, brief flicker of hope died and he wished there was a way to deafen himself to Marcas's words.

"Forgive me for not fighting for you. For my pride and my cowardice. It has haunted me since the day you left Town Blair, and I wish everyone to hear it from my own lips, now. I didna do right by you. I didna do right by this town. I didna do right by our neighbors, the Carsons. I am no better than Archibald. I am not this town's rightful chief. But we—hear me well, all you Blairs—we alone canna hope to defy this man who has invaded our home not once, but twice. We canna do it."

He dropped to his knees, and when next he spoke, his voice broke. "Forgive me my failings, son. It perhaps would have been easier if I had not loved you as my own, but I did. I still do. Lachlan, my son. Forgive me, and trust me this final time, I beg you. We will not fail you again."

Lachlan's throat constricted. It no longer mattered. It didn't matter what Marcas had done or failed to do. Even if he could not save him, Lachlan still loved him, too.

"I do," Lachlan said.

Marcas nodded, and his eyes grew hard as his hand disappeared inside his shawl. "Drop the letter, son."

Lachlan's fingers opened without hesitation, and the pages written by Thomas Annesley swirled as if caught in time, twirling, floating, and then sliding into the flames, where they shimmered into red and black and yellow nothing.

"*No!*" Vaughn Hargrave roared.

And then all hell broke loose in Town Blair.

* * * *

Finley watched with her stomach in painful, stabbing knots as Lachlan stood near the balefire, what appeared to be sheets of parchment clutched in his hand.

"Oh my lord," Kirsten breathed at her side. "Oh, my lord, Dand is alive."

"Shh," Finley said, watching Rory Carson closely now from where she and Kirsten peeked out from behind the corner of a house.

The Carsons were just coming into place around the perimeter of Town Blair's green on quiet Highland feet, with their great swords, their daggers, their axes and staffs. Hargrave's guards were not paying any attention to the darkness beyond the ring of houses, didn't see the scores of Carson men surrounding their positions, waiting, waiting...

"Come on," Finley whispered. She crouched and ran across the alley separating the houses, and then stepped up on a water barrel, hoisting herself up onto the low, sloped roof. She reached down and pulled Kirsten up, and then the two women crawled to the low peak of the house, looking over from the darkened backside. Finley reached down to ensure she'd not lost the blade attached to her shawl.

Marcas Blair was standing in the center of the green, speaking words Finley could not quite hear.

From the corner of her eye, she saw her father raising a fist in the air.

Then Marcas Blair went slowly, deliberately, to his knees.

Lachlan dropped the pages he was holding into the fire.

The frightening cry of Carson warriors filled the bowl of the green as they charged forward, taking the foreign guards by surprise. Marcas flung the small dagger he withdrew from his shawl, striking the guard nearest Lachlan in the neck, and then he raced to where Blairs roiled from benches and tabletops like the water going over the falls, diving for the pile of confiscated weapons. They came aright and at once sprinted to the perimeter to engage the English guards.

Crossbows twanged, metal on metal rang in the air, screams and grunts and wails sprang up like a fortress wall around the center of the green, where now Marcas Blair and Lachlan, swords in hand, circled slowly, opposite each other. In their midst stood Vaughn Hargrave and Harrell Blair, back to back.

A score or more of the English guards lay dead on the green already, and several were now fleeing—running, limping eastward from town, and Finley remembered the carts waiting in the dark. Was the cargo more weapons? Perhaps even the explosive fire used on Carson Town thirty years ago? If the escaping men were allowed to reach it, if their loyalty to Hargrave was true, they could destroy the populations of both towns in one devastating moment.

Finley raised up, trusting in the commotion below to mask her movements. She could see the shape of the horses in the distance, five or six houses away.

"I've got to reach the carts, Kirsten," she said.

"Fin, if you're caught, they'll kill you!"

"If I don't, everyone here could be in even greater danger. Both towns this time, Kirsten. I can't let that happen."

Kirsten stared at her with pleading eyes for a moment and then pulled Finley into a tight embrace. "You're my best friend," she whispered.

After a moment, Finley squeezed Kirsten to her. "And you are mine." She pulled away and went to her stomach, sliding from the roof to land on her feet with an *oof.*

She slipped her blade from its sheath, crouched, and ran around the house, sticking to the shadows of the overhanging eaves, trying to shield herself from the sounds and sights of battle. One house, two…she paused, pressing her back flat against the wall as an English soldier lurched from between the houses, staggering, falling, his crossbow crashing to the ground. It fired, and the arrow whizzed toward Finley with a sick whine.

She screamed, felt a tug on her sleeve, and her blade fell to the ground as a slow, spreading ache bloomed in her arm. She looked to the right and saw her sleeve ripped open, her upper arm split in a line of fleshy red, the shaft of the arrow still lying against her, where the tip had opened the side of her arm.

She jerked away reflexively, and the arrow remained stuck in the wall behind her. But the pain spread up into her shoulder just as quickly as the blood flowed down her arm. She bent and picked up her dagger with her left hand and then pressed it and her palm against her wound as she struck out once more toward the makeshift corral, staggering into the middle of the widening street, blinking away tears.

The corral ropes had been torn down. Many of the able soldiers had mounted horses and bolted down the road, leaving the dead and dying behind, and Finley was grateful for the mercenary tendencies that prompted them to self-preservation over duty. Riderless horses milled about the track in a dusty panic, the torches sputtering in the road. Finley dodged the spooked beasts and ran toward the nearest cart, where she strained to lift the edge of the thick, heavy covering hiding the cargo to see the shadowy shapes of rows of padded earthen jugs, nestled together and affixed with corks. Finley squeezed beneath the tight canvas and reached in with a hiss at her burning arm to pull at one of the stoppers until it came free. She slipped from beneath the canvas and brought the cork to her nose and sniffed. The sharp odor took her breath, and set her nose and eyes running.

Finley looked around her, fighting the dizziness that suddenly swarmed over her like bees.

Hornets. *Remember the hornets in Dove Douglas's bed? Someone had to stand up to him, teasing all the girls so.*

She sheathed her blade before struggling to loosen the cart horses with only one arm. She slapped their rumps, sending them galloping off into the darkness, the cart shafts drunkenly tipping up in the air, the earthen jars giving hollow thunks and rattles.

She shook her head to clear it. Now that the beds of the carts were raised, it was easy to retrieve a corner of the covering and pull it over the side, holding it down by her waist to twist it into a tight, spiraling point. Then she shoved the makeshift wick into the uncorked jug until it was wedged deep inside the neck of the bottle. Finley tipped the jug onto its side and smelled the volatile liquid as it began creeping up the tightly woven fabric and into the maze of batting.

Finley turned around, staggering on her feet for just a moment as her vision cleared, then took her dagger in her bloody hand once more before shuffling toward a flickering torch lying in the road. She felt so strange, she nearly toppled over when she bent to pick it up, but managed to stand aright and face the cart once more. They were lined up, side by side, like dead bugs, or women, she thought. Women with their legs up in the air and their skirts over their heads, waiting patiently.

She laughed aloud, thinking Kirsten would appreciate the joke. Finley's right hand felt cold and she looked down and saw her fingers dripping red. But rather than scare her, it cleared her mind of the fear- and pain-induced hysteria that had seized her.

Fire in one hand, her blade in the other, already coated in her own blood, she was a Carson tonight. As brave as any man—any son—of her town's fine, as fierce as any clan chief's wife. And she was fighting.

Finley hurled the torch with an enraged cry into the bed of the closest cart as if it were a javelin. At first, she thought the flame had gone out, but then it bloomed like a hazy sun on the surface of the canvas and began to creep like a wave beneath sand. Finley backed away, slowly at first, and then some instinct warned her to run. *Run.*

She stumbled back, turned, ran toward the green. The air pushed around her suddenly, heavy and hot, and then an explosion that shook the ground beneath her feet. Then another. And another. And another.

She ducked behind the side of the closest house and the wall opposite her was lit up as brightly as if it were midday.

Finley smelled noxious smoke. A burning piece of cart fell into the street with an explosion of fat droplets of fire. She dashed to the right, into the thickness of Carsons and Blairs, her dagger still clutched in her hand.

Lachlan. She must find him and warn him. Murdoch—

* * * *

"I ken it's the only reason ye didna kill me," Geordie said when Murdoch's weeping had quieted. "Why ye gave me leave to the old house, and kept my secret." He paused. "Ye couldna squall about it to nae one else, could ye? Ye knew I'd never tell that it werenae the Blairs' fault at all, what happened to Carson Town. Any Carson'd seen me would have cut me throat at first sight."

"I doona know that they would have done," Murdoch said quietly, his words almost a whisper.

"Aye," Geordie agreed with a hearty nod. "But that's what ye wanted me to believe, innit?"

Murdoch's reply was a whisper now. "Aye."

"An' I did believe it. I know I'm nae clever." He pulled out his small dagger from his pouch, its point already broken off when his father had given it to him years ago. Then he chose a stick near his side and rolled it between his thumb and forefinger, scraping off the flaky, dried moss. "Tommy saved me and Edna the day the men came up the ben. He held 'em off while we ran. If it werenae for him, we'd a' been killed. There'd been no bairn. No Lachlan Blair."

"If Sal would have stayed up the beach," Murdoch muttered. "If Andrew would have just let the goddam ships go…"

"None of this is nae one's fault but yer own, Murdoch," Geordie spat. "Yours an' that English bastard down there now." He stood and tossed the stick back to the ground as the ring of Carsons surrounding the Blair green in the darkness grew still in anticipation.. "Why do ye nae go down and say hallo to yer mate, Murdoch? May be he'll take you with him this time."

Geordie started down the hill.

"Geordie, wait!" Murdoch called out. "Doona go down there—you're dead if ye do. Doona leave me!" When Geordie only kept walking, Murdoch demanded, "Do ye even know which side ye'll fight for?"

The battle cry rose up then, causing Geordie to flinch, but he did not hesitate in his advance. He swiped at his nose with the back of his hand, still holding his knife.

"I'm nae on a side," he muttered.

Chapter 17

"You'll hang for this, Hargrave," Lachlan said, circling the pair of men pinned together, Marcas on the far side. "For what you've done. You as well, Harrell."

Marcas's harsh chuckle was clear. "They'll nae last for a hanging, lad, have I any say for it."

Hargrave appeared wary but not quite flustered by his current predicament. "What crime have I committed for which you think I should hang, pray tell, Master Blair?"

"The slaughter of Carson Town. The murder of the two men yonder," Lachlan clarified.

"Ah, no," Hargrave replied. "You have absolutely no witnesses against me for the unfortunate incident thirty years ago. I arrived—as I have yet again—seeking nothing more than to locate the man who murdered my daughter. I had reliable intelligence that Carson Town was harboring that very fugitive. And as for those two men, why, I certainly didn't kill them. Ask anyone here."

Lachlan refused to let Hargrave draw him into debate. "Your hired men are either dead or fleeing. Coin will only buy you so much loyalty. But just look around you, Hargrave; what do you see? Blairs and Carsons fighting together. Fighting you."

"Only temporarily, I'm sure," Hargrave said with a sly smile. "Your kind can't keep from resorting to barbarism for long."

"Da!" The voice came from behind Lachlan, but he wouldn't take his eyes from the Englishman. "Da!"

Searrach ran past Lachlan and threw herself on Harrell. Her gown was torn and filthy, her long, dark hair snarled with dirt and leaves. "Da! Finley Carson tried to kill me!"

Finley was here? In the midst of the fighting?

"Where is she, Searrach?" Lachlan demanded.

Hargrave tsked. "Oh-oh, lovers' quarrel?"

"I hope she's dead," Searrach screamed at Lachlan over Harrell's shoulder. "I'll rip out her throat myself if I see her!"

In that moment, Lachlan didn't know how he ever could have desired the twisted-faced, dumpy, sullen woman before him. She was like the dark, murky water left in a puddle compared to Finley's bright, fiery spirit.

"Dand! Behind you!"

The woman's voice seemed to somehow come from over Lachlan's head, and he noticed Marcas's face going slack as he stared across the green. Lachlan turned and saw his brother stumbling backward over a fallen body, while two English soldiers advanced on him with swords drawn. Dand's back was to a longhouse wall; there was nowhere for him to run. He held his sword before him, ready to fight. He looked younger than his age, then, despite his brave face.

"Marcas, go!" Lachlan shouted.

His foster father hesitated only a moment and then sprinted toward Dand as Harrell took the opportunity to attempt to pull Searrach toward Archibald's dark, old house through the void left by Marcas's departure.

She struggled against him. "I'm nae staying here, Da! I'm going to be married! Lord Hargrave said I'll—"

"You'll come away before you get us both killed!" Harrell slapped Searrach's face and then attempted to take advantage of her shock to haul her from the fray, but she shoved the spindly man with a shriek.

"I'm going!" She struggled against her father's flailing embrace.

Lachlan dismissed Searrach to lock eyes with Vaughn Hargrave. "It's just you and me now, Hargrave."

"Precisely as I'd hoped." The Englishman twirled his own weapon expertly in his hand, then crouched down with a grin. "I've not done this in so very long. I believe I've rather missed it. Come on with you, then, *boy.*"

They ran at each other, both swinging their blades. There were no blows landed at first, but the wind sang with each mighty thrust, youth and experience, desperation and righteousness springing up from the green around them like ancient spirits. Hargrave's blade caught Lachlan's shawl, sending his brooch flying with a sharp ting of metal; Lachlan nicked

Hargrave's forearm, doing more damage to the man's velvet tunic than the flesh beneath it.

"So slow, Lachlan. Shall I stop toying with you?" Hargrave taunted.

"I've not even st—"

An explosion ripped through the air, then another, and another. The underside of a tree beyond the green went up in flames, and the blasts still did not stop, taking everyone on the green by surprise.

Everyone, apparently, save Vaughn Hargrave.

He turned and drew his blade across the back of Harrell's knee in one swift motion, causing the man to scream and fall to the ground. There didn't seem enough time for him to seize hold of Searrach by her hair, twisting his hand with a practiced motion so that her head swiveled back on her neck, but he did. She shrieked, and her hands went to her scalp, but she did not struggle as the Englishman dragged her over the green, flaming bits of detritus falling from the sky like giant, flaming snowflakes.

Hargrave waved his knife. "I do not wish to kill her."

A Blair man ran down the length of a house toward Hargrave and seized Searrach's arm. Hargrave swung around in a graceful, powerful arc and drove his blade into the underside of the man's chin. He jerked it free just as quickly, releasing a shower of blood over the gasping, whimpering Searrach.

In a blink, they disappeared between two houses.

"Searrach!" Harrell cried, attempting to drag himself along the dirt, one hand grasping at his wounded leg. "My daughter! Someone help her! She canna go alone with him!"

Lachlan ran in the direction in which Hargrave had gone, but his intention was not to save Searrach. He wanted Vaughn Hargrave dead. Dead for what he'd done to both towns, dead for what he was trying to do to Thomas Annesley and everyone Lachlan's true father had ever known.

But then there was Finley, staggering onto the green from the next alley, one sleeve of her otherwise light gown black with blood. Her hair was orange as the flames rising behind her, her face bloodless around wild eyes.

"Lachlan," she sobbed and stumbled toward him.

He ran to her, catching her just before she fell forward. He saw the deep wound in her arm, looked over her head on his chest at the blackened holes all along the back of her gown, like spots of ermine.

"Finley, did you—?"

"He was going to do it again," she said, looking up at him with wide eyes. "Town Blair, this time. I couldn't let him."

Lachlan pulled her to him once more. "You saved us," he murmured into her hair.

"Lachlan, Murdoch is missing," Finley said. "I think he's—" She broke off, and her eyes grew even rounder as she looked past him, her pale lips parting.

Lachlan turned and recognized the loping gait of the man striding deliberately across the green. He wore an old leather skullcap, a long, old-fashioned tunic, and boots that had been made with inexpert hands. In his fist he wielded a blade not much larger than an eating knife. He reached the center of the green and stopped, looking all around him.

The explosions had ceased, leaving only the constant crackle of the flaming lower branches of the tree and the house beneath it. The only English soldiers left on the green were dead or dying. Blairs and Carsons alike stared at the strange old man, until Marcas walked out to meet him.

"Geordie?" Marcas called hesitantly. "Geordie, is that you?"

Harrell had been lying on the ground, sobbing into his arm, when he heard Marcas's hailing. He raised his face, and his expression was that of one who beheld a specter.

"Aye, Marcas," Geordie said. "'Tis me." Geordie's gaze roved the green until he found Lachlan and Finley. He gave his swooping nod. "Edna's son."

Lachlan nodded back. "Geordie."

Marcas raised an upturned palm, then dropped it in a helpless motion. "Where've ye been, Geordie?"

And Lachlan was transported back to that day in the cache. *Where've ye been, Tommy?*

"Yer dead," Harrell blurted out.

Geordie turned and looked down where Harrell lay. "Sure, and perhaps I've been ta hell. But I'm nae dead anymore, Harrell. Nae anymore, I'm nae."

Harrell turned onto his back, looking around frantically, as if for someone to agree with him. "*Yer dead,*" he said again, his voice raising to a higher register. "Why are ye here? Why are ye here and none have saved my daughter? Searrach? *Searrach!*"

"Geordie," Marcas said in a quiet voice. "Archibald died."

"Aye." Geordie continued staring at Harrell, who was becoming increasingly agitated, scooting himself backward in the dirt with his uninjured leg, leaving a trail of blood. "I'm glad o' that, Marcas."

"Nay," Harrell said in a quavering voice, stopping short against the body of a fallen English guard. His hands groped beneath the corpse's arm, pulling out a long, wooden object and swinging it around. It was a crossbow.

"Harrell, nay!" Lachlan shouted, holding Finley away and then running across the green. He knew he'd never get there in time. "Geordie, get down!"

Harrell struggled in fitting the foot of his unwounded leg in the stirrup, pulling back the crossbow, fumbling to set the arrow. But it was only a moment before he had pointed the weapon at the old man. "You should have stayed dead, Geordie-boy."

* * * *

As soon as Lachlan pulled away from her, Finley sank to her knees in the soft, cool dirt of the green, the scene before her tilting, going blurry. It was too much to take in, and shock caused reality to twist: the cottages turned black, the outline of the treetops white. The cool night air became too sweltering to take in as breath.

Lachlan sprinting across the green, pushing fragile old Geordie to the ground. And then it was only Lachlan standing there.

The sound of the crossbow was as loud as cannon fire, and it deafened Finley, making the world silent, the arrow's path graceful and slow.

She remembered her wedding day. Her wedding day on this green...

She would never be able to recall precisely from which direction Murdoch appeared. Some would later say that he ran in from the north, stepping in front of Lachlan at the last moment, and that could have been why Finley hadn't seen him. And yet others would insist he had come from the west, from the path leading to the falls. No one could agree, and so it would remain a mystery, a legend in both towns from that day on, how Murdoch Carson appeared and stepped between the Blair and an arrow already fired from only twenty yards away.

Finley was glad she could not hear the sound of the bolt striking the Carson chief in the chest; could not hear the cries of the Carsons as they sprinted across the green; could not hear Lachlan shouting *Murdoch, Murdoch*, although she could read his lips as he caught the man under his arms and Murdoch slid down, down...

Finley slid down, too, and her eyelids fluttered closed, shuttering the horrifying scene from her already overtaxed mind.

But hands were grasping her, pulling her back hatefully, shaking her without mercy.

"Fin! Finley!"

Her cheek was struck, and she cried out in indignation as she opened her eyes, her fingertips testing her jaw.

"Did you just hit me, Kirsten Carson?"

"Oh, thank the lord," Kirsten gasped and pulled Finley into an embrace, and Dand Blair knelt on the other side of her.

"Lachlan?" Finley asked of no one, of everyone, even as she struggled free of Kirsten's hold to see for herself around the shapes of the legs blocking her view. "Lachlan!" she screamed.

"Doona try to get up, Mistress," Dand advised. "You'll only find your seat again. He's coming."

And Dand was right: There was Lachlan, pushing through the crowd, rushing to her side and gathering her into his arms once more.

"Are you hurt?" she asked, running her left hand over his chest, up to his face, searching his eyes with hers.

"Nay," he said with a shake of his head.

She didn't want to ask—she already knew—but... "Murdoch?"

"Your arm needs tending. Kirsten, Dand, take her to Mother Bl—"

"Nay," Finley said. "I'm not leaving. Harrell—"

"Oh my lord," Kirsten breathed, and everyone's attention was drawn to the edge of the green once more, where Harrell Blair still lay.

Marcas pulled the crossbow from Harrell's hands and flung it to the ground behind him, and now he stood over the blubbering, pleading, wide-eyed Harrell, who held up his palms before his face.

"I wasna trying to shoot Lachlan, Marcas. I wasna," he rushed.

Marcas's voice was icy, monotone. "The only reason you didna is because Murdoch Carson gave his life to protect my son." He stared at him. "You would have killed *my son*. Instead, you killed the Carson chief. And for that—and so many other wrongs you have committed—you will pay. You will pay now."

"There has to be a council," Harrell stammered. "The fines must be called. They will decide my fate. It's the law, Marcas! It's the law!"

"*I* am the law," Marcas said, and he brought his sword before him, tip pointing toward the earth, both hands wrapped around the hilt. He raised his clenched hands above his head.

Harrell screamed. "Nay! *Nay!*"

Lachlan pulled Finley's face against his chest. An instant later, Harrell's scream ended.

When Finley looked again, Marcas was turning away from the body of Harrell Blair, his bloodied sword tip dragging the ground as he faced the crowd of shocked, grieving Carsons and Blairs gathered on the green.

"*It's over,*" he cried out hoarsely in the eerie silence, and flung his arm about. "Do ye hear? It's all over, as of now. What I said earlier, that I am not Town Blair's rightful chief; it is truer than I realized." He walked to the center of the green, where Geordie Blair and Finley's own father knelt at the side of Murdoch Carson's dead body. Once there, Marcas laid down his sword carefully and then straightened, his hands going to the ties of the old shawl. As his fingers worked at the knot, Geordie Blair rose to his feet.

"What's he doing?" Lachlan murmured.

But Finley knew in the instant before Marcas once more began to speak.

"Geordie Blair, firstborn child and only son of Archibald Blair, this belongs to you, by the laws of our clan." Marcas draped Archibald's old shawl around the man's neck.

Beneath her hand, Finley felt Lachlan still. She looked up at him. "He's Edna's brother, Lachlan," she said. "Don't you see? It's why he wept when he learned who you were. He's your uncle. Your family."

Lachlan's handsome face, sweat- and dirt-streaked, was drawn into a pained frown. He said nothing, only looked back to the center of the green, where Geordie Blair's odd, bulging eyes were already watching him closely.

"Me father never wanted aught to do with me," he said. "Archibald. Was ashamed of me. I reckon he had reason. Never was clever." He glanced down at the body of Murdoch Carson, whose face Rory had covered with the man's shawl.

He looked back up at Lachlan. "You saved my life, Edna's son. My Edna's son. Me own little sister. Reckon you didna ken who I was."

Lachlan shook his head slightly.

"Edna'd be proud," Geordie said with his bobbing nod. "Tommy, too, I reckon." His gaze roamed around the green for a long, quiet moment, as if he wanted the people gathered there to have a good, long look at him. "They'd nae be proud of what's gone on here, though. By neither o' the clans. Marcas's right: It ends now. It must. We canna put right everything that's happened. But, sure, we can be right going on." Geordie began walking toward where Lachlan and Finley held on to each other.

Finley felt an expanding of her chest—pride perhaps—but then a chill rushed in as Lachlan again moved away from her.

Geordie stood before Lachlan. "As the Blair," Geordie announced loudly, and then his toothless mouth crooked in a self-conscious grin, "I call Lachlan Blair, me own nephew, chief of Town Blair." Geordie removed Archibald's shawl and draped it around Lachlan's neck. He patted it in place over Lachlan's wide shoulders almost tenderly.

Lachlan stood with his head lowered for a long moment, and when he looked up, Finley could see the glistening in his eyes—the emotion, the triumph. He held out his hand, and Geordie clasped it.

Lachlan had gotten what he wanted.

He turned to look at her, and Finley thought her disappointment must have been clear on her face, for his brows knit together, breaking the moment for him.

She didn't care; her heart was breaking in the same moment.

"Finley," he said, turning to her and taking her hand, pulling her against his side to support her. He whispered into her hair, "Let's get you to the chief's house so that one of the mothers might tend your arm."

This time it was Finley who pulled away. She went to Kirsten, who slid her arm around her waist without hesitation, taking some of Finley's burden, which was not entirely physical.

"I release you, Lachlan Blair," Finley said. She turned her head to locate Marcas and addressed Lachlan's foster father. "I release him from our vows. We have not known each other. He is free."

"Finley," Lachlan said, his face a mask of confusion. "I thought...I thought we cared for each other."

"We do," she said. "Sure, we're friends."

"We're more than that."

She shook her head. "Nay. You've made your choice—the same one you told me at the very first you'd make. You're only keeping your promise. And so I'm keeping mine." She dropped her eyes and said to Kirsten, "Take me to my da, please. I want to go home."

"Wait," Lachlan turned to call to her as she passed. "Stay with me. Here, at Town Blair. I want you to be my wife, here." He reached out to touch her, but it was her injured arm and so Finley flinched away, although he hadn't truly pained it.

"This is not my home," she said, and then turned away from him. "And you are not my husband anymore."

She lifted her chin as she made her way through the crowd, and gritted her teeth as, one by one, both Carson and Blair warriors honored her with a bow as she passed.

Her father was waiting to take her into his arms. "My gel, my gel. I'm so proud."

"Take me home, Da," she hiccoughed into his chest.

And he did.

Chapter 18

Lachlan was the Blair.

A month had passed since that terrible night of *Lá Bealltainn*, the night the ben had nearly run red again. The night Vaughn Hargrave had escaped, and Murdoch Carson had died. The night Geordie Blair, Archibald's son, had come back from the dead.

The night Finley had left him.

He'd spent his days finding his way once more in a town that was at once familiar and foreign. Before Lucan Montague had ventured into the vale on his fine black horse, Lachlan would have stepped into the chief's place with nary a blink. But now—so much more had happened than could be reconciled to the mere passing of time, and it was an awkward return for Lachlan in more ways than one. They buried the dead and moved on, though.

Well, most everyone moved on. Kirsten Carson had returned to the place of her birth along with her friend, but Dand made the trip to Carson Town nearly every day now, openly wooing the blond Carson woman with both fine's blessings. There would be a wedding after the autumn butchering. They thought it fitting to celebrate the salmon run with it, both towns together. A healing.

Lachlan hoped he'd be healed by then, too. Healed in his relationship with Marcas, still strained and awkward, though neither one wished it that way. Healed of the pain of betrayal. He'd hoped it could return to the way it was before he'd left. But there was a shadow now between him and everyone else in the town. Not quite visible, nothing anyone could put name to, not ominous. But there.

Dand never spoke to Lachlan of Finley, although Lachlan had overheard bits of gossip that Carson Town had thrown her a fete, and had offered to send her to Edinburgh to make a match there. Just like Myra Carson... Myra Annesley. There was more than one murmur that several of Lachlan's own townsmen had their eye on the spirited Carson lass who had saved Town Blair from a fiery fate.

Finley Carson, who used to be his friend.

Lachlan's every waking moment was filled with thoughts of her wavy red locks, the delicate freckles on her nose. Her long legs that could nearly match his, stride for stride, in a foot race. The way she'd kiss him passionately, and then in the next moment laugh at him, fight with him, her sparkling blue eyes enchanting him with her fairy charm.

Every word she'd said to him on the beach the night of *Lá Bealltainn*, when she'd begged him to stay at Carson Town, rang in his head like a haunting, tinkling song.

He thought, too, of the friends he'd made at the town on the bay—the families who had accepted him and helped him, even knowing the truth of who he was, even with the past of his clan following him nearly to their ruin once more. Did they hate him now? Lachlan thought they had every right to.

Lachlan sat at the table in his grandfather's house after a short meeting of the fine. Everyone had left straightaway afterward; none had stayed for a drink like they used to in the old days. Harrell Blair was dead. Searrach was gone—probably dead as well. Lachlan had no intention of marrying again, perhaps ever. Who would have him, in truth, the Blair or nay? He poured himself another cup of the last of the Irish and sipped it in the light of the single, smoky lamp as it flickered over the brooch on the tabletop.

Mother Blair had found it on the green and returned it to him without meeting his eyes. "I thought you might want this," she'd said gruffly, and then snatched her shawl tighter over her chest and left him staring at the wedding brooch given to Ina by Andrew Carson. Given to Lachlan by Finley.

Were any of the people of Town Blair happy he'd returned? Marcas and Dand said they were, but Lachlan thought perhaps Dand was the only one who claimed it with any truth. Marcas...Marcas was tired. Tired and bitter from his struggle with and against Lachlan, his troublesome foster son. Perhaps he was more than a bit humiliated, too; defeated by the role that was taken from him not once, but twice. Was Lachlan only a reminder of the dark clan secrets that had been aired before all the valley to their great shame? Were they happy to have Lachlan as chief?

Am I happy to be chief? he asked himself suddenly. He'd sought justification for so long that, once he'd gained it, he'd never thought to question it before that night, sitting alone in his grandfather's house, wearing his grandfather's shawl. This was the future he had secured for himself—fought and nearly died for. Leading these people, living in this house, this town, for the rest of his life. He'd won.

But rather than victory, why did it feel like he'd sentenced himself to a long, cold mourning for what could have been?

Lachlan drained the cup, then blew out the lamp to hide his shaking hands in the dark.

* * * *

A pounding on the door woke Marcas Blair from his sleep. His head ached from too much mead, too many bad dreams of death and fire and blood. He pulled himself from the bed in the early dawn light and trudged to the door, his flesh prickling with the chill. He opened the door and saw one of the old wives, the hem of her skirts wet with dew.

"Marcas," she panted. "It's the Blair."

"Lachlan?" He rubbed his eyes.

"Aye, look!" The woman pointed a thick arm over the green.

Marcas squinted and then saw the blurry outline of a fluttering cloth on the side of the Blair's longhouse. It was like looking into the past, only months ago, when Archibald had died.

Marcas ran from the house in his bare feet, across the green toward the flapping cloth. It was the shawl, of that there could be no doubt. He crashed against the door, throwing it open and bursting inside.

"Lachlan!" He looked around the long, wide room. Everything was as it should have been, except there were no boots on the floor, no satchel on the peg. No knives on the table, no fire in the center hearth. The room was cold.

Marcas walked back outside and stood before the old, threadbare shawl nailed to the longhouse wall. It was a clear message: Lachlan didn't care who the Blair was anymore. He didn't want the law of it. He didn't want them. He was gone.

Lachlan had gone home.

Marcas leaned his forehead against the old shawl, the rough wall beneath poking through the thin material into his flesh, but he didn't care. He wept bitter tears of regret.

* * * *

Finley came out of the house in the misty morning light, pulling her shawl more tightly around her. She wobbled in her slipper, realizing she hadn't put it on properly, and stood in the dooryard, bent over, fighting with it. There.

She raised up, but froze in place as she heard the echoing clatter of metal on metal coming from the barn. She sighed. It was either Da, changed his mind about letting her take over all the chores in truth, which he'd promised not to do—again—or it was yet another of the townsmen, intent on wooing her with work. She'd found a Blair lad, at least five years her junior, in there last week.

Finley trudged up the path wearily. Taking care of the farm would be a lot less work if everyone would just let her get on with it.

She walked into the barn and saw a man in the shadows, turned away from her and bent at the waist, propping the fork against the wall. He straightened, and Finley noticed that he was missing his shirt. Her heart skipped, recognizing at once those shoulders, the line of his spine. He turned.

"Lachlan," she breathed.

"Good morning," he said. "How's your arm?"

"As if you care. What are you doing?"

He looked around the aisle pointedly, then back to her. He shrugged. "Working."

"Why are you here?" she demanded.

"I left Town Blair." He put his hands on his hips, blew out a breath while looking at the ground for a moment, then raised his eyes to her again. "I'm sorry. I made a terrible mistake, Finley."

She nodded vaguely. "Aye. That you did. Several."

He took a step toward her. "I love you—"

"Stop." Finley held up a hand. "You stop right where you stand, Lachlan Blair. I doona want to hear another word. You can just…you can just put your shirt back on and go home." She turned and stalked from the barn, hot tears leaking from her eyes. She flung them away with her fingertips.

"Finley!" She heard his footsteps behind her, running down the path.

"Go away, Lachlan!"

He grabbed her arm and turned her on the path, and Finley lashed out with her other hand, striking his bare skin with a loud smack. But it didn't deter him. He pulled her into his arms and kissed her. She struggled, but it was as if her tears had made her weak, and when he did not relent, she surrendered to the feel of him, the smell of him. Oh, how she had missed his face, his voice, the touch of his hands.

But the way he was touching her now, it wasn't like before he'd left. This was insistent, urgent. His hand went to her breast; he lifted her against him.

"I love you," he said against her mouth. "I loved you the day after we were married, only I was too stubborn and prideful to admit it."

"Did they throw you out again?" she asked, her voice cool even as she clung to the warmth of him.

"What?" he asked, and then laughed. But then he framed her face in his palms, leaned his head near hers, and looked into her eyes. "I left on my own. Because I'd rather live a hundred lifetimes in the old house alone, as Geordie did, if I canna spend the rest of my life with you. You are the very beating of the heart inside my chest, and I have longed for you as the restless sea longs to retire upon the shore."

She pulled away and glared at him with all the distrust she felt, even though his romantic speech had caused her chin to flinch, her throat to constrict. "You're so sure I'll have you, is that it? After you humiliated me?"

"I'm not sure at all you'll have me," he said. "And I didn't humiliate you. I humiliated myself. I have done nothing but show everyone who's ever known me what an idiot I am. You—Finley, you're everyone's darling; their hero. Surely you know that."

"They want to send me to Edinburgh," she admitted. "To make a match."

He shook his head, pulling her to him once more with a frown. "Nay. Doona go. You canna go. Not if you love me." He kissed her again. "Say it."

"We're friends," she said, turning her head.

He stooped and scooped her into his arms and walked toward the house.

"What are you doing?" she demanded, although she hooked her arm around his neck. Just so she wouldn't fall, she told herself.

"Taking you inside to bed you, so you have to marry me again," he said. "Door."

Finley reached down and disengaged the latch.

He stepped inside and kicked the door closed, and the room was dark. He walked toward the back of the house, stubbed his toe on a chair that had been moved since last he was in the house, and cursed. Turned her sideways to enter the bedchamber and then laid her on the single bed that now occupied the room. She put up no resistance when Lachlan loosened her shawl and the ties of her apron and slid them from her. Finley watched him in the gloom as he bent to address his boots, stepped from them, and then knelt on the bed.

He pushed her gown up to her hips, then up to her ribs, over her small breasts. He paused there, kissing each one in a leisurely fashion. Finley pulled her arms from the sleeves, and Lachlan lifted the gown from her head. She gave up all pretense, then, opening her legs to him as he reached down to his breeches. She wasn't afraid of his body. In fact, the greatest fear she'd had these past weeks was that she would spend the rest of her life without feeling his body again.

He took her slowly at first stroke, and it was just right for her. He was careful, gentle, until she had become ready for him, and then Lachlan worked his body atop hers, timed his strokes, his rocking, until Finley was panting beneath him.

"That's it," he encouraged. He drove into her in a steady, increasing rhythm, and leaned his face close to hers to whisper in her ear. "I'm going to put a baby in you. My baby."

Her peak took her by surprise, expanding her body and then collapsing the entire world to one pulsating point, and Lachlan stilled, his hips pushing his promised seed deep inside her.

After a moment, he rolled away from her, flopping onto his back. Finley curled into his side.

"I almost forgive you."

"Good." He pulled her close to him and rested his cheek on her head. "I love you. Do you love me?"

"I suppose."

He gave her a squeeze. "Will you make me a bannock, then? I've nae had a proper meal in days."

Finley shrieked in outrage and swiped the pillow from beneath his head to press it over his face. He tossed her off easily and pinned her to the mattress.

"Fine, fine!" he consented. "You win. I'll bed you once more. But then I really must have something to eat."

This went on for quite a happy while.

* * * *

They walked into town together at midday, and Finley knew they caused considerable stir as several of the wives ran off to summon the rest of the town. Lachlan grinned at her with a shy blush and shook their joined hands.

This was a different man beside her. Same in all the ways she had missed, but with a gentleness now, a slowness he'd never before possessed.

A certainty.

Everyone gathered at last, even Geordie Blair, who was wearing proper clothes and living in the little cottage that had been meant for Rory and Ina Carson. He was a Carson now, and part of Carson Town. He'd more than earned it.

Rory and Ina had taken up residence in Murdoch's old house, and until the fine decided otherwise, Rory had agreed to act as clan chief.

Lachlan squeezed her hand and then stepped into the center of the crowd alone. "Thank you for letting me speak," he said. "I come here to ask once more for the charity and mercy of Carson Town. I have forsaken my place as chief of Town Blair. Because I realized it was in Carson Town that I learned the meaning of friendship. The meaning of working for the good of all. I learned about forgiveness, and family. I learned how to drag in nets." Here, everyone chuckled. "And I realized that when I think of my future, of a family of my own, I can only imagine it being here. With all of you, if you will have me."

He turned to look at Finley, and his gaze burned to her soul. "If Finley will accept me as her husband. I've never wanted anything more in my wildest dreams than a family with this woman. Raising our bairns as she was raised. I can learn to be a better man here. I will learn. I promise you." He looked back at the town.

"If you refuse me, as is your right, I will bear you no ill will. But I willna return to Town Blair. More than one person in this town told me that it was nae my home, and they were right." He turned to Finley again, facing her fully.

"Finley Carson, will you be my wife?"

Finley nodded and answered quietly, "Sure, I will."

A shout rose up in the crowd, and Lachlan and Finley were swept up in happy embraces and handshakes until at last they were pushed together.

"Give us a kiss to seal it!" someone shouted.

"It's nae as if this is a proper wedding," Finley scolded as she felt her cheeks heating under the close but smiling scrutiny of the entire town.

Lachlan grinned down at her. "We do things better our own way." He leaned his head toward hers.

Eachann Todde chimed in. "I believe this happy occasion calls for a sonnet. "Again, my lo—'"

"Nay!"

"Boo!"

"Leave off, Todde!"

Finley and Lachlan laughed, their foreheads leaned together.

Then the sound of hooves rang foreign in the warm afternoon air, and all turned to regard the dusty cloud entering the town.

Black horse, black rider.

Lucan Montague slowed Agrios to a trot, but came right up to where Lachlan and Finley stood in the shocked and wary silence. Without a word, he reached into his black doublet and withdrew a folded packet of parchment, tied with a blood red ribbon.

Lachlan took it, read it, and then looked into Finley's eyes.

Epilogue

Vaughn Hargrave read the letter thrice over, and then folded it back neatly into its former shape. He retied the ribbon carefully and placed the letter in his desk. Then he rose and quit his chamber, making his way through the maze of corridors and stairwells that made up Darlyrede House; its cold marble floors, its muraled walls filled with sparkling, gilded frames and spotless tapestries.

Down, down, he went. Smiling at the servants he passed. Pausing to say this or that to a particular one. He walked to the end of his wife's wing, stood before her door for a moment. Even raised his hand to rap on it, but changed his mind. He looked around to ensure no one was watching, then entered the secret corridor to the narrow, damp stone stairs that led down, down, down even farther into the bowels of Darlyrede.

He could hear her panicked skittering as he unlocked the gate. She wasn't crying, and Hargrave was heartened. She was of robust stock, and tonight she would be rewarded.

Rewarded greatly.

"Are you awake?" He came around the corner and saw her, her skin so pale as to be nearly blue. He came to stand over her.

"Searrach. Hallo."

She didn't smile.

He leaned down. "I have a job for you. How do you like that? Are you ready to go upstairs?"

She nodded, her movements like a hummingbird's, her eyes sunken like warm stones dropped in a snowdrift.

"Well, let us see. I'm going to place great trust in you. You will need to obey me completely. Can you do that?"

Again, the anxious nod.

"Stand up, then," he encouraged in a kind voice. "Here, let me help you. Careful, you'll be a bit wobbly on the stem for a moment. Better?"

She stared up into his face, her sharpened features wary. No trace of the plump, mouthy Highland wench he'd taken from Town Blair.

Town Blair. Carson Town. Myra Carson…Myra Annesley. Tenred.

Thomas.

Thomas.

The letter.

"Very well." He turned and pulled a long robe from a peg. "Put this on. You may follow me upstairs to my rooms to be cared for by my servants until you are well enough to be of use. It shall be just in time, too, I think, with such important visitors en route to Darlyrede House even as we speak. Why, just look at you, poor bird, having traveled so far from your home to seek work. Set upon by bandits, were you not? They have infested our wood, I'm afraid."

Searrach pushed her arms through the sleeves without question.

Yes, she would do.

Printed in the United States
by Baker & Taylor Publisher Services